Check into the Pennyfoot Hotel...
for delightful tales of detection!

Room with a Clue

The view from the Pennyfoot's roof garden is lovely—but for Lady Eleanor Danbury, it was the last thing she ever saw. Now Cecily must find out who sent the snobbish society matron falling to her death . . .

Do Not Disturb

Mr. Bickley answered the door knocker and ended up dead. Cecily must capture the culprit—before murder darkens another doorstep . . .

Service for Two

Dr. McDuff's funeral became a fiasco when the mourners found a stranger's body in the casket. Now Cecily must close the case—for at the Pennyfoot, murder is a most unwelcome guest . . .

Eat, Drink, and Be Buried

April showers bring May flowers—when one of the guests is found strangled with a maypole ribbon. Soon the May Day celebration turns into a hotel investigation—and Cecily fears it's a merry month . . . for murder.

Grounds for Murder

The Pennyfoot was abuzz when a young gypsy was hacked to death in the woods near Badgers End. And now it's up to Cecily to find out who at the Pennyfoot has a deadly axe to grind . . .

A PENNYFOOT HOTEL MYSTERY

CHECK-OUT TIME

KATE KINGSBURY

BERKLEY PRIME CRIME, NEW YORK

CHECK-OUT TIME

A Berkley Prime Crime Book / published by arrangement with
the author

PRINTING HISTORY
Berkley Prime Crime edition / March 1995

ISBN: 0-425-14640-5

Berkley Prime Crime Books are published by
The Berkley Publishing Group,
200 Madison Avenue, New York, NY 10016.
The name BERKLEY PRIME CRIME and the BERKLEY PRIME CRIME
design are trademarks belonging to Berkley Publishing Corporation.

PRINTED IN THE UNITED STATES OF AMERICA

10 9 8 7 6 5 4 3 2

CHAPTER

❊ 1 ❊

London was not the best place to be in the summer of 1908. The prolonged heat wave took everyone by surprise, causing even husky laborers to stagger under the merciless rays of the sun.

The managers of the fashionable stores along Bond Street complained bitterly about the lack of business. Most of their wealthy patrons had followed the example of their flamboyant king, deserting the smoke-belching motorcars and fetid fumes from horse droppings to seek relief in various parts of the British Isles and Europe.

Thus it was in August of that year that the Esplanade in Badgers End had more than its usual share of visitors. Phoebe Carter-Holmes, who normally managed to appear cool and collected under the most trying of circumstances, found both the unaccustomed heat and the bustling crowds along the seafront quite irritating to say the least.

So much so that she had stayed longer than she had intended at the Pennyfoot that afternoon. Her visit with Cecily Sinclair, the owner of the hotel, had been delightful. The arrangements for the Midsummer Ball, to be held at the end of the week, had been dealt with in a most satisfactory manner.

Phoebe was in charge of the entertainment for the event and had secured the presence of a juggler, who performed amazing feats with water jugs and chamber pots. Phoebe had been a little doubtful about the chamber pots, but Cecily had assured her that in this instance they would not be considered bad taste. Phoebe could not abide a lack of taste in any context.

She had enjoyed a light lunch of salmon and cucumber sandwiches, followed by an exquisite sherry trifle. The snack had done wonders for her frayed nerves. In fact, seated in the cool shade of the conservatory, she had almost nodded off on occasion.

Phoebe was most reluctant to face the long walk back to the vicarage. Her son, Algie, would no doubt be in the church, trying to maintain some kind of order with those dreadful choirboys.

Phoebe never understood how they could resemble such perfect angels at times and yet take so much delight in tormenting the vicar.

Even she had to admit, however, that Algie was an excellent target. Now, if it were she who was dealing with the little horrors . . .

She left the thought unfinished as she emerged from the cool shadows of the foyer into the blinding sunlight. The white stone steps dazzled her, and for a moment or two her vision was quite blurry.

Blinking the stinging tears from her eyes, she saw a shadow move in front of her, and her heart skipped. She knew, even before she heard the voice, who it was who stood before her.

"Well now, if it isn't the most beautiful lady I ever did set my eyes upon," a rich, baritone voice declared in tones that set Phoebe's heart fluttering like the wings of a dove.

Arthur Barrett, the Pennyfoot's new doorman, had to be the most handsome man Phoebe had ever seen. Not that she would ever admit that, of course. A lady of her standing wouldn't stoop to acknowledge so much as a smile from a lowly hotel employee, although Phoebe found it most difficult to think of Arthur as lowly.

As she took a quick peek at him now from under the massive brim of her hat, her breath seemed to catch in her throat. She had to look up quite a ways to see his face. And what a wonderful face it was.

His light blue eyes sparkled with warmth and laughter, and his smile could melt the coldest heart. His imposing build and thick white hair only added to his charm, but it was his voice that made Phoebe's pulse race at a rate most unbecoming in a lady.

To listen to Arthur's soft Irish brogue was to be swept away like a summer breeze to some exotic land, basking in the admiration that colored every wonderful word he spoke. Not only that, he could sing like an angel. In fact, had he not been employed as the hotel doorman, Phoebe would have begged him to sing at the ball.

Even the aristocrats seemed to take to him immediately—the ladies responding to his flattery, the men enjoying his jovial comments and jokes that ordinarily would have been deemed disrespectful coming from someone of lesser stature.

Phoebe found it a constant struggle to appear unaffected by Arthur's smooth comments. For the most part she hid it under a veneer of cool indifference, with an occasional scathing glance of outrage to keep him in his place.

This afternoon, however, she found herself alone with him, in a manner of speaking, at the top of the steps leading down from the Pennyfoot's main doors. That was something that didn't happen too often.

In fact, more often than not, Mrs. Chubb, Cecily's rotund housekeeper, was hovering somewhere in the background.

Phoebe had the distinct impression that Altheda Chubb had more than a passing interest in the new doorman, a fact that made Phoebe appreciate all the more an opportunity to enjoy him all to herself. Even if she could never let him know of her pleasure.

So, instead of sweeping past him as was her custom, she allowed her eyelashes to flutter just a little, and whispered a trifle breathlessly, "Good afternoon."

"It is indeed, sweet lady, if it affords me the very great pleasure of hearing your delectable voice. Would you be giving me a smile now, just to make my day complete?"

Glancing up at him, Phoebe caught the full impact of his laughing eyes. The sight so unnerved her, she quickly averted her gaze, intending to restore some sense of decorum to the situation.

As she did so, a movement high up above the street caught her attention. She momentarily forgot the seductive voice of the doorman. The sight that met her eyes shocked all coherent thought from her mind.

She blinked twice, convinced the blinding sun and oppressive heat were causing illusions. Part of her mind heard Arthur ask if she was feeling unwell. She couldn't answer him. She was beyond speech. All she could do was shake her head in disbelief at the scene her eyes recorded.

Each suite on the upper floors of the Pennyfoot had a balcony with a wrought iron railing guarding the outer edge. At the very top, four floors above the street, Phoebe saw a man balancing on the narrow rim of the railing, one foot waving precariously in midair above the street.

She pressed her hand to her mouth to suppress a scream. The man's arms waggled up and down while he attempted to step forward, walking the narrow edge as if it were a tightrope.

At her side Arthur uttered a muffled exclamation, followed by a yell as he dashed past her down the steps.

For once Phoebe's attention was not on the doorman. Though every instinct she possessed urged her not to look, she could not seem to tear her horrified gaze away from the figure of the man swaying violently so high above the pavement.

As she waited, her heart thumping in terrified anticipation, the figure suddenly executed a strange little dance. The jerky movement toppled him off balance. For a moment he hung suspended in space, arms flailing and one wobbling leg apparently searching frantically for a foothold. Then, without a sound, he plunged like a wounded pheasant to the street below.

Phoebe's stomach lurched at the dreadful thud as the man hit the ground. He landed almost at Arthur's feet, just as the burly doorman arrived at the spot. That was the last thing Phoebe remembered as darkness swooped over her and swallowed her up.

"Baxter, I do believe you are putting on weight," Cecily declared as she faced her manager across the library table.

Baxter stood respectfully by the door, though he immediately pulled in his stomach and lifted his chin, adding another half inch to his height.

"It is the waistcoat, madam," he said stiffly. "I think it must have shrunk. Mrs. Chubb cleaned it for me, and it has never been the same since."

Cecily smiled. "If you say so, Baxter. I should hate to see you acquire a belly like some of our more prominent guests. I find it most distasteful to look at."

Baxter swiveled his eyes in her direction. "I wasn't aware that a lady would be at all interested in viewing that particular portion of a gentleman's anatomy."

"One can hardly miss it on some gentlemen." Cecily leaned back in her chair and drew on her cigar. "I wonder why most men consider a large belly an inevitable symptom of aging. Look at Arthur, for instance. He is approaching sixty, and yet his body is as fit and trim as a man thirty years younger."

This time she got the reaction she had expected. Baxter's snort of disgust was most satisfying.

"If I might be permitted to say so, madam, Arthur Barrett would do well to take care of his tongue as well as he does his physique. And, I must add, I find it most uncomfortable to discuss this sensitive subject with a lady."

Cecily blew a stream of smoke through pursed lips. "Oh, come now, Baxter. I was under the impression that you and I could discuss anything, within reason."

"Within reason, it seems to me, would preclude the personal attributes of your employees."

Cecily sighed. "I do hate it, Baxter, when you get so deplorably stuffy."

"Yes, madam."

She leaned forward to stub out the cigar in the silver ashtray and she looked up just in time to see the look of disapproval on Baxter's face. He had never been able to accept her smoking habit, deeming it highly unsuitable for a woman, although he was the one who supplied her with the thin cigars that she enjoyed so much. Albeit reluctantly, and upon her insistence.

Deciding it was time to change the subject, she said lightly, "I haven't seen much of Michael since he came home from Africa. I'm disappointed in him. I quite thought he would have paid us a visit before now."

"He is most likely busy with the George and Dragon, madam. Your son took on a great deal of work when he bought the inn. From what I hear, Scroggins did not take good care of the building and allowed it to become quite dilapidated."

"So I understand." Cecily glanced up at the portrait of her dead husband, which hung above the marble fireplace. "I remember when James and I bought the Pennyfoot. It needed so much work, and the cost of repairs was quite horrifying. I sometimes wonder if I shall ever get the loans paid off. I can understand how Michael must feel, particularly since business at the inn has dropped off so drastically."

"A new owner always finds it difficult to establish a business," Baxter said, rocking back on his heels.

Cecily regarded him with a stab of irritation. No matter what she said to him, how much she pleaded with him, he would not unbend on his stand of complying with proprieties.

Just once she would love to have a heart-to-heart discussion with him, but it was impossible when he insisted on standing at attention at the door instead of sitting with her at the long mahogany table that dominated the library.

"I think establishing a business might be even more difficult in Michael's case," she said carefully. "Some customers might well be uncomfortable in the presence of Michael's wife."

She watched Baxter's face to gauge his reaction. So far she had avoided the subject, but she desperately needed to talk about the situation, and she couldn't think of anyone she would rather discuss the problem with than Baxter.

Cecily needed an impartial ear, an understanding ear. She fervently hoped that Baxter would be able to provide her with one.

After a moment he said a little hesitantly, "I am quite sure, madam, that the presence of Mr. Sinclair's wife is not the reason for the lack of customers."

As always, Cecily found it impossible to judge his expression. Baxter had a formidable practice of hiding his feelings and emotions. "I wish I could be as certain," she said, continuing to study his face. "I admit I was upset with Michael for not telling me he was bringing home a bride. I was very disappointed not to be present at his wedding. That is, until he described the ceremony." She paused, feeling again her resentment. "Simani may be of African descent," she said, "but I hardly think a primitive ceremony in the jungle, presided over by some sort of witch doctor, constitutes a legal and binding marriage."

Baxter raised an eyebrow but chose not to comment. Frustrated, Cecily added, "I might have felt better if I'd known about it beforehand. Springing a surprise like that on me was most inconsiderate. Particularly since Simani is not . . ." She hesitated, trying to find a delicate way of saying what was on her mind. "She doesn't exactly fit in here," she finished lamely.

Baxter's faint look of disapproval gave her a twinge of guilt. "Not that I'm prejudiced, of course," she added quickly. "We are all God's children, no matter the color of one's skin. No one should know that better than I, having spent so much time in the tropics when James was in the military. But after all, one has to think of the children of such a union, and the kind of consequences with which they might have to deal."

Not a muscle in Baxter's face moved. Feeling a trifle desperate, though Cecily had no idea why she should feel that way, she said with just a hint of defensiveness, "It just takes some getting used to, that's all. And you are right, of course. I'm sure the local customers will come back, once they get used to the idea."

"Yes, madam."

She had to acknowledge the fact that Baxter was not prepared to discuss the issue. She was about to change the subject when he said abruptly, "I have a complaint to make, madam."

She straightened her back, wondering what to expect. Baxter rarely complained, usually taking care of any untoward incidents himself.

"It's the new doorman, madam. I must object to the liberties he takes with the guests. Why, only the other day I heard him tell the Duchess of Morden that he admired her hair. It was most fortunate her husband did not overhear, or we would have had to deal with quite a nasty scene."

"I'm sure Arthur meant well," Cecily said, trying not to

sound defensive. "And I have heard no complaints from the guests. Quite the contrary, I have heard some very nice things about him."

"His familiarity with the aristocracy is deplorable," Baxter said, his neck turning red, warning Cecily he was upset with her. "I find it unacceptable that a common doorman should take such liberties. I have spoken to him about it, but he pays no attention to me. Perhaps you should have a word with him yourself."

Cecily shook her head. "I have to disagree with you, Baxter. Arthur is not just a common doorman, which is the precise reason I hired him. His voice is cultured, and his manner, which I admit is perhaps a little more free than we are used to, is never disrespectful.

"The guests seem to enjoy it, and personally I think his jovial attitude is just what we need. Our guests are staying here for pleasure, after all, and such good humor is a wonderful introduction to the Pennyfoot Hotel's hospitality."

"There are means of issuing a welcome without being impertinent," Baxter muttered, but Cecily paid no attention, for at that moment a light tap sounded on the library door.

Baxter opened the door to a robust young woman whose dark eyes glittered with suppressed excitement in her flushed face. The manager tutted at the sight of the housemaid's pleated round cap, which hung at a rakish angle on her unruly black hair.

One strap of her spotless white pinafore had slipped from her broad shoulder, and her long skirt gathered slightly in the front to accommodate the gentle swelling of her belly.

Although Gertie was six months pregnant, her ample girth and height helped to diminish the physical evidence of her condition. At times Cecily had trouble remembering that her housemaid carried a baby inside her. Gertie's strength and energy was as formidable as ever.

"Do tidy yourself up," Baxter muttered irritably. "Your condition does not excuse such slovenliness."

Gertie's hand flew automatically to her head. "Strewth, I'm sorry, sir. I never can keep the bloody thing straight on my head at the best of times, and I was in such a blooming hurry to get here—"

"Is something wrong?" Cecily asked, sensing a certain urgency behind Gertie's rapidly paced words.

"Wrong? It's a bleeding catastrophe." Gertie advanced into the room, ignoring Baxter's muffled protest. "There's been a death, that's what."

Cecily's cry of dismay mingled with Baxter's soft and quickly smothered oath as she braced herself for the worst. "Who has died? What happened?" Her only hope was that the volatile housemaid was overreacting as usual and had muddled the message.

"Well, mum, all I know is he fell from his balcony. Mrs. Chubb says as how you should come at once."

Getting to her feet, Cecily exchanged a glance with Baxter. His expression mirrored her own thoughts. Not another death. That's all they needed right now, in the middle of the busiest season the Pennyfoot had seen in years.

"I'll come at once," Cecily said, and the housemaid bobbed a curtsey, flashed Baxter a cheeky grin, and disappeared.

"I will come with you, if I may," Baxter murmured, looking sympathetic.

"I wish you would." Cecily glanced up at the portrait once more. "I'm afraid poor James would turn in his grave if he knew how many tragedies we have witnessed here."

"I shudder to think what he would say if he knew." Baxter opened the door for her and stood back. "He would be devastated to know his beloved wife was involved in such dastardly goings-on."

Cecily gave him a tired smile. "Oh, I think he would be comforted by the knowledge his good friend is taking such great care of me. That was indeed a gallant promise you made to him on his deathbed, Baxter. I wonder, had you but known what was in store, if you would have been so prompt in your granting of his request."

"I would indeed, madam. And I only hope I can continue to keep my word to protect you." He stood back to let her pass, and she stepped out into the hallway.

"I have no doubt, Baxter." She glanced up at him, troubled by his serious expression. "Another death at the Pennyfoot," she murmured. "Let us pray that this time it is an unfortunate accident. Though even that is unlikely to bode well for the hotel."

For once his answer failed to comfort her. "I'm afraid you may be right, madam, especially since the victim apparently fell from one of the balconies."

"I can't imagine how, unless he climbed over the railing. I had them all inspected at the beginning of the season." She led the way down the hallway, wondering just what kind of new trouble was brewing for the Pennyfoot.

CHAPTER

❁ 2 ❁

The sight that met Cecily's eyes when she entered the lobby filled her with dread. Arthur stood just inside the main door, and she couldn't mistake the still figure of the woman he carried.

Phoebe's elegant pale violet gown trailed on the floor, while the bright pink feathers in her large hat drooped dismally over his shoulder. In front of him, Mrs. Chubb stood with her arms crossed, demanding he set his burden back on her feet this instant.

"Sure, and I would now," Arthur said, his voice carrying clear across the lobby, "if the lady had her eyes open. If I put her down, unconscious as she is, she'll topple over like a crumpled rose."

Mrs. Chubb snorted loudly. "I'm sure she'll manage quite nicely. Phoebe is not nearly as weak-kneed as she would have you believe. And I'm sure the weight of her must be breaking your back."

"Ah, but she's as light as a feather," Arthur said, giving the housekeeper a broad smile. "Am I not strong enough to hold her, do you think?"

Having reached Mrs. Chubb's side, Cecily looked at Phoebe's white face with concern. In spite of her doorman's levity, she had the frightening impression for a moment that Phoebe could be the dead person Gertie had been talking about. Then she remembered the housemaid had said the victim was a man.

"What happened?" she demanded, shaken by the lifeless appearance of Phoebe's delicate features.

"I'm afraid Mrs. Carter-Holmes has had a nasty shock," Arthur said just as Phoebe let out a quiet moan and stirred in his arms. "The lady had the misfortune to watch Sir Richard Malton plunge to his death from his balcony."

Relieved that at least it hadn't been Phoebe's demise, Cecily let out her breath. "How did it happen? Was the railing defective?"

"No, ma'am." Arthur uttered a soft grunt as Phoebe opened her eyes and dug her elbow into his midriff. Slowly he lowered her feet to the ground and steadied her, while Mrs. Chubb looked on with a disdainful sniff.

"It appeared to me," the doorman went on, "that Sir Richard overbalanced while attempting to walk across the rim of the railing."

Behind her Cecily heard Baxter's muffled oath. She ignored it, her attention fully on the doorman. "Sir Richard Malton was trying to balance on top of the railing?"

A loud wail from Phoebe interrupted her. "Oh, Cecily, it was dreadful. One minute the poor man was balanced up there on that narrow strip of metal, the next he was falling at Arthur's feet."

She gave a little moan and sagged against the doorman, who put a protective arm around her. Phoebe seemed not to notice, but Mrs. Chubb, having apparently reached the end of her patience, took a firm hold of Phoebe's arm.

"I'll take care of her," she said firmly. "It's nothing that a good strong cup of tea won't cure in an instant."

"One moment," Cecily said sharply. "I need to ask some more questions."

Baxter murmured something she couldn't catch, but she could guess what it was. Before he could voice his objections more loudly, she glanced up at him and said quietly, "Just to find out what happened, Baxter."

Without waiting for his approval, she turned back to Phoebe, who stood swaying in Mrs. Chubb's grasp. "Did you see him climb up onto the railing?"

"No." Phoebe clutched her throat and gave a pitiable moan. "He was already attempting to walk along it when I saw him."

"Did you see anyone else there?"

Phoebe shook her head. "If someone was in the room, he wasn't out on the balcony. As far as I could see, Sir Richard Malton was quite alone."

She paused, shaking her head so that the feathers and ribbons on her hat shimmied in the light from the gas lamps. "Oh, my, I shall never forget the sight. He did this strange little dance, though I can't imagine why. He had enough trouble keeping his balance as it was. Anyway, the dance put him right off balance. He swayed back and forth for a moment or two, then down he plunged, with not so much as a whisper from him."

"He must have wanted to die, that's for sure," Mrs. Chubb said, sounding upset. "It's the only thing that makes sense. He must have wanted to kill himself."

A muffled gasp sounded from the stairs, and the housekeeper called out sharply, "Gertie? Is that you? You'd better get back to the kitchen, my girl, before I catch you. What have I told you about nosing in on something that doesn't concern you? Whatever next!"

"It's all right, Mrs. Chubb," Cecily said, laying a hand on

the housekeeper's plump arm. "Perhaps Gertie could fetch us a blanket."

She looked back at Arthur. "I presume the body is still lying out there?"

Arthur nodded, his face now grave. "I didn't want to move it, madam. Not until the constable has seen it."

Cecily groaned. "The constable. Of course. Yes, you are quite right, Arthur. Just cover it up for now, until we can get hold of Police Constable Northcott. I'll send Samuel right away. I only hope the man can get here as soon as possible. No matter how it happened, the sight of a dead body lying in front of the building is not too reassuring to our guests."

"I would suggest that Sir Richard might have been inebriated," Baxter said as Mrs. Chubb hurried over to the stairs to give Gertie her orders. "I can't imagine why else he should attempt such a strange act. He did not strike me as the kind of person who would engage in such foolhardiness."

"Precisely," Cecily murmured uneasily, having reached the same conclusion.

"Begging your pardon, ma'am," Arthur said, "but I don't think the gentleman had been drinking. I couldn't detect a smell of booze on him, and as sure as the grass is green in Ireland I would have done so had he had a drop to drink."

"I don't doubt that at all," Baxter muttered.

Ignoring them both, Cecily studied Phoebe's face, relieved to see that some color had returned to the delicate features. "You didn't hear him say anything?" she asked.

"Not a word," Phoebe said, shuddering visibly. "That was the odd thing. Not even when he fell. You would expect him to scream or something, wouldn't you?" She laid a fluttery hand on her breast. "Oh, my, I do believe I am going to faint again. The shock of it all . . ."

"No, you are not," Mrs. Chubb said firmly, arriving back to grab Phoebe's arm. "You are coming with me for that hot cup of tea." The housekeeper glanced at Cecily. "That's if you are finished with the questions, mum?"

Cecily nodded absently, her mind still questioning the odd behavior of a sedate aristocrat like Sir Richard Malton.

Gertie appeared at the top of the stairs, carrying a blanket. At the same moment, the main door opened to allow in a whoosh of hot air.

Arthur hurried forward, prepared to deliver his usual hearty greeting, but as the woman and boy came forward, he pulled up, apparently at a loss for words.

Cecily's heart sank when she recognized the woman. With all the commotion going on, she had forgotten about Lady Lavinia. The dead man's wife, apparently sensing something in the doorman's face, paused and laid one hand protectively on the head of the eight-year-old boy at her side. Stanley Malton jerked his head away in sulky defiance.

Unless they had already seen the body, Cecily thought with despair—and they looked far too calm to have done so—someone would have to break the news to them. And she was very much afraid that the task would be up to her.

"Cor blimey, I tell you," Gertie said with relish as she stood at the kitchen sink later, "you could have heard a farthing drop when Lady Lavinia and Master Stanley came through the door. I could see no one wanted to tell them. Not as I blame them. It must be dreadful to have to tell a woman her husband just died."

Ethel, the second housemaid and Gertie's best friend, seemed preoccupied. She stood drying the wineglasses with a slow motion that drove Gertie crazy. Gertie liked to get things done as quickly as possible, so that at the end of the day she could relax a bit and take it easy. Ethel took so long to do every task that Gertie knew they'd still be there come midnight.

"What's the bloody matter with you, then?" Gertie said with more irritation than was warranted. Since her pregnancy her back had been killing her, and she resented the extra time she spent making up for Ethel's lack of enthusiasm.

Ethel looked up with a start. "Nothing," she muttered in a tone that said everything was the matter but she didn't want to talk about it.

Gertie decided to ignore her friend's despondency. "Course," she said, plunging her arms into the hot, soapy suds, "Stanley didn't look too upset by the news of his father's death. He looked at his mother as if she was blinking daffy when she started to cry."

"Mmmm," Ethel murmured, intensifying Gertie's impatience.

Grimly she gritted her teeth. "Not that you'd expect Stanley to think of anyone but himself. I never saw such a bloody horrible kid as that one. If he gets any fatter, his belly is going to explode. Gets too much of his own way, that's the trouble. And if he doesn't stop playing all those bleeding nasty tricks on everyone, he's going to be the next one to cop his lot, I can tell you."

She had finally succeeded in getting Ethel's attention. The housemaid gasped and said in shocked tones, "Gertie Rossiter, what a dreadful thing to say."

Gertie spun around, her skirt twirling around her ankles. "'Ere, I'm Gertie Brown, remember? Me and Ian was never married, so I can't be Mrs. Rossiter."

Ethel dropped her gaze back to the wineglass in her hand. "Sorry," she mumbled, "I keep forgetting. But it seems to me you might as well have kept the name until after the baby is born. Makes it seem more proper like, doesn't it?"

Gertie made a rude noise. "I never had the name in the first place, seeing as how he was already married to someone else. Bleeding farce that were, going through a wedding ceremony and him with a wife already. Good job me old man didn't find out while he was here. He'd have bleeding murdered him, he would."

"Seems such a shame, your poor baby growing up without a father." Ethel sighed loudly. "You'll have to find someone else to marry, to take care of it."

"Not so bloody likely," Gertie said with gusto. "I ain't

never going to get near another flipping man as long as I live. Just me and the baby, that's all I need. I just hope it don't grow up to be a fat monster like Master Stanley Malton. I can't stand that bleeding kid. I tell you, if he plays one more trick on me, I'll shove him headfirst down the bleeding lavatory, I swear I will."

She looked over her shoulder at Ethel, who sat staring at the glass as if she could see her future in it. Apparently she hadn't heard what Gertie had said.

"Are you going to tell me what's wrong with you or not?" Gertie demanded. She wasn't about to admit to her hurt feelings, but she and Ethel had always exchanged confidences before. They'd never had secrets between them, and Gertie couldn't imagine what it was that Ethel was keeping from her now. "'Ere," she said suddenly as a thought occurred to her, "you ain't bleeding pregnant, are you?"

Ethel looked up, and Gertie was shocked to see tears shining in her friend's eyes. "No. I'm not bleeding pregnant. Trust you to jump to the wrong conclusions. I have a big decision to make, that's all. And I don't want to talk about it. I need time to think about it, to decide what to do."

Shrugging, Gertie turned back to the sink. "Suit yourself," she muttered. "I was only trying to help." She didn't even turn her head when she heard Ethel leave the room. She knew when she wasn't wanted. And she'd be blowed if she was going to ask Ethel again what was wrong. Though she couldn't help worrying about it just a little.

Cecily had accepted Arthur's offer to escort the bereaved woman and her son to their suite, giving her time to take a quick look at the body before Baxter covered it up with a blanket. Leaving Arthur posted at the spot until the constable arrived, Cecily then hurried back to speak with Lady Lavinia.

"Please accept my sincere condolences," Cecily said, her heart going out to the weeping widow. "If there is anything I can do at this time, please don't hesitate to ask."

Lady Lavinia fumbled in her pocket for a handkerchief. "Most kind of you. I'm sorry, this has all been such a shock."

"Yes, I'm sure it has."

It would be only a matter of time before the news spread all over the hotel, Cecily thought gloomily. She could only hope that P.C. Northcott arrived as quickly as possible. A dead body lying in that heat outside for any length of time was going to attract a good deal of attention. Arthur had been posted to watch over it until the police arrived. Not an enviable task for the new doorman.

"Would you like me to stay with you for a little while?" Cecily said quietly. "I have sent word to Dr. Prestwick. He could no doubt give you something to calm your nerves when he gets here."

"That would be most kind," Lady Lavinia managed to say between sobs. "I would like to know what happened."

Seated on a padded velvet chair, she uttered a low moan. "Whatever am I going to do without him? How am I going to manage Stanley on my own? Your kitchen staff have kindly offered to take care of him for now, but sooner or later I must decide what to do about him." The last word was smothered by a fresh bout of weeping.

Cecily patted her shoulder. "Perhaps I should fetch my smelling salts," she suggested, but Lavinia shook her head.

"I need to know exactly what happened." She delicately blew her nose and made a visible effort to pull herself together.

"I'm afraid I can't tell you very much," Cecily said, thinking back to what Phoebe had told her. "Apparently, for some reason, your husband attempted to walk the balcony railing. Like a tightrope, Mrs. Carter-Holmes tells me. He then tried to dance on it and lost his balance. It seems he died at the moment he hit the pavement."

Lavinia emitted a loud moan. "Poor Richard. I can't imagine what got into him. Such a foolish thing to do. Not like him at all."

Remembering Baxter's comment, Cecily said carefully, "Was Sir Richard in the habit of enjoying a glass of spirits, by any chance?"

Lavinia lowered her handkerchief, her eyes blazing with resentment. "I can assure you, Mrs. Sinclair, my husband had not been drinking. He never took a drink. He suffered greatly from ulcers, and any kind of alcohol burned his stomach. He couldn't even manage one mouthful."

She shuddered, blew her nose again, and added bitterly, "Besides, I'd left him just a few moments before his death. I intended to take Stanley to see the Punch-and-Judy show on the sands. The show had been canceled, however, due to the performer's illness, and Stanley and I returned to the hotel to find . . . this . . ." Once more she succumbed to her tears.

Cecily waited until the sobbing had subsided before asking, "Did you husband appear normal when you left him this afternoon?"

Lavinia took a while to answer. When she did, it was with a strange inflection in her voice that quickened Cecily's pulse. "As a matter of fact," she said slowly, "he was acting rather strangely. That was the main reason I returned immediately to the hotel."

"Strangely?" Cecily leaned forward, intent on the answer. "In what way?"

Lavinia shrugged her slim shoulders. "It's difficult to describe. He seemed distant, uncertain of what he was doing. He moved very slowly, as if he had trouble controlling his actions, and when he looked at me he didn't seem to see me or hear what I said, yet he answered me quite lucidly when I spoke to him."

"Did you ask him if he was feeling unwell?"

Lavinia nodded. "He said he felt quite well. Never better, he told me." She paused, frowning. "In fact, he said that he was invincible and capable of doing anything he set his mind to do. It's all a matter of control, he said."

"And that was unusual?"

"Most unusual. My husband was the kind of man who questioned his every action, weighed every decision. He was not a man of confidence by any means."

Cecily hesitated, but the question was important. "Was he by any chance concerned about financial problems?"

Again Lavinia bristled with indignation. "My husband was a wealthy man, Mrs. Sinclair. If he had any problems at all, I can promise you lack of money wasn't one of them. And even if it were, Richard was not the kind of man to take his own life. He was too God-fearing to do such a thing."

"I'm quite sure you are right," Cecily hastened to say. "But I should mention that these are the kind of questions the police constable will be asking when he gets here."

Lavinia groaned. "Oh, dear Lord, I don't think I can face such an ordeal. Can't you tell him I am too ill to answer his questions? I certainly don't feel well at all."

"I'm afraid he might insist. It's a normal part of the procedure at times like this." Cecily rose, giving the other woman a sympathetic smile. "I'm sure he will be as brief as possible. There's just one more question I have, if you will permit me?"

"What is it?" Lavinia said wearily.

"I was just wondering if perhaps Sir Richard could have taken a wager of some kind. Some people will do outrageous acts in order to win a wager."

Lavinia violently shook her head. "Not my husband, Mrs. Sinclair. Richard was a strong man in many ways, but he would never have risked his life for a mere wager. He was too afraid of dying."

Cecily's response was forestalled by a firm tap on the door. Lavinia lifted her handkerchief to her face, muttering, "Oh, I hope it's not the constable. I don't want to see anyone while I am looking like this."

"I'll take care of it." Cecily rose and opened the door.

Baxter stood there, concern written all over his face. "I do beg your pardon for the interruption, madam, but the police constable is here and wishes to speak with you."

"Thank you, Baxter. And Dr. Prestwick? Has he also arrived?"

"Not yet, madam."

Cecily looked back at Lavinia, who sat huddled in her chair, a picture of abject misery. "I have to leave," Cecily said, wishing there was more she could do for the stricken woman. "But I will send Dr. Prestwick up with one of the maids when he arrives. I'm sure he'll be able to prescribe something that will make you feel more comfortable before talking to the constable."

Lavinia nodded speechlessly, waving a hand in dismissal.

Quietly Cecily closed the door behind her, then looked up at Baxter. "You are not going to like this one little bit, Baxter," she said softly, "but I have a feeling in my bones that all is not as it appears."

Baxter's frown creased his forehead. "I do trust, madam, that you will not undertake any more investigations into circumstances that are none of your business."

"As I've told you many times," Cecily said firmly, "the hotel is my business. So is anything that happens under its roof."

Baxter lifted his gaze to the ceiling and groaned. "And that, madam, is what I dread hearing the most. At least this time we can be reasonably sure that it isn't murder."

Cecily's smile felt a little strained. "Can we, Baxter?" she said softly. "Can we, indeed?"

CHAPTER

✤ 3 ✤

Police Constable Northcott stood in front of the marble fireplace in the library, his hands clasped behind his back as he rocked slowly back and forth. His small brown eyes roamed around the room, over the tall shelves of books, across the French windows, up and down the oak paneling, settling anywhere but on Cecily's face.

"Per'aps you could fill me in on all the pertinent details, then, ma'am," he said, his deep voice pronouncing every word as if it were a precious command from the Almighty.

Cecily did so, as briefly as possible. She was interrupted more than once by the constable, who appeared to have a great deal of trouble keeping pace with her as he laboriously scribbled down notes on a dog-eared notepad.

When she described the little dance that Sir Richard

Malton had executed, the constable glanced up at her for a second before switching his gaze back to his report.

Baxter, as usual, stood stiffly at attention, his scorn for the police officer only too plain on his face. Remembering what he had told her about his relationship with Northcott, Cecily felt a moment of sympathy.

It couldn't be easy for Baxter, having to associate with the man who had stolen away his only love. Although it had happened many years ago, Baxter made it obvious that he had never forgiven the constable.

Cecily had often wondered how any woman could have chosen P.C. Northcott over Baxter. The policeman was several inches shorter than her manager. In fact, he was at least two inches shorter than she. While it was entirely possible that he had not yet acquired his protruding belly when he courted the young lady, Cecily could not imagine even a much younger P.C. Northcott being considered attractive.

His bulbous nose dominated his face, and the police helmet perched atop a mound of bushy brown hair gave him a somewhat comical air. Even the luxurious mustache, waxed to extend beyond his ruddy cheeks, failed to add even a hint of charm.

Baxter, on the other hand, with his strong features enhanced by crisp dark hair with its silver wings, and a physique that must make any man envious, was a striking figure. Even if he was past forty.

Unexpectedly Baxter's gaze met hers, momentarily unsettling her. She was thankful when P.C. Northcott cleared his throat, thus capturing her attention.

"Yes, well, a very h'unfortunate tragedy, ma'am, seeing as 'ow it took place on your property, like. Most h'unfortunate, I must say." He closed his notebook with a loud snap that brought forth an audible sigh from Baxter. "I 'ave h'examined the body, and no doubt you will be pleased to hear that the corpse 'as been removed to the proper vicinity. I will report my findings to my superior, Inspector Cranshaw. Though it's an open-and-shut case, I would venture to say. Most definitely a suicide, by my reckoning."

Cecily nodded, her expression deadpan. "I am inclined to agree with you, Constable. I feel deeply sorry for the widow. It must be twice as hard to bear, knowing her husband took his own life."

Baxter made a small sound in the back of his throat, but she ignored him. "I expect you will want a word with her?" she blithely continued. "I must warn you, Lady Lavinia knows very little about the circumstances. She was out of the hotel at the time the tragedy happened. I'm afraid she will have nothing to add to my testimony."

The constable shook his head. "I won't disturb the bereaved widow at this time. I shall refer the case to the h'inspector, who will no doubt wish to question everyone involved in the situation."

Cecily exchanged a resigned glance with Baxter. She had expected as much, but heartily wished it could have been avoided. The inspector was a dour man, who possessed all the charm of an ill-tempered skunk. He made it clear he considered Cecily a willful busybody who was doing her best to disrupt the constabulary of the entire south of England.

"Will that be necessary, do you think?" she murmured, clinging to a last faint hope. "You said yourself it was a simple case of suicide, and I have told you all the details as we know them."

P.C. Northcott drew in a breath and expanded his chest like a winter robin. "Yes, well, I'm sure you are aware, ma'am, in a case like this we have to h'explore every avenue. Although I am positive the h'inspector will agree with my findings, he will want to make his own investigation, no doubt."

"No doubt," Baxter echoed dryly.

P.C. Northcott shot him a suspicious glance, but Baxter's face remained impervious.

"Well, if he must, he must," Cecily said hastily. "I shall

make every effort to accommodate him, and I will see that my staff are available for questioning. As for Lady Lavinia, I'm not sure when she plans to return to London. Perhaps I should suggest she stay until the inspector has conducted his investigation?"

"I would be most grateful, Mrs. Sinclair. Thank you." Northcott glanced at the clock on the mantelpiece. "I must be off now, ma'am. It's a long ride back to the village on my bicycle. Gives one quite an appetite, that it does."

He slapped his belly with the flat of his hand, causing Baxter's eyebrows to arch with indignation.

Acknowledging the broad hint, Cecily smiled. "Perhaps you would care to stop by the kitchen on your way out, Constable," she said pleasantly. "I'm sure Mrs. Chubb would be happy to offer you some refreshment to help you on your way."

The constable touched the narrow brim of his helmet. "Thank you, Mrs. Sinclair. Much obliged, I'm sure." He edged toward the door and opened it. "I do hope this tragic h'incident will not disrupt your guests. If I may say so, you have had more than your fair share of ill luck in the past."

"We have indeed, Constable. Thank you for your concern."

The constable nodded. "And how is young Mr. Sinclair faring at the George and Dragon?"

Baxter cleared his throat, managing to sound threatening.

"Michael is doing very well, thank you," Cecily said, sending a warning look at her manager. "His father would have been so proud of him. It is really sad that James could not be here to enjoy his son living so close by."

"Yes, well, I'm sure you are enjoying that very great pleasure. It must be most comforting." P.C. Northcott nodded his head several times then backed out through the door and closed it.

Baxter let out an explosive sound of outrage. "The gall of that pompous ape!"

"Why, Baxter," Cecily murmured, "that is a little strong,

don't you think?" She watched a deep red hue creep slowly up his neck.

"Please excuse me, madam, but I become concerned when you allow too many liberties from people of lesser station. Mr. James would be most distressed."

"Oh, piffle, Baxter. Stan Northcott was simply being polite, that's all. I imagine that Michael's homecoming must have raised quite an amount of speculation. Especially since the George and Dragon is the focal point of the village. People are bound to be curious."

"That's as may be. It does not, however, give a mere policeman the right to act so chummily with a lady of the house. 'Most comforting,' indeed. What, may I ask, does he suppose you have been doing all the time your sons were in the tropics?"

Somewhat taken aback by this uncharacteristic outburst, Cecily said quietly, "What every mother does when she has sons in the military. Wait for them to come home. I only wish Andrew could have come home with Michael."

She was happy to see a sheepish expression flit across Baxter's face. "I do beg your pardon, madam," he said, his voice a trifle stiff. "My concern is unwarranted, I can see. Please excuse my comments."

Cecily smiled and reached out to pat his arm. "Thank you, Bax. I do appreciate your concern. But as I've told you before, society is not what it used to be. We are rapidly changing our ways and relaxing our standards of protocol."

"Thanks to that pretentious gadabout on the throne."

She drew back, pretending to be shocked. "Why, Baxter! That amounts to treason. I thought you were an avid Royalist."

"I was once, before the Prince of Wales inherited the crown. It was a sad loss for the country when Queen Victoria, God rest her soul, was laid to rest." He laid a hand on his chest and gazed up at the ceiling.

Cecily burst out laughing. "Baxter, you are an unabashed fraud. Why don't you just admit that this attitude of yours came about simply because you cannot abide P.C. Northcott and would find fault with him were he to lay down his life for me?"

Baxter growled in his throat. "That pretentious idiot wouldn't lay down his coat for you, much less his life."

"But you would, no doubt?"

She'd meant to tease him, but the gaze he concentrated on her face disturbed her, and her smile faltered.

"Yes, madam, I most certainly would trade my life for yours. I sincerely trust that you are assured of that."

She made an attempt to make light of his softly spoken words. "I am quite sure that the promise you made to my husband will be honored. I certainly hope that you are never forced to the extreme of risking your life for mine."

"I echo your sentiments, madam." For a moment his intent gaze engrossed her, then he cleared his throat, stretching his neck against his stiff white collar. "Speaking along those lines, I feel I must warn you."

"Warn me?" She found it uncommonly difficult to recover her composure. A little annoyed at him for causing that effect on her, she added a little sharply, "What is it you are afraid I shall do now?"

"I heard you agree with Northcott that the death of Sir Richard appeared to be suicide. Earlier you expressed doubts as to that conclusion, which leads me to suspect you intend to conduct your own investigation. Am I correct?"

"I have very little to base any assumptions on at present."

"I have known you to base assumptions on far less, if I might say so." He rocked forward on his toes and looked down his nose at her. "I trust you do remember the strong chiding you receive from Inspector Cranshaw every time you interfere in police business?"

She sighed and lifted her gaze to the crystal chandelier above the table. "How could I possibly forget? It was for that precise reason that I agreed so readily with P.C. Northcott that Sir Richard committed suicide. I was hoping to avoid a confrontation with the inspector."

"Might I suggest that you allow the police to conduct their own investigation? Then you won't have a confrontation at all."

She looked back at him and shook her head. "Baxter, I don't think I have to remind you that we have had more than one police investigation here at the hotel. You are also well aware of the reason so many of the aristocrats choose our hotel over the larger ones in Wellercombe."

"I am indeed, madam. Due to your insistence that the staff turn a blind eye to their nefarious deeds, these shallow, self-centered wastrels are free to gamble and drink the night away to their hearts' content. That's if they're not cavorting in the boudoirs with someone else's spouse."

Cecily cocked an eyebrow at him. "Those self-centered wastrels help to pay the bills, Baxter, as you well know. Without their business I would not be able to keep up the payments on the loans. And I'm very much afraid that if we get too many more visits from Inspector Cranshaw, our customers will feel their privacy is threatened."

"I understand your concern, but a police investigation seems unavoidable when there is a death. Especially one of such bizarre circumstances."

"I agree, Baxter, which is why I must try to find out more about the situation before the inspector arrives to form his own conclusions. If my suspicions are correct, this is no suicide. Nor do I believe it to be an accident. If I can present Inspector Cranshaw with a solved case, so to speak, then he will have no need to question anyone."

There followed a long pause while Baxter appeared to digest this argument. "And I take it that you expect me to assist you in your investigation?" he enquired at last.

Cecily gave him her best smile. "That would be most comforting, Baxter. I should sorely miss your help if it were not there." She got up and moved over to touch his arm. "There have been many times when I could not have done it without you."

He avoided her gaze, but a faint flush brushed his cheeks.

"I'm not sure I should feel pleased about that. I feel I am only encouraging you in your perilous escapades."

"You know very well that I should continue without you," Cecily said, this time earning a cool look. Baxter's light gray eyes could convey a frigid blast now and again.

"In that case, madam, perhaps you should tell me why it is you are so certain Sir Richard's death was neither an accident nor suicide."

"I had a brief conversation with his widow." She repeated Lady Lavinia's account of her husband's rather odd behavior that morning. "She was adamant that her husband had no reason to take his own life," Cecily added as Baxter listened attentively. "She was just as positive about her assertion that, given her husband's personality, he would not have attempted something as foolhardy as balancing on a railing."

"From what I know of Sir Richard, I have to agree with her on that point."

"Neither was he drinking, according to his wife. In fact, Lady Lavinia was quite offended that I mentioned the possibility." Cecily gazed up at the portrait of her own dead husband. "She assured me that he was incapable of consuming liquor. I found it touching that she so passionately jumped to his defense."

"I am quite sure you would have done the same thing, madam, had it been your husband."

Cecily gazed at the painted face of James for a long moment. "I would indeed. James and I had something very special. It saddens me a great deal to see that same devotion in the eyes of a new widow. I know how very painful and lonely these next months will be for Lady Lavinia."

Baxter's voice sounded gruff when he answered. "Yes, madam. I fear you know only too well."

Summoning a smile, Cecily turned to look at him. "It does get easier, Baxter. Time takes care of a good many things."

He didn't answer, but she saw sympathy in his eyes as he

looked at her. Feeling a need to break the tension that still seemed to hover between them, she said brightly, "I think I will pay a visit to Michael this evening. I want to see for myself how he is faring as an innkeeper."

"I would be happy to accompany you," Baxter said, moving to open the door for her. "I have a meeting scheduled with the chef, but I can postpone it. There are several matters I need to discuss with him. His breakages, for one. If he were not such an excellent cook, I should suggest sacking him. He has cost us a small fortune to replace the items he has damaged, not to mention the brandy he consumes."

Cecily crossed the floor to the door, her long cotton skirt billowing behind her. "Please don't worry, Baxter. Have your meeting with Michel. I can have Samuel take me in the trap."

"I do worry, madam. The George and Dragon is no place for a lady to go unaccompanied."

Pausing in the doorway, she looked up at him. "Now that my son is the proprietor, Baxter, I think you can relax a little. I shall come to no harm."

"It isn't so much your safety I'm concerned about, but your reputation."

She frowned, pretending to take offense. "Are you suggesting that my son would own an establishment of ill repute?"

Baxter cleared his throat a little too loudly. "Not at all, madam. I assure you I was merely passing comment on the possible attitude of some of the customers."

"I hardly think that anyone is likely to look unfavorably upon a mother visiting her son."

"Quite so."

Not sure if she'd won the argument or not, Cecily decided to change the subject. "Do try not to be too hard on Michel. I know he has a problem or two, but he has done much to enhance the reputation of the Pennyfoot. A good chef is difficult to find in these parts, and Michel is very good."

"Yes, madam. As you wish."

She left, feeling a little put out and not quite sure why.

"Aw right, aw right," Gertie muttered, "keep your bleeding hair on. I'm going as fast as I can."

Mrs. Chubb heaved a massive sigh. Whatever she was going to do with this girl she just did not know. "I've told you three times, Gertie, to get that tray of silverware back into the dining room. Ethel will be having a pink fit, that she will. How is she going to get the tables laid in time for dinner if she doesn't have the silverware?"

"Ethel ain't going to blooming know if it's there or not." Gertie picked up the tray and balanced it on her solid hip. "She's in a bloody dreamworld lately, going around with that dopey look on her face. I don't know what's the matter with her, I don't. Strewth, you'd think she'd be happy now that she's finally got a blinking man to grab hold of."

Mrs. Chubb tutted in disapproval. She wasn't about to admit it, but she'd been a bit worried about Ethel herself. The girl just wasn't acting normally. She never had been as lively as Gertie and sometimes moved at a snail's pace, making Mrs. Chubb feel like screaming. But she'd always been dependable. Give Ethel a job and she'd get it done, albeit in her own time.

But lately the girl had been dithering about so long that half the jobs hadn't been completed. Mrs. Chubb had finished them herself, hoping the lapse was only temporary. It was time she had a talk with the young lady, she thought, watching Gertie stride to the door.

Just as the housemaid reached it, the door flew open, narrowly missing the loaded tray. "'Ere," Gertie yelled indignantly. "What's your bleeding hurry, then?"

Michel bounced into the kitchen, waving his fist in the air. "He 'as the nerve to complain about breaking ze dishes," the chef announced in his fractured French accent. "*Moi*, the most superb cook in the whole of the British Empire. How can I create ze masterpiece if I 'ave to worry about ze dishes, *s'il vous plaît?*"

"Oh, blimey, he's orf again," Gertie muttered, lunging through the door and letting it swing to behind her.

Mrs. Chubb winced as Michel grabbed a saucepan and crashed it down on the cast-iron stove. If it wasn't one thing, it was another. Sometimes she wondered why she kept working at the Pennyfoot at her stage in life. Surely there was an easier way to make a living. Then she thought about Arthur Barrett. There were some compensations, after all.

She wondered if the new doorman had ever been married. A man as handsome as he was surely must have had scores of women after him. She'd ask him. The very next opportunity she got.

The thought of talking to Arthur again gave her so much pleasure she actually smiled when Michel threw a colander onto the tiled floor, no doubt putting a dent in the side of it.

She didn't smile, however, when she carried a sack of flour across the kitchen, pouring a white trail from the hole cut in the bottom. When she picked up the jug of fresh milk in the larder and found a dead mouse floating around in it, her yell of wrath echoed across the kitchen yard.

Master Stanley Malton was up to his tricks again. He deserved a smacked bottom. Her hand itched to do just that. She should feel sorry for the child, she knew, him having just lost a parent. Apparently his father's untimely demise, however, had not affected the child's penchant for mischief.

She could only hope that someday the little scalawag would grow out of his ill behavior before he did something really terrible and caused someone harm.

Shaking her head, she began clearing up the mess, determined to put Stanley out of her mind and dwell on a more pleasant subject. Like Arthur Barrett, for instance.

CHAPTER

✤ 4 ✤

The George and Dragon had stood for more than two hundred and fifty years on the sharp curve of what was still called the Dover Road, so named for the route the stage-coaches took in the mid-nineteenth century.

Although the more modern horse-drawn carriages and traps had replaced the coaches, and the years had added height to the oaks and elms that shaded the roof, the interior of the inn had changed little since the Cavaliers raised their tankards in support of Charles I.

The same solid oak beams still supported the ceiling, hung with tankards, jugs, and assorted brass pots, making it treacherous for a man of above average height to cross the floor without bowing his head. In fact, more than one man had received a crack on the noggin when a belly full of ale had dimmed his eyes and his attention.

Sir Frederick Fortescue was no exception. Some said that it was due to the constant bashing of his head that the colonel was off his rocker. Others more charitably attributed the man's decidedly bizarre behavior to extreme pressure under gunfire while serving in the army during the Boer War.

Whatever the reason, the colonel was blissfully unaware of his condition and was often amazed when misunderstood by his acquaintances.

Cecily felt a certain sympathy toward the man, having been witness to many of the tragedies associated with war. She also tolerated the colonel's unpredictable behavior, since he was a constant guest at the Pennyfoot and one of her most valued customers. As long as he didn't exactly drive anyone crazy, she was happy to welcome him any time he chose to stay at the hotel.

Even so, when she saw him seated in a corner of the lounge bar, she was inclined to postpone her visit for another time. Conversations with the colonel tended to be lengthy and highly unproductive. Upon occasion, however, he had accidentally provided a valuable clue in his bumbling manner to help her solve a perplexing puzzle.

Not that she expected any help from him this time, she thought ruefully as she ducked her head to avoid the low portal. The colonel had arrived just that morning and would know nothing about Sir Richard or his family.

Since it was yet quite early in the evening, only a half dozen customers sat in the lounge. As Cecily crossed the creaking floor, she caught sight of her new daughter-in-law standing at a corner table talking with two of the pub's patrons.

Simani was the daughter of an African chief and had received a British education from the missionaries. She spoke perfect English, with only a trace of an accent. At the moment it seemed that Simani was doing most of the talking. The two men were simply nodding, and both appeared to be most uncomfortable.

Cecily could hardly blame them. Her daughter-in-law was a striking young woman, tall and slender, with smooth black skin that gleamed in the sunlight slanting across the room from the narrow paned windows.

Her short, bushy black hair emphasized her majestic features, while her large, dark eyes, framed with long, thick lashes, dominated her face. Huge gold-and-black-enameled orbs swung from her ears, gracing her amazingly long neck.

Her dress was equally dramatic and quite startling. Wrapped tightly in a brilliantly hued fabric from bosom to knee, her bared shoulders and arms would have seemed quite natural in the jungles of Africa. Here, in a secluded English country inn, the amount of flesh she revealed was definitely scandalous by British standards. One simply did not expose that much ankle, much less naked calves.

As much as Cecily sympathized with the new Women's Movement, even she drew the line at some things. Although she hated to admit it, even to herself, part of her secretly envied her daughter-in-law's freedom of expression and apparent unconcern for public approval.

Had Cecily been thirty years younger, she might well have emulated the bold young woman, though with a great deal more discretion, of course. She just had to keep reminding herself of the difference in cultures and that it would take time for Simani to conform.

Simani looked up at that moment, and Cecily exchanged a tight smile with her before turning her attention to the counter. Michael stood behind it, holding up a pint of ale and examining it with a critical eye.

She was about to call out to him when she heard a scandalized voice exclaim, "Mrs. Sinclair! Whatever is the world coming to? A lady of your station entering an establishment such as this without an escort? What? What?"

The colonel's ruddy face seemed to glow as he stared at her, his eyelids blinking rapidly like the fluttering of a moth's wings.

Forcing a smile, Cecily paused by the table. The colonel,

remembering his manners, sprang to his feet. His elbow caught the glass of clear liquid sitting in front of him and spilled the contents across the table.

"Oh, dear," Cecily murmured. "I'm so sorry, Colonel. I didn't mean to startle you."

"Startle me? My dear lady, you have shocked me. If you needed an escort, pray, why wasn't I approached? I would be happy to offer you my protection. Indeed I would. Honored. Yes. Most definitely honored."

His head nodded up and down so vigorously that Cecily became alarmed. "Please do not upset yourself, Colonel. You may have forgotten that my son now owns the George and Dragon. It is quite proper for me to visit Michael, is it not?"

"Your son? Good Lord! Does he, by Jove! I wonder, does he know his mother is wandering around a public house unescorted?"

"He will very shortly," Cecily said, casting a hopeful eye at the counter, where Michael still seemed absorbed in the ale.

The colonel leaned forward, raising a hand to shield his mouth, which was almost completely hidden by a luxuriant white mustache. "I say, old bean," he whispered. "You had better warn him. We have an intruder in our midst."

Anticipating the reason for the colonel's alarm, Cecily tried to reassure him. "If you are referring to the young lady, she happens to be Michael's wife. They were married in Africa a few weeks ago."

"Married?" He drew back with a look of horror on his face. "My dear lady, you must do something at once. He has obviously bewitched your son."

Cecily frowned. "He? To whom do you refer, Colonel?"

The colonel nodded vigorously across the room to where Simani still chattered with the customers. "There, in the corner. See him? Looks like a woman, doesn't he?" He leaned forward again, covering his mouth once more. "That, old bean,

is a witch doctor in disguise. Mark my words. I can spot one
a mile off."

Cecily did her best to hide a smile. "I think you are
mistaken this time, Colonel."

Fortescue lifted his eyes to the ceiling in despair. "Oh,
good Lord. The evil is spreading already." He dropped his
chin, his eyelids flapping furiously. "Dear lady, I tell you
that woman is the epitome of evil—a fiend transformed.
Yes, indeed. You must protect yourself from his black
magic, I implore you. That friend of yours, Miss
Penglove . . ." He waved a hand in the air. "Whatever it
is."

"Pengrath," Cecily said, casting an anxious eye at Simani
in case she could overhear this ridiculous conversation,
"Madeline Pengrath."

"Ah, that's the ticket, yes. Miss Pengrath. Super with the
plants, you know. Does wonders with weeds and such.
Dashed marvelous, I must say. Why, I heard she can even
give a man something to make him more virile . . . you
know . . . with the ladies—"

He broke off, apparently warned by Cecily's expression
that he'd said too much. Harrumphing a good deal, he
cleared his throat, his eyeballs rolling around in his head.
"Er . . . sorry, old bean. Got a little carried away there.
Dreadful of me, of course. Forgetting my manners, what?
What?"

"That's quite all right, Colonel." Cecily caught Michael's
eye and lifted her hand in greeting. "Ah, I see my son. I
must have a word with him."

"Yes, yes, of course. Jolly good show, that, what?" The
colonel reached for his glass and lifted it. "To your son's
success with his new venture."

Apparently forgetting he had spilled the contents, he
touched his lips to the empty glass, then held it up in front
of him, a look of astonishment on his face. "By Jove," he
muttered, "I must have drunk that one fast. Didn't feel a

thing. Dashed disappointing, that is. Don't make booze like they used to, you know."

"Let me get you another," Cecily said, seizing the excuse to leave. "Michael will be happy to oblige, I'm sure."

She left the colonel muttering to himself, his glass still held in midair.

Michael's smile seemed forced as she approached him. Even though she had been prepared for his return, the sight of him gave her a pang of bittersweet nostalgia. Her eldest son was so like his father, even without the army uniform, which Michael had now discarded in favor of becoming an innkeeper.

He had James's handsome features, though Cecily liked to think her son had inherited her wide smile. Michael wasn't smiling now, however, and Cecily viewed him with concern.

"Everything is well with you, I hope?" she enquired as Michael wiped his hands on a bar towel.

"As well as could be expected, I suppose." His voice held a note of resignation, so at odds with the enthusiasm he had displayed when first opening the pub for business.

"You are not ill, I trust?" She studied his face, dismayed to see the worry lines at the corners of his mouth.

He shook his head and sent a glance over to where his new wife still chatted with the customers. "No, Mother. Just tired, that's all. I never realized just how much work goes into this business. It's a long way from those last days in the tropics, hunting down tigers and knocking back the gin on a warm night."

"And, if I remember, you were thoroughly bored with the life."

Michael gave a rueful nod of his head. "That I was, Mother. That I was. Damned brattish of me, I know. This is what I wanted, and I shouldn't be complaining if things are not going the way I expected. They will in time, I'm sure. I just have to keep the stiff upper lip and all that rot."

"It could be worse. At least you are home, safe and

sound." Cecily suppressed a shudder. "You don't know how many nights I lay awake worrying about you and Andrew out there."

"I know. I know how much you must miss the pater, too. That was a hard blow. It was one of the reasons I wanted to settle down here on the coast."

Cecily's eyes misted. "I do miss your father, Michael, but it's a great compensation to have you here in Badgers End. Though I do hope you are not here solely on my account. You can't live your life for others, you know. You must live it for yourself."

She felt a great deal comforted when Michael patted her hand. "Don't worry, Mother dear. The peace and quiet of Badgers End suits me very well at present, though I daresay one of these fine days I shall be off searching for new horizons."

Cecily had not the slightest doubt about that. "What about Simani?" she asked, sending a glance over her shoulder. "Is she settling down here? I was hoping you would pay us a visit to the hotel. She has been there only once since you arrived."

"I'm sorry, Mother, we've just been so busy with the George, and Simani is not one to go visiting on her own. I think she feels just a little self-conscious. People do tend to stare at her, you know."

Before she could answer, Colonel Fortescue's voice boomed across the room. "I say, old bean, what about my gin?"

"Oh, dear heavens, I quite forgot," Cecily muttered. "Would you please give the colonel another drink, dear? I'm afraid I caused him to spill the last one."

"I don't think he needs another one," Michael said, reaching for the gin bottle anyway. "That gentleman is absolutely bonkers. Every time he comes in here he starts talking rubbish. Sometimes I even find myself answering him. By the time he leaves, I'm wondering if I'm the crazy one."

Cecily watched him pour a measure of gin. "He's harmless enough," she said, stretching out her hand to take the glass. "He just gets confused sometimes, that's all."

"Confused?" Michael shook his head in disgust. "He should be locked up, if you want my opinion. People like that can be dangerous."

"Not the colonel, I can assure you." She paused as Simani's hearty laughter rang out. Apparently the gentlemen were beginning to relax. "I'll be right back."

She carried the glass to the colonel's table and set it down in front of him. "There you are, Colonel. I hope this one will taste better."

"Thank you, dear lady." He reached for the glass and lifted it to his lips. "You shouldn't have waited on me, however. That fellow behind the bar should have brought it to me. New chappie, he is. I've never seen him before."

"That's my son, Colonel," Cecily said, with more patience than was warranted. "Remember, I told you he had bought the George and Dragon?"

"Oh, gad, yes. How could I forget that?" The colonel swallowed a large mouthful and smacked his lips. "Now *that's* what I call gin."

"I'm glad you like it. Now, if you'll excuse me—"

"Did you warn him about the witch doctor?"

Behind her, Cecily heard Simani bid farewell to the two men, who had got up to leave. "Yes, I did, Colonel," she said quickly. "Please don't worry, he will take care of everything."

"Just keep the blighter away from me," Fortescue mumbled. "You get mixed up with one of those, you might as well be dead."

Cecily hurried back to the counter, where Simani stood talking to Michael. She arrived just in time to hear her daughter-in-law say, "Michael, I do not have the time to visit your mother, even if I were to be made welcome."

Something in Simani's tone of voice prompted a stab of guilt. "I should certainly hope you would feel welcome at the Pennyfoot," Cecily said warmly. "I would be happy to send the trap for you, should you find an hour or two to spare for a visit."

Simani's smile was distant. "Thank you, Mrs. Sinclair. But there is so much I have to do here. Actually I have things to take care of right now. If you will please excuse me?" She glided away, disappearing through the door that led to the private quarters.

Cecily met Michael's disapproving look. "I do hope I haven't said something to offend her," she said.

"I think she has the impression that you are not exactly enamored of our marriage."

"Michael, I have no right to make judgments on your decisions. If I am unhappy about anything, it is that I was not invited to the wedding."

His short laugh was without mirth. "Take my word for it, Mother, you would not have enjoyed it at all. It was quite primitive by your standards."

She couldn't help the flash of resentment. "I am not unfamiliar with primitive surroundings. I endured extremely uncivilized conditions when I traveled the world with your father. And I had the added responsibility of two small boys, if you remember."

His expression suggested that she had no idea what she was talking about. But all he said was, "Quite. So, what brings you down to the George? You must be rushed off your feet at the hotel. And where is your faithful escort? Don't tell me he had something better to do this evening."

Again Cecily had to hide her resentment. Michael had made no effort to conceal his mistrust of her manager. He had actually accused Baxter of having a mercenary interest in her.

Had Cecily not been so amused at the thought, she would have set Michael straight and sent him off with a flea in his ear.

As it was, the idea of Baxter having designs on the hotel was ridiculous. He knew full well that the Pennyfoot was deeply in debt, thanks to the extensive costs of renovations, and it would be years before the loans could be paid off.

She saw no reason to concern her son with her problems, however. He had enough of his own. So, as usual, she ignored the barb and said instead, "I wanted to see you, for one thing. Since you won't come to the hotel, I have to come here."

His expression softened. "I'm sorry, Mother. But you know how it is when you have a business . . ." He waved a hand at the near-empty room.

"I do, indeed." Cecily refrained from pointing out that there didn't seem to be much business at the inn. "I also wanted to tell you, before the rumors got started, that we have had an unfortunate accident at the hotel. One of our guests, Sir Richard Malton, fell from a fourth-floor balcony this afternoon."

After a moment of stunned silence, Michael asked in a strained voice, "He's dead?"

"Yes, I'm afraid he is. Such a tragedy. He has left a young wife and son. One can only hope that he has provided for them—" She broke off, staring at her son in surprise. Michael actually looked happy at the news.

He quickly changed his expression to one of polite concern, but Cecily could not have mistaken the look of relief that had crossed his face at her words.

"Have you met Sir Richard, by any chance?" she asked, and was disconcerted when Michael averted his gaze.

He began busying himself by hanging up the tankards on the hooks above the counter. "He's been in here," he mumbled.

Cecily did her best to sound casual. "Oh? When was that?"

This time the pause stretched even longer. Vaguely she heard the colonel call out a good night, but her attention was on her son, who seemed to be having a great deal of trouble meeting her eyes.

"Two days ago." Michael's expression changed again, to

one of defensiveness. He slapped a tankard down hard on the counter, making Cecily jump. Her surprise turned to consternation when he added fiercely, "I'm not sorry the bastard is dead. In fact, I was tempted to slit his throat myself."

CHAPTER

❖ 5 ❖

"Perhaps you had better tell me about it," Cecily said, trying to ignore the flutter of fear that his words had produced.

Michael shrugged. "It isn't a secret. There were a half dozen customers in here at the time. I had a few words with him, that's all."

Cecily rested her hip on one of the bar stools, earning another look of disapproval from Michael. Pretending not to notice, she demanded, "So tell me what it was about."

"He was an absolute pig," Michael said, hanging the tankard on its hook. "He saw Simani and made some beastly derogatory remarks about her dress and the color of her skin. Loud enough for everyone to hear."

Cecily leaned across the counter and covered his hand with hers. "Oh, Michael, I'm so sorry. I know how distressing that must have been for you."

He looked at her the same way James had looked at her when she'd said something thoughtless. "As well as for Simani," he said deliberately.

"Of course, for both of you." Inwardly cursing herself for her insensitivity, Cecily added, "I can quite see why you had words with him. He most certainly deserved them."

"I was incensed that he should speak about my wife that way. Of course, he didn't know at the time she was my wife, but even after I protested quite vigorously, he refused to apologize. I told him to leave."

"In those words?"

Michael looked a little sheepish. "Well, no. If you must know, I used stronger language than that, of course. I wanted to physically throw the blighter out, but I didn't want to upset the other customers."

"That was probably wise. What happened then?"

Michael reached for another tankard and started twisting it around in his hands. "Well, he got really angry and began waving his fists and yelling that he was going to close down the inn. Said he was quite capable of doing so, and that it wasn't the first time he'd closed down an establishment for causing him grief."

Cecily sighed. "And then?"

"And then he left. Still shouting threats at me."

"Had he been drinking?"

Michael shook his head. "No, apparently he doesn't drink. In fact, that's what started the entire fiasco. He'd ordered milk, and a couple of the farmers in here began sniggering. One of them said something that amused Simani, and she laughed out loud. You know what a hearty laugh she has."

Cecily nodded, remembering the belly laugh that seemed so incongruous coming from that graceful, statuesque figure.

"Well, anyway, that's what got Malton's goat. The blasted coward turned on Simani, rather than face down the laborers. It was fireworks from then on."

"And you threw him out."

"Like a shot. That's when he started threatening me with closure. I don't mind admitting it, Mother, I was worried. With his connections as a barrister and his influence with some of the wealthiest men in London, he could easily have put me out of business. Not that business is that great, anyway."

Cecily wriggled off the stool. "Well, you won't have to worry about Sir Richard and his threats anymore. As for your customers, they'll come back once the word gets around that the George is open for business again." She gave him a reassuring smile. "Don't worry, darling, it will all turn out for the best, I'm sure. Please say goodbye to Simani for me, and tell her I look forward to her calling on me sometime soon."

Michael nodded but didn't look too optimistic. Cecily left him, wishing heartily that Michael had chosen someone a little closer to home to marry. Baxter could say what he liked, but she couldn't help thinking that maybe there would be more customers patronizing the George if they didn't have to contend with Michael's new wife.

She was barely outside the door before she chided herself for her intolerance and prejudice. At least one question had been verified, she thought, as she allowed Samuel to help her into the trap. Sir Richard Malton had ordered milk at the bar. Lady Lavinia had not been mistaken when she stated that her husband did not drink alcohol.

Frowning, she thought about Michael's confrontation with the dead man. How serious had Sir Richard's threats been? she wondered. And what would have happened to Michael's business if the wealthy barrister had not met with his unfortunate demise? Shaking off her morbid thoughts, Cecily settled back in the trap and prepared to enjoy the drive back to the hotel.

The summer had brought a kaleidoscope of colors to the hedgerows and fields. Bright red poppies, pink foxglove, and mallow crowded with yellow tansy and tiny blue forget-me-nots at the sides of the road.

Passing under the leafy branches of an ancient beech tree, Cecily felt the salty sea breeze brush her cheeks and gently lift the ribbons on her hat. How she loved this season, when the gardens in the Pennyfoot were lush with roses, and the lawns echoed with the smack of a tennis racquet and the hard whack of a croquet ball.

This had been James's favorite season, too, in spite of the extra work it brought with the influx of visitors. And this year was turning out to be no exception.

Cecily's smile faded. How long, she wondered, could they keep the business if they continued to endure the misfortune that seemed to plague the Pennyfoot? Though generally everything invariably seemed to turn out all right in the end, the constant appearances of the constabulary could well be a deterrent to the wealthy citizens who escaped the heat of London to enjoy their privacy at the seaside hotel.

In future, Cecily decided, if, heaven forbid, something else untoward happened, she would have to make every effort to resolve it herself, before sending for the police constable. She was quite sure Baxter would have more than a few words to say about that.

The steady clip-clop of the chestnut's hooves calmed her worries, and she turned her thoughts to the colonel, whose stout figure she could see farther on down the narrow lane that crossed the grassy slopes of Putney Downs.

It would be a shortcut for him, since he was on foot, though sometimes she feared that one fine evening he might wander off the trail and fall over the cliff to the rocks below.

The colonel usually took great pains to ensure he was back at the hotel by nightfall, but there had been an occasion or two when he had forgotten the time and had been forced to walk back in the dark.

Sometimes she wondered how he found his way back at

all. There were even times when, in his confusion, he had
trouble finding his way around the hotel.

Cecily tucked her wrap closer around her shoulders as the
breeze freshened. The colonel's remarks about Simani still
hovered in her mind. Quite ridiculous, of course. Even so,
some people might actually believe the ludicrous state-
ments. Perhaps she should have a word with him and try to
convince him he was mistaken about her daughter-in-law,
though convincing the colonel of anything was a major
undertaking.

She smiled when she remembered his comments about
Madeline. *Miss Pengrath. Super with plants, you know.
Does wonders with weeds and such. Dashed marvelous, I
must say.*

He was right about that. Madeline's expertise with
healing herbs and flowers was quite remarkable. Cecily felt
a pang of guilt when she realized how long it had been since
she'd seen her friend. On impulse, she leaned forward and
called out, "Samuel, I've decided not to go straight back to
the hotel. Would you please take me up to Miss Pengrath's
cottage instead?"

"Yes, ma'am." Samuel touched his hat with his whip, and
Cecily sat back, anticipating with pleasure her visit with
Madeline.

Gertie paused for a moment in the backyard, watching the
sun sink behind the high slopes of the Downs. As the last of
the gleaming yellow globe disappeared behind the hills, the
sky above it darkened to a deep red, then purple. Bloody
beautiful, it was, she thought with a sigh of satisfaction.

Gertie never tired of watching the sunset, though she
would prefer to do it somewhere other than the backyard
behind the kitchen of the Pennyfoot Hotel. Nowadays she
always felt an ache in her heart as she watched another day
fade away.

The baby inside her stirred, and she absently patted her
swollen belly with her free hand. The other held a scuttle of

coal for the stove. In less than four months now, the baby would be born.

Gertie lifted her face to the sky and cursed. Trust her to get bleeding lumbered the very first time she did it. Married in February, and by May Day she'd found out she was bloody pregnant.

Too bad she hadn't waited three months. Too bloody bad she hadn't found out that Ian already had a wife before she'd married him. Too bleeding bad. Now she was stuck with a baby, while he was back in the Smoke with pregnant Gloria, the wife he hadn't bothered to tell her about until he'd given her a flipping bun in the oven.

Gertie sighed, a long drawn-out sound of abject misery. Gloria should be just about ready to drop her baby. Lucky bugger. At least she had a husband.

Not that Gertie particularly wanted a husband. Finished with men, she was. Besides, no one would want her now, not with another man's baby to feed and clothe. No, she was stuck, good and proper. Thanks to that bleeding bastard she'd married.

Scowling, she turned to go back inside. Then her entire innards seemed to turn inside out. Right in front of her was the most horrible sight she'd ever seen. And she'd seen a few. Gertie dropped the bucket of coal, spilling the nuggets across the ground. Then she put her hands over her face and screamed at the top of her lungs.

Madeline opened the door at the first sound of Cecily's rap on the knocker. "I heard the trap," she said, smiling. "I hoped it was you. It has been so long since I've seen you."

"Yes, it has. Much too long." Cecily stepped into the cluttered living room and climbed over baskets of silk flowers, bags of embroidery, and a beautiful needlepoint footstool in order to reach the one armchair in the room.

Madeline made a sparse living creating handmade souvenirs for the tourists and used her living room as a workshop. Stepping into Madeline's house was like walking into an arts bazaar crammed with exquisitely crafted items, from tea cozies and tablecloths to dolls and baby clothes.

Cecily never knew what to expect when she entered the tiny cottage, but each visit brought something new and wonderful to exclaim over and enjoy.

"Can I take your wrap?" Madeline asked as Cecily set her parasol down at her side and gazed around at the bounty of craftwork.

"Thank you, but I'll keep it on for now." She felt a shiver touch her back and couldn't be certain if it was a chill or the memory of Colonel Fortescue's whispered accusation. "It is a little cool in here," she added as if to reassure herself.

"I've had the door open all day." Madeline clasped her hands together, her lovely face wreathed in smiles. "Isn't this the most perfect weather? Clear summer skies and still nights. I just adore it. I can smell the night-scented stock from the bedroom window, and when the breeze is off the sea, I awake to the fresh fragrance of sand and seaweed. Wonderful."

Her low laugh seemed to ripple across the room, and Cecily gazed at her friend with the sense of wonder that never deserted her.

Madeline's youthful appearance belied her age by at least ten years, sometimes more. Her graceful figure and long, flowing black hair belonged more to a young girl than a woman past forty.

There was not too much difference in their ages, but Cecily felt positively ancient compared to her friend. Maybe it was the hair, though Cecily couldn't imagine letting her own long tresses loose from the bun to fall about her shoulders that way.

Yet on Madeline it seemed so natural—if there was anything natural about Madeline. There were many who swore she was a witch, or at the very least a gypsy, possessed of strange and incredible powers.

There was no doubt that Madeline exhibited unusual capabilities, seemingly impossible at times. For some reason a vision of Simani popped into Cecily's mind. It took her a moment or two to heed the question Madeline asked her.

"I'm sorry." Cecily stared up at her friend. "What did you say?"

"Well, well, you look positively bewitched." Madeline peered closer at her. "Are you feeling unwell? Can I get you some herb tea? You look as if you need something to relax you."

"When have I not?" Cecily answered lightly. "I'd love tea, but plain black Ceylon, please. I never did enjoy that brew that you are so fond of."

"Much better for you." Madeline seemed to float across the room, managing to look regal in a soft blue cotton gown that had long ago faded from being hung so many times in the sun to dry. "Herbs can cure so many ills, you know." The bead curtain serving as a door rattled as she passed through, then slowly settled back into place.

Cecily leaned back in the chair and closed her eyes until Madeline returned with a loaded tray in her hands.

"I'm sure you haven't had dinner yet," Madeline said, "so you must be hungry. Help yourself to a Cornish pasty or sausage roll. I picked them up from Dolly's Tea Shop today, so they are quite fresh."

"No, thank you, just the tea." Cecily took the cup and saucer from her. "I'll be dining as soon as I get back to the hotel. I won't stay long this time. I must get back, or Baxter will begin to worry."

"It must be wonderful to have a man to worry about you." Madeline lowered herself to the floor in one fluid movement and tucked her bare feet under the fabric of her voluminous skirt.

Cecily took a sip of her tea before answering. "Oh, you know Baxter, he worries about everything. He's an old fussbudget, but he means well, I suppose."

Madeline's dark eyes rested on Cecily's face. "One day, Cecily, my dear, you will know what is in your heart and in your mind. Don't wait too long, for devotion is only too fleeting and can disappear in a twinkling if neglected."

Well used to Madeline's flowery speeches, Cecily took little notice of the words. "Well, I have more to worry about right now than Baxter's supposed devotion. I'm afraid we've had another death at the hotel."

Madeline's eyes widened. "No one I am acquainted with, I hope?"

"Not unless you were on personal terms with Sir Richard Malton."

"Sir Richard? I know who he is, of course." Madeline replaced her cup in the saucer and wriggled closer. "Tell me what happened. Don't leave out a thing."

Cecily recounted the dramatic death, while Madeline's gaze remained fastened on her face. "Poor Phoebe saw the whole thing," Cecily said after she'd described the fall. "Arthur had to carry her back into the hotel."

Madeline sniffed. "Phoebe always did like to be melodramatic. She falls in a dead faint if a horse steps too close to her."

"Well, I suppose it was more than a little upsetting for her." Cecily shook her head. "I just can't imagine why someone as staid and predictable as Sir Richard would attempt to dance on a railing four stories above the street."

"Well, he wouldn't, of course. Maybe he was bewitched." Madeline leaned forward. "I'm not the only witch around here, you know. There are rumors that the gypsies are back, though no one has seen them."

"Anyone who thinks you are a witch needs his head examined. Knowing how to heal certain ills with plants does not make you a witch. People are always so swift to condemn what they don't understand."

Madeline smiled. "Dear Cecily. Always coming to my defense. Someday I shall repay you for your loyalty. When the time is right."

"Well, I'm not so sure I deserve your benevolence." Cecily stared down at her cup for a long moment. "I'm afraid I should be practicing what I preach. I am as guilty as anyone else for my prejudices."

"You?" Madeline's laugh rang out. "You are the most fair and just person I know."

Feeling a strong urge to share her misgivings, Cecily looked up. "I've just come from the George and Dragon," she said quietly. "I had a talk with Michael. Simani was there, and I'm afraid I might have offended her in some way."

Madeline's response to her confession was totally unexpected. She climbed to her feet, and her voice sounded harsh when she said, "That woman? I loathe and detest her."

Dismayed and bewildered by this adverse reaction, Cecily put her cup down loudly in the saucer. "I'm sorry, I wasn't aware that you had met my daughter-in-law."

"Once." Madeline began pacing around the room, her jerky movements completely at odds with her usual graceful glide. "I met her only once, but that was all that was needed. I knew what she was the moment I set eyes on her."

The flesh on Cecily's arms began to prickle. "Whatever do you mean, what she was?"

Madeline swung around suddenly, making her jump. The younger woman's face seemed contorted in the dancing flames of the gas lamps. "I warn you, Cecily. Get rid of her. As soon as possible. She will bring you and your son nothing but trouble."

"Madeline—" Cecily started to rise, but sat down again when Madeline put a palm up in the air.

"Listen to me, Cecily. If you love your son, you will rid him of this woman. She brings trouble with her. Of the most evil kind."

"I cannot let you say something like that about a member of my family without demanding an explanation," Cecily said firmly, though inside she was shaking like warm jelly. "No matter how great a friend you are, I must ask you to please tell me what you mean by those unkind words."

"Unkind?" Madeline's wide mouth pulled into a grimace

"Cecily, you have no idea what danger Michael could be facing. I beg you, get rid of her. I will help, if you wish."

Cecily's voice trembled when she answered. "I must know why you feel this way about Simani. Please, Madeline, if you value our friendship."

Madeline's mouth tightened. "I cannot tell you how I know what I know. I wish I could. I have no wish to harm our friendship."

"Very well." Cecily straightened her wrap and picked up her parasol. "I must leave now, Madeline. I wish we could have parted on a more pleasant note."

"I'm sorry, Cecily. Please believe me." Madeline pulled open the door. "I hope you will forgive me once you realize that my words are true."

Sitting in the trap a few minutes later, Cecily tried to banish Madeline's voice from her mind. Normally she would dismiss the words, putting them down to Madeline's fanciful notions and her constant talk of spirits and myths.

But this was too close to home. This was threatening her own son. To make matters worse, Cecily herself felt extremely uneasy whenever she was near Simani, though she hadn't been able to determine why.

Much disturbed, she failed to enjoy the trip along the Esplanade as she usually did. Her mind dwelled elsewhere, on Madeline's words and on Michael's relief when he had heard that Sir Richard Malton was dead.

In spite of her efforts to prevent it, the word *witchcraft* kept creeping into her thoughts over and over again.

CHAPTER

6

Mrs. Chubb heaved a loud sigh of relief as she closed the door of Gertie's bedroom. The poor girl had been quite hysterical after the fright she'd had, and it had taken near on an hour and two cups of warm milk heavily spiced with brandy before exhaustion had finally quietened the sobs.

Gertie now lay gently snoring, and Mrs. Chubb could turn her attention to the cause of all the uproar. Taking hold of her skirts, she marched up the stairs to the lobby.

Halfway across the foyer she saw the new doorman sitting behind the reception desk, his nose buried in *The Evening News*. Mrs. Chubb's anger subsided. The culprit could wait.

The foyer was deserted, with most of the staff and guests occupied with the evening meal in the dining room. Unlikely to be interrupted, Mrs. Chubb could foresee a golden opportunity. Patting her hair to make sure no stray wisps escaped from the knot on the crown of her head, the housekeeper swept across the carpet on flying feet.

Arthur Barrett looked up as she reached the counter, and her heart skipped with excitement when his twinkling eyes, the color of a morning sky, smiled upon her face.

"Well, if it isn't the princess herself come to pay me a visit, to be sure," he said in his marvelous rich voice. "What can I be doing for you this fine evening, me fair lady?"

His fair lady. She felt her heart fluttering like a young girl's. Indeed, she felt exactly like a young girl facing a beau for the very first time. Reminding herself that she was a middle-aged woman well past the prime of life, she did her best to calm her silly notions.

"I just wanted to thank you, Mr. Barrett, for coming to Gertie's rescue like that. I don't know what the poor girl would have done had you not been there to take care of her."

"Ah, 'twas nothing, I can assure you. I heard her screaming like a banshee on an Irish moor, and I did what any fine gentleman would do. I rushed out to see what was ailing the poor girl. A strong shoulder to cry on as I led her inside was all that was needed."

Feeling more than a trifle envious of Gertie, Mrs. Chubb said warmly, "Well, she is most grateful, as I am sure she will tell you herself tomorrow when she is feeling a little better." She allowed a smile to peek through. "Perhaps later on, when the night porter arrives, you would care to come down to the kitchen for a spot of tea before you leave?"

The doorman tilted his head to one side and gave her one of his devastating grins. "Well, now, I might be tempted by that gracious offer. Especially if you could see your way clear to adding just a drop of fine Irish whiskey to the brew?"

Mrs. Chubb clasped her hands together to stop them shaking as she pretended to think about it. "I might be able to manage a drop of Scotch whiskey, if that would do?"

Arthur Barrett sighed. "Ah, to be sure, beggars can't be

choosers now, can they? That will be just fine, Mrs. Chubb. Very nice, indeed. Thank you most kindly."

"Oh, not at all, Mr. Barrett. I shall look forward to it." She nodded at him several times, at a loss as to what to say next, while he continued to smile at her in a such a way that she thought she would never catch her breath again.

Then he captivated her completely by saying in a soft voice, "Please, my dear, call me by my Christian name, the way everyone else does. Arthur it is, as you well know."

"I do indeed . . . Arthur. Until later, then." She spun around so fast she almost tripped over the hem of her skirt. Steadying herself, she cast a glance over her shoulder. Arthur still sat there, smiling at her with the face of a Greek god.

"I would like it very much if you would call me Altheda," she said breathlessly.

"Altheda," he repeated, making her name sound like the most romantic word ever invented. "'Tis a pretty name, to be sure. I will be honored and delighted to hear it tripping from my lips. That I will."

"Oh!" Titillated by the thought of anything tripping from his lips, Mrs. Chubb found herself incapable of answering him, which was not like Altheda Chubb at all. She fled instead, across the floor to the stairs, completely forgetting the reason she had come up them in the first place.

When Cecily arrived a few minutes later, Arthur was back at his post by the door. He greeted Cecily with a cheery "Good evening," giving her a roguish smile that might have turned her head twenty years ago. His charm certainly went a long way toward restoring her good spirits. Until he told her what had transpired since she'd left the hotel earlier.

"Lady Lavinia has taken to her bed, ma'am," he said. "She is stricken with grief, poor lady, and is unable to cope with anything. She has left orders not to be disturbed."

"Oh, dear, I was afraid of that." Cecily pulled her wrap from her shoulders and folded it over her arm. "Perhaps I should call the doctor to tend to her. The shock must have been devastating for her."

"I'm sure it must have been, ma'am. But if you'll pardon me for saying, it isn't milady you should be worrying about."

Cecily wrinkled her brow. "Something else has happened?"

"Yes, ma'am." Arthur glanced around the lobby as if making sure they were alone. "It's not my place to be carrying tales, but no doubt you will hear of it sooner or later."

Becoming alarmed now, Cecily said sharply, "What is it, Arthur?"

"It's the boy, Master Stanley Malton, ma'am. He's being a holy terror, begging your pardon."

"What has he done now?"

"I daresay, it's not all his fault, mind. With his father lying dead and his mother taken to her bed, there is no one to discipline the lad. I would venture to say he's had little enough of that as it is. He appears to show very little respect, or grief for that matter. Maybe it hasn't sunk in yet that his dear father has departed to heaven and will not be coming back."

"Maybe so," Cecily said with a touch of impatience. "But I would like to know what the boy has been up to."

"Yes, ma'am." Arthur lifted his hand and began counting off on his fingers. "Well, now, let me see. He ran water into the kitchen sink so that it overflowed. He stuffed newspaper down the lavatory and blocked it. He smeared black boot polish all over the drawing room windows. Then he took the bearskin rug from the floor, draped it over himself, and gave a good many ladies in the hotel an attack of the vapors when he crawled down the corridors growling and snarling like a hungry lion."

"Oh, good Lord."

"That's not all, I'm afraid, ma'am."

Cecily groaned. "There's more?"

Arthur solemnly nodded. "He cornered Gertie in the kitchen yard. He had the bearskin rug over him, and he clutched a baby doll between his teeth. Gertie thought it was a real baby, her being so close to motherhood herself, so to speak. Mrs. Chubb had to calm her down and put her to bed."

"Where is he now?" Cecily asked grimly.

"Locked in the suite with his mother, though how the poor woman will put up with him, her being so ill and all, I shudder to think."

"So do I." She glanced at the grandfather clock in the corner, its face barely visible in the dim light from the gas lamps. "It's too late to do much tonight, but tomorrow I'll have a word with the boy. Maybe we can get someone to keep an eye on him."

"That sounds like an excellent idea, though who will agree to take on that formidable task, I can't imagine."

Cecily shook her head. "Someone will have to do it. I'll take care of it in the morning."

"Perhaps Mr. Baxter can be persuaded to do it," Arthur said, amusement coloring his voice.

A harsh voice rang out behind them, making Cecily jump. "No, Mr. Baxter will most definitely not be persuaded to do it."

She swung around to see Baxter advancing toward her, his face looking like the onset of a thunderstorm.

"I think I hear the trap," Arthur said and stepped smartly through the main door, closing it behind him.

Cecily wrinkled her nose at his desertion, then said brightly to her manager, "I hear there has been some excitement here tonight."

"If you are referring to that brat of a boy," Baxter said stiffly, "then your information is correct. Since you seem to have discussed the matter thoroughly with the doorman, however . . ."

He'd said "doorman" in the tone of voice one would use to describe cow manure.

Cecily winced. "Arthur was merely giving me the details," she said, meeting his brittle gaze with a defensive frown. "As owner of this establishment, I am entitled to be informed, am I not? I really think it matters not who gives me the information. Since Arthur was directly involved with the incident concerning Gertie, I asked him for an explanation. But why I should feel obliged to explain myself to you, I have not the faintest idea."

Baxter stood there without answering, his gaze steady on her face, a muscle twitching in his temple. "I don't like the way he addresses you with such familiarity," he said finally.

Annoyed with herself for allowing him to intimidate her, Cecily said crossly, "Oh, piffle, Baxter. You are just being finicky, and I can't imagine why. If you had been here when I arrived, naturally I would have relied upon you to inform me of the problem. As it was, Arthur was the first person I saw. Now, if you have some quarrel with that, I am sorry, but I have no wish to deal with it tonight. I am tired and I am going to bed."

She waited for what seemed like an eternity. Finally, in a voice so low she could barely hear it, he muttered, "Good night, madam. I trust you will sleep well."

She watched him stride across the floor, his coattails flapping furiously behind him, and she felt a deep ache of regret. How she hated arguing with him. Now she would have to wait an entire night before making peace with him.

She had Stanley Malton to thank for that, she thought as she stomped up the stairs to her suite. Tomorrow she would deal with them both. Baxter and Stanley. And out of the two, she was looking forward to dealing with Baxter the least.

When she awoke the next morning, Cecily decided to tackle Stanley first. Reaching the bottom of the stairs on her way to breakfast, she caught sight of Gertie crossing the foyer, and called out to her.

The housemaid bobbed a clumsy curtsey as she reached her. "Good morning, mum."

"Good morning, Gertie." Cecily peered closer at her flushed face. "Are you feeling better? Arthur tells me you had a nasty scare last night."

"I bleeding did, mum. That little bugger stopped me 'eart, he did. I thought it was a real baby he was chewing on. I'll never forget it. I never saw nothing so 'orrible in all me born days. I could kill the miserable—"

"Gertie!"

The irate voice echoed across the foyer from the direction of the stairs, and Gertie groaned. "I swear that Mrs. Chubb has eyes in the back of her head. Begging your pardon, mum, but I'd better scarper before she has me liver for dinner."

"One minute, Gertie." Cecily raised a hand to detain her. "I don't suppose you know where Stanley is now, do you?"

Gertie drew her eyes together to meet across her nose. "At the bottom of the sea, I wish. Last time I saw him he was scampering out the back door, on his way to the gardens. Probably going to dig up all the bleeding roses, I shouldn't wonder."

Again Mrs. Chubb's voice bellowed up the stairs, and Gertie flinched. "Will that be all, mum?"

Cecily nodded. "Thank you, Gertie. Tell Mrs. Chubb I kept you talking if she complains."

Gertie grinned. "Don't you worry about Mrs. Chubb, mum. Her bark is a lot worse than her blinking bite." She marched off across the foyer, muttering loudly, "Aw right, aw right, keep your bleeding wig on. Cor blimey, there ain't no bleeding peace for the wicked, that there ain't."

Thankful that Mrs. Chubb couldn't hear the housemaid's words, Cecily hurried down the hallway to the gardens beyond.

A loud chorus of birds greeted her as she stepped outside into the cool morning air. Dew sparkled on the smooth lawns and on the branches of the topiary bushes so carefully maintained by John Thimble, the Pennyfoot's amiable gardener.

Cecily glanced fondly at the shrubs, then halted, her eyes widening. The two at the far end of the row had something hanging from them.

Hurrying toward them, Cecily shaded her eyes from the sun to get a better look. She hadn't imagined it. Groaning, she surveyed what could only be the latest handiwork of Master Stanley Malton.

Tied to a lower branch of one bush, a lady's corset swung gently from its laces. The other bush was lavishly adorned with various items of ladies' underwear. A pair of pale orchid drawers flapped in the fresh sea breeze, and silk stockings clung to several branches, like garlands on a Christmas tree.

Gritting her teeth, Cecily headed for the Rose Garden, trying to remind herself that the boy was going through a traumatic time after the death of his father.

She saw John Thimble as soon as she passed beneath the archway. He stood bending over a white rosebush, carefully snipping at it with a pair of shears.

She greeted him warily, wondering how she was going to tell him about the lingerie clinging to his shrubs. John was fanatical about his gardens. He cared more for his plants and shrubs than he did for people. His work was his life, and he lived for nothing else. Cecily decided she wouldn't want to be in Stanley's shoes when John saw what he'd done to his precious topiary bushes.

He answered her greeting with a nod of his head and touched the floppy brim of his hat. John rarely spoke unless it was absolute necessary.

"Have you seen Master Stanley Malton anywhere about?" Cecily asked, not really surprised when John shook his head.

"Haven't seen anyone, m'm."

"Well, never mind. I'm sure I'll find him." Cecily hesitated, then murmured her thanks and left. She would find Stanley and make him remove the articles of clothing, she decided, since he was the one who put them there.

Poor John had never been married. He would be mortified if faced with that array of unmentionables. Stanley was exceptionally devious.

She had almost reached the fish pond when she heard the sound of voices—a shrill young voice, echoed by a deeper hoarse tone that sounded quite desperate.

"Get out of here, you filthy swine! Down boy, down! Stay under cover. By gad, I'll have them!"

Barely recognizing the colonel's voice, Cecily quickened her step.

"There they are, Colonel! Look, over there," the young voice exclaimed.

"Where? Where? Let me at 'em. By George, I'll massacre the rotten blighters."

Again the shrill voice. "Over there, over there, look, look!"

"Where? Great Scott, they are fast little buggers."

"Over there, Colonel. Look out! One of them has a gun!" The shrill words were followed by an agonizing scream.

Cecily broke into a trot and burst through the bushes just as the colonel howled, "Now see what you've done, you despicable degenerates. You've killed him. By God, I'll see you hung, drawn and quartered for this, you damn butchers."

Cecily took in the scene with one swift glance. Stanley lay flat on his back, looking like a bleached whale. Rolls of fat bulged above the waist of his knickerbockers, while a horrible grimace distorted his features and one hand clutched his chest. His eyes were closed tight, and not a muscle in his body moved when the colonel bent over him and patted his cheek.

"Oh, dear God, they've killed him," the colonel moaned, sounding close to tears. "Whatever shall I tell his poor, dear mother?"

Cecily compressed her lips and marched forward. "Stanley," she ordered in her fiercest voice, "get up this instant. I want a word with you, young man."

Stanley opened one eye and hastily closed it again when he saw Cecily glaring at him.

The colonel apparently had not noticed the slight movement. "My dear lady," he yelled, waving his arms about in wild gestures at the woods behind him, "get down, get down! The ugly brutes are in there, getting ready to attack. They've already felled the boy, poor little chap!"

"Colonel—" Cecily began, but the man spun around and, with his back to her, started advancing on the trees.

"Have no fear, old bean, I'll protect you!" Leaping and dancing, he charged forward, emitting a bloodcurdling scream.

A loud snort captured Cecily's attention. Stanley had both hands pressed over his mouth, while his rotund body shook with silent laughter.

Cecily leaned over the sputtering boy and firmly took hold of his arm.

"Ow!" Stanley yelled, much more loudly than was warranted.

"Get up," Cecily said, managing to put a great deal of authority into her quiet tone.

"I am, I am. Let go." He glared at her, his eyes looking too small in his chubby face.

Cecily released her hold, and the boy scrambled to his feet. Anticipating his intentions, she took hold of his arm before he could run. "If you go back to the kitchen now," she said, fixing him with a stern look, "you can ask Mrs. Chubb to give you some blancmange. Tell her I said you could have it."

Stanley's surprised look turned to one of delight. Without another word he lumbered off, his mind apparently on his favorite subject—food.

With a sigh, Cecily went in search of the colonel. She could hardly leave him rushing around the gardens in that state. Heaven only knew what he would do if he encountered one of the guests. She would have to deal with Stanley later, she decided, trying not to feel too murderous toward the boy.

The colonel wasn't terribly difficult to find. Cecily just followed the crashing noises reminiscent of a rhino on the rampage. When she caught up with him, he was bent almost double, brandishing a long stake at a thicket of brambles.

"I can see you, you nasty little devils. Come out and fight, I say. Ghastly cowards, that's what you are, the bloody lot of you."

"Colonel—"

The colonel yelped and jumped back several feet. "Good Lord, madam, whatever are you doing here? Don't you know you are in deadly danger? These little fellows can drop you at fifty feet. They've already got that poor Malton boy. First his father, now the child. That poor, poor woman. Whatever shall I tell her?"

"Colonel, Stanley is perfectly all right. I'm afraid he was playing a trick on you. There's no one here, look."

She began walking toward the brambles, but he thrust an arm ahead of her. "Madam, I implore you."

It took Cecily the best part of an hour to convince him that Stanley had been having a game with him, and that there were no enemies hiding in the woods to kill him or anyone else.

When she finally felt it was safe to leave him, he was pacing up and down muttering that he was going to buy a spell from Madeline Pengrath and turn Stanley Malton into a toad.

Cecily was tempted to help him cast the spell.

CHAPTER

❦ 7 ❦

Stanley was seated at the huge scrubbed wood table when Cecily arrived back at the kitchen. His red face perspiring with the heat from the stove, the boy had both hands around a hunk of bread and cheese, while his jaws worked on the massive bite he'd taken out of the thick sandwich.

In front of him sat a bowl of pink blancmange, and Stanley's eyes remained fixed on the tempting sight while he struggled to finish the mouthful.

At least he was quiet for now, Cecily thought, as she turned her back on him and confronted Mrs. Chubb.

The plump housekeeper seemed more cheerful than usual. Her round face beamed, and her eyes positively sparkled above her flushed cheeks. Even her voice had a lilt in it as she greeted Cecily.

Wondering what had caused this transformation, Cecily

said brightly, "It's nice to see you in such good spirits, Mrs. Chubb."

"Thank you, mum. I am feeling very well at present."

Michel, who was standing at the stove a few feet away, sniffed in a derisive manner. Mrs. Chubb sent him a look that would have stopped an elephant in full charge.

"I have a big favor to ask of you," Cecily said hastily. "Lady Lavinia has taken to her bed, and it might be a day or two before she recovers sufficiently to take care of Stanley."

Mrs. Chubb's smile faltered a little, and a look of wariness crept into her eyes. "Yes, mum?"

"I was wondering if you and your very efficient staff could keep an eye on the boy, just until his mother is feeling a little more capable of handling the task."

"That'll be bleeding never," Gertie muttered, splashing dishcloths into the soapy water in the sink.

From the stove came a loud crash. "*Sacre bleu*," Michel muttered and promptly dropped the saucepan lid to join the pot on the floor.

Mrs. Chubb sent an icy glare over to Gertie, then another at Michel. "We'll be happy to take care of Master Stanley, mum," she assured Cecily, albeit through clenched teeth.

Feeling guilty for saddling the busy staff with such a chore, Cecily left the kitchen to the tune of Michel's crashing and banging. The noise didn't quite drown out the high-pitched giggle from the boy at the table.

"Strewth," Gertie said, as the door closed behind Cecily. "I hope you ain't bleeding expecting me to take care of the little horror. Gawd, in my state of health it would be enough to kill me, that it would."

Stanley turned his head and stuck out a tongue coated with half-chewed bread.

Gertie moaned and put a hand over her belly. "Oh, blimey, I think I'm going to be sick." She gave Mrs. Chubb a pathetic look, but she might have known the housekeeper would take no poppycock from anyone.

"Not on my clean floors, you're not," Mrs. Chubb said

crisply. "So you'd better hold it in until you go outside to get the coal."

At the table Stanley snorted, while Gertie felt a growing urge to pour the dirty dishwater over the bloody kid's head. "Ah, come on, Mrs. Chubb," she said, patting her belly. "Look at me. I ain't got the health and strength to run after the bleeding little twit, honest I haven't."

She winced as Mrs. Chubb folded her hands across her ample breast and in her sergeant major's voice barked, "I'll thank you, Gertie Brown, to watch your tongue in the presence of a child. That kind of gutter language is more suited to the back streets of the slums, and innocent ears should be treated with respect. Especially when they belong to a child of Master Stanley's background."

Stanley swiveled his head around and licked his lips. "So there, wobble belly. Shut your mouth."

Gertie lifted a hand. "Why, you—"

"Gertie!" The housekeeper's warning was drowned out by Michel as he slammed a frying pan down hard on the edge of the stove.

"How am I supposed to create a superb soufflé with all this caterwauling going on?" he demanded, nodding his head so fiercely his tall chef's hat slipped sideways. Straightening the cap, his dark eyes flashed fire at Mrs. Chubb.

Gertie took the opportunity to stick out her own tongue at Stanley, who reciprocated by putting both thumbs in his mouth and pulling down the corners. He then crossed his eyes and waggled is tongue up and down until Gertie quite seriously thought she would chuck her innards up all over the floor.

She snatched her gaze away as Mrs. Chubb said heavily, "I'm sorry, Gertie, but you are the only one I can spare right now to watch Master Stanley. Ethel is busy with the dining room, and in any case she is so scatterbrained lately I wouldn't trust her with the boy."

"I'll do her job," Gertie offered hopefully, but she wasn't too surprised when Mrs. Chubb shook her head.

"No, I want Ethel where I can keep an eye on her." For a moment she looked almost apologetic. "Look at it this way, Gertie. It will be good practice for you."

Michel uttered a short laugh. "*Mon Dieu*, the shock of it will probably be enough to make her give ze baby away to ze very first gypsy that passes by, *non*?"

"Wee," Gertie said with heavy emphasis.

"Nonsense." Mrs. Chubb reached up to the shelf above her head and took down a jar of pickled eggs. "I really don't know what you're both making so much fuss about, so help me I don't. Master Stanley is only a child, after all, and just needs a firm hand."

She gave Gertie a look that was supposed to be inspiring. "Now, I know you are quite capable of doing that, my girl. So don't go giving me any of that drivel that you can't take care of an eight-year-old boy."

Gertie puffed out her cheeks. "Eight-year-old, be blowed. This little monster has enough bloody mischief in him to be eight hundred years old." She turned back to look at Stanley, and instead saw an empty chair. A hasty glance around the kitchen assured her that the boy had left the room.

"Bloody hell," she said. "He's bleeding gorn."

Michel threw his hands up in the air. "Hallelujah."

Gone?" Mrs. Chubb looked wildly around as if she thought the child was hiding somewhere. "Where could he have gone?"

"He must have snuck out when we weren't looking," Gertie said helpfully.

"Then go and find him. I promised madam we'd keep an eye on him. For heaven's sake, find him before he gets us all into trouble."

"Cor bleeding blimey," Gertie muttered as she wiped her hands on her apron. "Why is it always me that 'as to go and do the dirty jobs?"

Mrs. Chubb clicked her tongue. "Just mind you watch that tongue of yours, my girl."

Gertie gave the housekeeper a dirty look as she passed, but Mrs. Chubb had already turned her attention to the pickled eggs. Heaving a sigh, Gertie went off in search of Master Stanley Malton.

"It really is very strange, Baxter," Cecily said, watching the smoke curl up from the end of her cigar. "If Sir Richard Malton did not commit suicide, as his wife is so sure he didn't, and if he wasn't attempting to win a wager, nor was he drinking, what on earth possessed him to balance on that railing?"

Baxter gazed at her across the gleaming library table. Despite the smell of cigar smoke, the faint scent of polish still lingered, mingling with the fragrance of the white roses that stood in a crystal vase in the center of the table.

"There is the possibility that any one of those three reasons could be true," he said, wrinkling his brow as Cecily took a long drag on the cigar. "Lady Lavinia could be lying or could simply not be aware of anything troubling her husband. It would not be the first time a man had kept something from his wife."

"Indeed it wouldn't." Cecily held the cigar over the large silver ashtray at her elbow and tapped it. A thick roll of white ash fell into the receptacle and disintegrated into dust. "In fact, I would venture to say that it is more the rule than the exception. For some strange reason, men are still ignoring the fact that women are human beings, with feelings and sensitivities, not chattels to be used and taken for granted."

Apparently unwilling to enter into an argument with her, Baxter said quickly, "Is it not possible that Sir Richard could have ended his life rather than allow his wife to discover a dreadful secret about him?"

Cecily stared at the roses, noting the way the petals curled so evenly, lovingly overlapping each other. "It's possible,

Baxter. But if Sir Richard did intend to take his own life, I would imagine he would not be feeling too cheerful about the prospect, am I right?"

"I would tend to agree with that, yes, madam."

"Then perhaps you could explain to me why, instead of simply throwing himself over, the usually staid and proper gentleman climbed up onto the railing and not only attempted to walk the length of it, but actually performed a strange little dance. Had it not been for that little jig, Sir Richard might well have survived the experience, so Arthur tells me."

Baxter stretched his neck against his stiff collar. "Arthur Barrett seems to know a great deal about everything."

Cecily sighed. "I really wish I knew why you have such an aversion to our doorman. He is such a pleasant man, always so cheerful. I don't think I've ever seen him without a smile on his face."

"Exactly. What does he have to smile so much about, that's what I want to know. As for the infernal humming and whistling—at times the foyer resembles an aviary."

She looked at him in astonishment. "Has Arthur said or done something to upset you, Baxter? If so, I do think you should tell me about it."

Baxter cleared his throat. "I object to the way he speaks to our guests. Entirely too familiar, in my opinion."

"Well, as long as the guests don't object, I don't see any need to be concerned." She leaned forward. "You're not jealous by any chance, are you, Baxter?"

She watched the flush tinge his cheeks. She had always been of the opinion that her manager looked more distinguished than most in his black morning coat and pin-striped trousers. The color suited him.

Sunlight fell across his face as he stood by the French windows, turning his gray eyes to silver. Eyes that could be so cold, yet they had looked at her on more than one occasion with a warmth that had so comforted and reassured her.

"Jealous?" Baxter said stiffly. "Pray, why in the world would I be jealous of a man like Arthur Barrett?"

"Because he is so popular. Everyone likes him and enjoys chatting with him."

He shrugged, avoiding her gaze. "Perhaps I don't share the public assessment of him. Everyone is entitled to an opinion."

Frustrated, Cecily ground the end of her cigar into the ashtray. "You are right, or course. But until I feel there is good reason to complain, I have no quarrel with Arthur. Now, back to Sir Richard. I do have to question why someone intending to end his own life would be so frivolous about it."

"If he had been drinking . . ."

"But Arthur insisted he could smell no alcohol on the man's breath." She saw Baxter roll his eyes up to the ceiling, and chose to ignore the gesture. "Besides, Lady Lavinia swore her husband couldn't consume alcohol because of his condition. And Michael told me that Sir Richard ordered milk in the bar, earning a great deal of ridicule in the process. Why would someone do that in a bar unless he didn't drink?"

"Why would someone go to a public house in the first place if he didn't drink?"

Cecily looked up at him. "He simply could have been looking for company. A game of darts, maybe?"

"That's possible."

Pleased that they seemed to be on amicable terms again, she smiled at him. "I'll have another word with Lady Lavinia just as soon as she recovers."

"I presume there would be no point in asking you to refrain until after the inspector has conducted his investigation?"

Her smile widened. "None at all, Baxter. We've already been over that."

He nodded. "That's what I thought."

"In any case, I want to speak with Lady Lavinia as soon

as possible." Cecily propped her chin on her hands and gazed at the roses. "I know she will have to stay here until after the investigation, but she will really have to do something about Stanley. I've asked Mrs. Chubb if she can have someone keep an eye on the boy, but I'm not happy about imposing on the staff when they have so much else to do."

"I'm sure Mrs. Chubb will handle matters for you. She is most efficient. Though I have been a little concerned about her lately."

"Concerned? In what way?"

"I can't be sure, but I have a suspicion it has something to do with our new doorman."

Cecily's sigh was pure exasperation. "Baxter, unless you have a legitimate complaint, I really do not care to hear one more word about Arthur Barrett."

Baxter's gaze had turned quite frosty when he looked at her. "Yes, madam. I shall endeavor to remember."

Why, thought Cecily miserably, did they always seem to argue over a member of the staff who had apparently done nothing to deserve Baxter's displeasure?

Her gaze drifted to her late husband's portrait. She stared at James's smiling face, realizing for the first time that she no longer felt the dreadful pain of loss when she thought about him.

She still missed him, of course. But she no longer thought about him a hundred times a day, asking herself what James would have thought about this or that. When had she stopped aching for him? It was hard to remember now.

"If you will excuse me, madam, there are chores that need my attention."

She nodded absently, still caught up in the revelation of her apparent recovery from James's death. She was vaguely aware of Baxter hesitating by the door, but she paid scant attention. Her gaze was on the portrait, and she barely heard the door close gently behind her manager.

*   *   *

Gertie looked up at the white clouds scudding overhead, driven by the fresh breeze from the ocean. It looked as if they might have a bit of rain before long, she thought, as she hurried across the grass toward the woods at the back of the gardens.

She didn't know a lot about eight-year-old children, but something told her that the trees would be a perfect place for a boy to hide while he planned some new mischief. And she was willing to wager her last bloody ha'penny that Master Stanley Malton was up to no good.

Finding him in the middle of all those trees wasn't going to be that easy, neither. She just hoped it didn't start bloody pouring before she found him and dragged him back to the hotel.

It must have taken her the best part of the afternoon before she found him. She'd searched the woods, shouting and threatening until she was hoarse, but had not seen hide nor hair of the flipping kid.

She had finally given up and was on her way back for a well-earned cuppa when she heard someone talking over by the fish pond. The voice caught her attention because it sounded so bleeding weird, like someone in a trance or something.

Creeping up to the bushes that shrouded the pond, she peered carefully around the corner. There was the bloody little horror, kneeling with his back to her, staring at something in the pond.

Her hands fairly itched to give him a good shove. Serve the little bugger right, it would. Him and his big mouth. Who the hell did he think he was, just 'cause his bloody father was a toff?

'Cept he didn't have no father now. Gertie's shoulders relaxed. Poor little bugger. It must be terrible to lose a father like that. All crumpled up on the pavement. It was a blessing Stanley and his mother hadn't seen the body when they came back from the beach. Couldn't have been a pretty sight, that.

Gertie narrowed her eyes as Stanley started mumbling again. She couldn't hear what he was saying, but he seemed intent on something in the pond.

Her lips tightened. Probably tormenting some poor fish or one of the blinking frogs. She'd bloody torment him, dead father or no dead father. Creeping forward, she edged along the side of the pond until she could see what he was doing.

She stopped short, intrigued by the sight. Stanley was leaning over the water, his hand outstretched. From his fingers dangled a gold watch on a chain, and it swung back and forth in a wide arc while the boy seemed to be repeating something over and over again.

He was still too far away for Gertie to hear the words, but for a moment a sharp memory of something sprang into her mind. She struggled with it for a second or two, but then it vanished, and she couldn't get it back.

Shaking her head, she advanced on Stanley, her feet making no sound on the thick grass. She came up behind him, but he was far too engrossed in what he was doing to notice her there.

Placing her hands on her hips, Gertie said loudly, "'Ere, what you up to, then, you bleeding little pest? I've been looking for you—"

She got no further, because Stanley, startled out of his wits, lost his balance and slowly toppled into the water. He landed with an almighty splash and the most piercing shriek Gertie had ever heard in all her born days.

CHAPTER

❊ 8 ❊

For a second or two Gertie stood transfixed by the sight of the boy howling and splashing around like a mad bull in a swamp. He screamed for help, water spitting from his mouth. "Save me! I can't swim! I can't swim!" He made a *glugging* noise, and his terrified face disappeared beneath the water.

Galvanized into action, Gertie leapt for the edge of the pond, leaned over, and grabbed a handful of hair. She gave it a hard jerk, feeling a grim satisfaction when Stanley let out a yell.

"You don't have to swim, you stupid little twit," she said, putting her face close up to Stanley's. "The water only comes up to your bleeding hips. Stand up, dummy, and you'll bloody see for yourself."

Stanley stopped crying and clambered to his feet. Water

poured from him in streams as he rubbed at his eyes with his fists. His normally curly hair lay plastered on his head and shoulders, and his face was streaked with mud, as were his saturated clothes.

"Cor blimey, look at you," Gertie said dismally as she dragged him up onto the grass. "I'll probably get merry hell for this. I'd better get you back to the hotel before you catch your blinking death of cold."

She grumbled at him all the way back, though part of her felt sorry for the little bugger. He never said a word, not even when she told him how bloody stupid he was to think he could drown in two feet of water.

Luckily they met no one in the foyer when they went in. There was no sign of Arthur, who must have gone down for his porridge.

Arthur ate porridge every afternoon. Gertie couldn't even eat the muck in the winter, leave alone in the middle of summer. But then, Arthur was different from any man she'd ever met.

She made it downstairs with the silent boy dripping water everywhere. She'd probably have to go and mop it up once Mrs. Chubb got an eyeful of sogging Stanley, Gertie thought as she pushed open the door to the kitchen.

Sure enough, Arthur sat at the table with a steaming bowl of porridge in front of him. But what surprised Gertie was the sight of Mrs. Chubb, leaning over him with her tits brushing his shoulder while she spooned brown sugar onto the oatmeal.

For a moment or two neither Arthur nor Mrs. Chubb noticed the two figures standing in the doorway. Arthur had his face tilted up, smiling into the housekeeper's flushed face, while she stared lovingly into his eyes.

"I hope that will be sweet enough for you, Arthur," Mrs. Chubb said in a voice Gertie didn't recognize.

"Sure now, won't it be every bit as sweet as the fair hand that sprinkled it," Arthur said softly.

Mrs. Chubb uttered the closest thing to a giggle Gertie

had ever heard from her. "You do have a way with words, Arthur. Enough to turn a lady's head, I'd venture to say."

"Well, it won't be for the want of trying, Altheda. A head as lovely as yours I'd delight in turning, to be sure."

Feeling like gagging, Gertie loudly cleared her throat. Mrs. Chubb sprang in the air like one of Father Christmas's reindeer. "Mercy me," she gasped, clutching her heaving chest. "How you startled me." Her gaze fell on Stanley, and Gertie almost laughed at the look of horror that spread across the housekeeper's chubby face.

"Good God Almighty," Mrs. Chubb cried, holding up her hands in dismay. "Whatever has he gone and done now?"

Stanley, who up until that moment had not uttered one sound, said succinctly and very clearly, "She pushed me into the pond."

Gertie glared down at his dripping head, fighting the urge to slap him one up the side of the ear. "I bloody did not, and you know it. You bleeding fell in."

Stanley's response was to promptly burst into loud and heart-wrenching sobs.

Mrs. Chubb clicked her tongue and bustled over to him. "There, there, ducks, don't cry. We'll soon have you dry. Go and stand by the stove, and I'll make you a nice fat ham sandwich. Would you like that, luv?"

Stanley nodded, his sobs subsiding into a disgusting spate of snorting sniffs. Obediently he slopped over to the stove, leaving a trail of muddy water all across the floor.

Mrs. Chubb folded her arms and fixed Gertie with a baleful stare.

"I didn't do it, honest I didn't," Gertie began. "He was kneeling by the bloody pond—"

"Haven't I already told you a thousand times not to use those repulsive words in front of the child? It's bad enough that *we* have to put up with it, but I will not allow innocent ears to be abused by that dreadful language."

"You ought to hear what he says sometimes," Gertie said hotly. "Bloody hell make your hair stand on end, it would."

"Ger-tay!"

Gertie recognized that tone of voice only too well. She sent a glare at Stanley, who stood with his back to the stove, watching the proceedings with great interest.

Secure in the knowledge that the housekeeper couldn't see him, he lifted his fingers to his nose and waggled them at Gertie.

"As for letting him fall in the pond," Mrs. Chubb went on relentlessly, "it is your fault for not taking better care of him. What madam would say if she saw him, heaven only knows. God help you when you get a child of your own, Gertie Brown. You'll have to have your wits about you then, that's for sure."

Behind her, Stanley was pulling the most horrible faces Gertie had ever seen. She looked over at Arthur for support, but he was watching the little bugger with a huge grin spread all over his face.

Gertie's resentment ignited into a hot fire of outrage. She compressed her lips and threw her shoulders back while Mrs. Chubb went on ranting and raging for several more seconds. Then, as if remembering whose almighty presence sat at her kitchen table, the housekeeper turned off the torrent of rebuke and lowered her voice.

"Well, the harm's been done, so it's too late to say anything now. Just get a mop and a bucket and clean this mess up. I suppose it's all the way across the foyer, too?"

Gertie nodded defiantly, her heart filling with revenge.

"I expect it to be spotless when I come and inspect it later," Mrs. Chubb snapped. Then she turned her back on Gertie and in a completely different voice said to the still-grinning doorman, "I'm so sorry, Arthur. Sometimes these girls are enough to try a saint, so help me. Please get on with your porridge before it gets cold, and I'll make you a nice cup of tea."

Released from her torment, Gertie stomped across the kitchen to the scullery to get a mop and bucket. *I'll make you a nice cup of tea,* she mimicked in her mind.

What about poor Gertie? she thought, slapping the mop inside the bucket with such force it threatened to put a hole in it. She didn't get no bleeding tea. No, what she got was a bloody tongue-lashing and most likely a backache from mopping the bleeding floor, that's what.

And it was all thanks to that flipping kid. Well, she was going to get even with that rotten, horrible Stanley if it was the last bleeding thing she did.

Conjuring up all kinds of torture in her mind, she trudged off to clean up the foyer.

Cecily climbed the stairs to the second floor, hoping that Lady Lavinia would not be too ill to see her. According to Mrs. Chubb, the woman refused to see a doctor, preferring instead to be left alone to handle her grief in her own way.

While Cecily respected that, there were one or two questions that remained unanswered, and time was of the essence if she were to make some sense of Sir Richard's death before Inspector Cranshaw arrived to question everyone.

Reaching the door of the Marltons' suite, Cecily gave the paneling a gentle tap. "It's Mrs. Sinclair, Lady Lavinia," she called out softly. "I just wanted to enquire as to how you are feeling and if you need anything."

After a pause a weak voice called out, "You may enter, Mrs. Sinclair. I'm in bed and can't come to the door."

Cecily pushed the door open and peeked in. Lady Lavinia reclined on the bed in a swirl of pink satin sheets. The lace curtains of the canopy were drawn back, allowing the sun to fall across the satin and lace bedspread, and a book lay open near her pale, fragile-looking hand.

"I'm sorry," Cecily said, advancing into the room. "I don't wish to disturb you, but I was a little concerned when I heard that you had declined to see a doctor."

Lady Lavinia shook her head. "I do hate being pulled around by doctors, especially ones I don't know." She made an effort to sit up, then fell back on the lace-edged pillows.

"I do hope Stanley isn't being too much trouble. He was getting very restless being cooped up in this room, and he promised me faithfully that he would behave if I let him play outside."

"Master Stanley is quite all right," Cecily assured her, crossing her fingers behind her back. "He is being looked after by the kitchen staff and seems to be enjoying the attention."

"I hope he isn't eating too much." Lavinia stared up at the roof of the canopy. "That boy seems to put on weight just by looking at food."

He does more than look at it, Cecily thought, remembering Stanley's demolishment of the bread and cheese. "I'm sure Mrs. Chubb will keep an eye on him." She pulled up a padded velvet chair and sat down on it. "I'm concerned about you, however. Have you been eating?"

Lavinia moved her head as if it weighed a ton. "I'm not interested in food right now."

"Perhaps if I sent up something light later on?"

"Perhaps." Lavinia sighed. "There doesn't seem much point to it all, does there?"

Cecily frowned. She felt a very deep sympathy for the poor woman, but Lavinia had a son to think about now. She just couldn't give up on everything.

"I mean," Lavinia went on, "when one thinks how easily life can be taken away from us, it makes one wonder why we struggle so hard to preserve it."

Cecily leaned forward, her ears suddenly alert. "Taken away from us?"

"Well, yes. I mean, there Richard was, hale and hearty and seemingly happy with his life, and in a few seconds . . ." She waved a limp hand. "Poof! He's gone. Like blowing out a candle."

Cecily tensed. "So what do you think happened?" she said quietly.

Lavinia's eyes looked feverish when she turned toward

Cecily. "Who knows what happened? Black magic, if you ask me. Something made him do it. I wish I knew."

"Did he meet with anyone the night before?"

Again Lavinia's head moved from side to side. "He was with me all evening. And in the morning, until Stanley wanted to see the Punch-and-Judy show. Richard hates . . . hated the sands. He always said it made him feel itchy for days. I wasn't going to go without him, but Stanley threw a tantrum, and Richard was so restless I thought it would give him an hour or so of peace and quiet."

"How was he restless?"

Cecily waited while Lavinia apparently considered the question.

"I don't know," she said at last. "Just the way he was acting. He kept looking at his watch, as if he had an appointment to keep."

"Was he planning on meeting someone?"

"No, I don't think so." Lavinia closed her eyes. "He never left the hotel, until he fell from the balcony. And there couldn't have been anyone with him. The door was locked from the inside. Mr. Barrett had to force the lock to open it for me."

She raised her head for a second or two then let it drop. "I suppose I should have the lock repaired," she murmured.

"I'll have Samuel take care of it," Cecily said, staring at the door. "Mr. Barrett must have forgotten to inform me the lock was broken."

"Oh, that's probably my fault." Lavinia's voice had softened to a whisper. "I told him not to worry about it. I didn't want anyone messing around with it and making a lot of noise. I just . . . wanted . . . to be . . . alone."

Quietly Cecily rose from the chair and crossed to the door. Leaving Lavinia resting peacefully, she let herself out into the hallway and gently closed the door again.

Noise or no noise, she would have to have the lock repaired, she thought as she descended the stairs. The guests and their property were her responsibility while they stayed at the hotel, and she couldn't take the chance of allowing something to be stolen from the room while Lady Lavinia slept.

Reaching the main floor, she went in search of Baxter, knowing she could put off no longer the need to reconcile their differences.

She finally found him out in the stable yard, discussing the condition of the traps with Samuel. The young footman doffed his hat as Cecily approached, then settled it on his head again.

"Samuel," Cecily said, without delay, "I understand the lock is broken on the door of suite five. Lady Lavinia is resting in her room at the moment, but after you have finished your chores here perhaps you could take Ethel with you and repair the lock? Just make sure you have milady's permission to work on it first."

"Yes, mum." Samuel looked worried. "What if she don't want me to work on it?"

"Then explain to her that it is the policy of this hotel to keep all locks in good working order. It is for her own protection, as well as her privacy. I don't think she will be too difficult about it."

"Very well, mum."

Cecily could feel Baxter's gaze on her face, but she continued to watch Samuel as he strode toward the stables where the horses were waiting to be fed and watered.

"I wasn't aware that the lock was broken on the Maltons' suite," Baxter said, sounding a little strained.

"Neither was I until a few minutes ago." She finally looked at him and found him regarding her with a grave expression. "So Arthur didn't say anything to you about it?"

He looked surprised. "No, was he supposed to say something to me?"

"Not particularly. I just wondered why he hadn't mentioned it to one of us, that's all, considering he was the one who broke it."

Baxter raised an eyebrow. "Are you telling me that Arthur

Do-No-Wrong Barrett actually neglected to report an infraction?"

Cecily gave him an exasperated look. "You are being childish, Baxter."

"Yes, madam."

"Arthur had no choice in the matter. The door was locked from the inside and had to be forced open."

"I understand, madam."

"I'm glad you do."

"I merely wonder why he didn't ask for the skeleton keys to open the door, instead of forcing it."

"He most likely did not want to leave Lady Lavinia standing there, since she was obviously overwrought at the time."

"That doesn't excuse him for failing to report the matter."

"Lady Lavinia requested that he not worry about it. She didn't want to be disturbed by the noise."

"I see, madam."

"I thought you would, Baxter."

"Was it not his place, however, to report the incident, as well as Lady Lavinia's concerns for privacy?"

Cecily stared at him in frustration for a full ten seconds. Then she saw the corner of his mouth twitch, and, in spite of herself, felt her mouth widening into a smile.

"Yes, of course, Baxter. You are right. I shall take care to chastise Arthur for his negligence in this matter." Warmed by his answering nod, she felt as if the sun had reappeared after a lengthy spell of cloudy skies.

"That will be most gratifying, madam."

"Don't get too smug about it," she said lightly. "It's not a criminal offense, and he still has a job here."

"Yes, madam." He sounded suitably quashed, but she could see a twinkle in his eye, and a smile still lurked at the corners of his mouth.

"The interesting point this matter raises is that there could not have been anyone with Sir Richard at the time of his death, since the door was locked from the inside," she said, feeling a great deal happier than she had all day.

"That would indeed appear to rule out the possibility of an intruder." Baxter stroked his chin, looking thoughtful. "And so that leaves us with what?"

Cecily shook her head. "I wish I knew, Baxter. I wish I knew. The more I learn about this case, the more puzzling it becomes. And I'm very much afraid that Inspector Cranshaw will come to the same conclusion, which means he will most likely be skulking around the hotel for days, poking into this and that and unsettling everyone with his questions."

"It would appear that way, madam."

"I have to solve this puzzle, Baxter. And as soon as possible." She looked up at him, her usual confidence deserting her. "The problem is, I just don't know where to look this time. I seem to have reached a dead end."

For once he could find nothing to say to console her. This time, Cecily thought dismally, it looked very much as if she had lost the game.

Unless something turned up very quickly, she might well lose some very well paying customers. Customers she couldn't afford to lose. The Pennyfoot Hotel, it would seem, was on very shaky ground.

"Can you bloody believe that little snot-nosed horror?" Gertie demanded as she and Ethel scrubbed the carpet in the foyer.

Actually Gertie had been surprised by Ethel's offer to help, seeing as how the girl was supposed to have the afternoon off. When Gertie had asked why she wasn't taking it, Ethel had made some casual remark about having nothing to do.

Gertie surmised that she'd had a row with Joe and wanted something to do to take her mind off it. Gertie was only too pleased to oblige, her needing someone to unload all her woes upon, so to speak.

She'd related the entire story to Ethel, who had nodded and tutted and made sympathetic noises in general at intervals. Gertie still had the feeling she didn't have her friend's full attention, however.

"I can't imagine what he was bloody doing by that pond," she said, thinking about the strange scene she'd witnessed. "Talking to himself he was, muttering like he was in some kind of trance." She paused and sat back on her heels, her scrubbing brush held poised in midair.

"You know, Ethel, there was something about that whole thing that reminded me of something, thought I can't for the bleeding life of me remember what it was."

She frowned, grasping for the elusive memory, then shook her head. "I tell you, this flipping pregnant business is making an old woman out of me. Can't remember me own name sometimes, I can't."

She looked at Ethel, who worked her brush back and forth as if she were trying to put a hole in the carpet. "You're not listening to me again, are you?" Gertie demanded.

Ethel stopped scrubbing and looked up. "What?"

Gertie sighed. "When are you going to tell me what's the bloody matter with you? Am I your best friend or aren't I?"

To Gertie's utter dismay, Ethel's face crumpled. Uttering a loud sob, she sprang to her feet, dashed across the foyer to the door, and fled through it, leaving Gertie staring open-mouthed after her.

CHAPTER

❖ 9 ❖

Inspector Cranshaw arrived at the hotel shortly after the dinner hour that evening. As usual, it had taken him an entire day to take care of business in Wellercombe, which he deemed far more important than anything that had happened in Badgers End. Ethel was sent up to summon Cecily, who was resting in her suite, her feet up on the ottoman and the latest copy of *The Tatler*, the society magazine, open on her lap.

Cecily was not happy to be disturbed. She had been engrossed in an article about suffragettes who were on a hunger strike in prison, and to have to leave it to meet with the police irritated her no end.

Inspector Cranshaw waited for her in the library. He was a tall thin man with a permanent disagreeable expression on his sharp features, and the moment he set eyes on her he stated crisply, "I would like a word with the widow." His tone of voice clearly indicated he would not listen to objections.

Even so, Cecily felt obliged to mention the fact that Lady Lavinia was resting in her room and did not wish to be disturbed.

"I do not doubt that, Mrs. Sinclair. This is a death with unusual circumstances, however, and as such must be investigated. That is the law." He looked down at her when he spoke, as if daring her to argue.

Realizing the futility of such foolhardiness, Cecily nodded. "Very well. Perhaps you would like me to accompany you as chaperon? I think Lady Lavinia would prefer my presence rather than one of the housemaids."

He regarded her suspiciously for a moment, while P.C. Northcott stood behind him, sniffing and shuffling the pages of his notebook in a vain attempt to look officious. Then, with a brief nod of his head, the inspector stalked out through the doorway, followed by the constable.

Baxter, who had stood by the door the entire time and had been totally ignored by both policemen, rolled his eyes in disgust.

Cecily smiled at him, knowing that her manager's contempt was for the ill manners of the policeman in preceding her. She gave a slight shake of her head as she passed Baxter, warning him to say nothing.

Outside in the hallway the inspector stood waiting, impatiently tapping his foot. P.C. Northcott gave her an anxious look, as if concerned that she would arouse his superior's ire and put him in a bad mood.

That wouldn't be too difficult to do, Cecily thought, as she led both men to the stairway. No one spoke as the three of them made their way up the staircase to the second floor.

Below in the foyer a group of guests stood laughing and chatting, having just finished their evening meal. Cecily looked down on them as she turned the bend in the staircase and caught a swift movement in the corner.

Stanley, for some reason, stood wedged behind the grandfather clock, staring intently across the foyer at the front door. Glancing across, Cecily could see no reason for his rapt attention. She continued on up the stairs, hoping fervently that the boy wasn't planning any more mischief.

Her light tap on the door of suite five went unanswered. After sending an apologetic look at the inspector, Cecily tried again, harder this time. "It's Mrs. Sinclair, Lady Lavinia," she called out. "I'm here with Inspector Cranshaw. He wishes to have a word with you about the circumstances of your husband's death."

She was rewarded with a faint sound from inside the room, which sounded more like a moan than an invitation. Just to make sure, she tapped again, while the inspector uttered an irritable sigh.

Once more the moan answered her knock. "I think she might be sleeping," Cecily said hopefully.

"Then I am afraid we must awaken her." Inspector Cranshaw peered down at her, his eyes looking hard and uncompromising in the flickering light of the gas lamps.

"Of course," P.C. Northcott echoed, nodding his head.

The inspector silenced his subordinate with one quelling glance.

Cecily hoped that Samuel hadn't repaired the lock yet, making it necessary for Lady Lavinia to climb out of bed to open the door. Carefully she twisted the doorknob and was relieved when it turned. She quietly opened the door and peered in.

Lavinia appeared to be suitably covered, and after announcing the names, Cecily opened the door wider for the inspector to pass through. Northcott followed him, looking decidedly nervous.

Cecily waited just inside the door as the inspector approached the bed. "I am deeply sorry for your loss, milady," he said, actually sounding it. "I regret the necessity to disturb you at this time, but there are some important questions I must ask. I hope you will forgive the intrusion?"

Irritated by this change of attitude in the presence of aristocracy, Cecily listened while the policeman questioned the widow. It soon became apparent that he would get nothing intelligent from her.

Lady Lavinia appeared to be rambling, uttering barely discernible, disjointed sentences, revealing nothing more than Cecily already knew.

P.C. Northcott seemed to have some difficulty jotting down notes, and Cecily felt sorry for him. Trying to follow that meandering voice was bad enough, but knowing he would get it in the neck for not getting everything down exactly as it was said was bound to be unsettling him.

Finally the inspector straightened. With a quick nod at the constable he left the room, again followed by Northcott. Cecily sent a worried glance over at the bed, where Lavinia lay restlessly moving her head from side to side and quietly talking to herself.

Her words were unintelligible, and after a moment Cecily left the room to find the policemen waiting for her.

"I should like to question the witnesses," Inspector Cranshaw said while the constable feverishly looked over his notes.

"You will find Arthur at his post at the front door," she told him. "I'm afraid you will have to talk with Mrs. Carter-Holmes at the vicarage." She couldn't help wondering what Phoebe would say when the police arrived on her doorstep. Phoebe's concern for her "image" was legendary.

After watching the policemen go in search of Arthur, Cecily made her way to the kitchen. She had one more task to take care of, and then she intended to pay a visit to Baxter's study. She very badly needed a cigar.

Gertie stacked another plate on the pile of dishes on the draining board, her mind still dwelling on Ethel's unexpected outburst of tears. It wasn't like Ethel to keep things to herself, especially from her friend. Something had to be wrong. Something between her and Joe, more than likely.

Gertie felt immeasurably sad. She knew what it was to lose the man you loved. She just hoped her friend and her man could patch things up again. She knew how much Ethel loved Joe. She'd seen them together. They had reminded her of Ian and herself, and how things used to be, before she went and got married and then found out he'd already got a wife.

A tear trickled slowly down Gertie's cheek and plopped into the water. She dashed at the trail it left with a soapy hand, swearing when she dabbed a lump of soapsuds on her face.

Behind her she could hear Mrs. Chubb rattling around in the pantry, while Stanley sat at the table, drawing on a slate with colored chalks. He was blessedly quiet for a change. Too bloody quiet.

She whipped her head around, just in time to see him creeping back to his chair. "'Ere," she demanded, "whatcha bleeding up to, then?"

He curled his lip at her. "I'll tell Mrs. Chubb what you said."

Gertie stuck a fist on her hip. "You do, you nasty little perisher, and I'll pull all your hair out."

"Yeah? Well, I'll cut off all your fingers."

"I'll cut your bleeding tongue out, then you'll have to shut up."

"You won't be able to because you won't have any fingers."

"I'll do it with my bleeding feet if I have to."

He stared at her, as if fascinated by the idea. "You've got soap all over your face," he said at last.

Gertie wiped her face with the back of her hand. "At least it's flipping clean."

Stanley screwed his eyelids almost shut. "My father always said that scullery maids aren't worth the dirt they walk upon."

"How would he blinking know? I bet he's never been near a scullery maid in his life."

"We have scullery maids at home."

"I expect you do. But you have a housekeeper, too, don't you? She's the one what tells the scullery maids what to do."

Stanley shook his head. "I have seen my father talking to them, lots of times. Mostly in the bedroom, when he showed them how to make the bed."

Gertie's eyes widened. "Go on," she said, intensely interested in this revelation. "How did they make the bed, then?"

"They lay on the bed to smooth out the sheets."

She burst out laughing. "Cor blimey, that's a good one, that is. Wherever did you hear that, then?"

Stanley's face got very red. "My father told me, and he knows everything. So there. He saw me looking one day, and he told me that's what they do."

"Fast thinking, that were." Gertie held her sides, laughing uproariously.

"Stop laughing," Stanley demanded, banging the table with his fist. "I'll tell Mrs. Chubb."

"You'll tell Mrs. Chubb what?" the housekeeper demanded from right behind Gertie's ear.

Gertie stopped laughing. "Don't ask," she said, turning back to the sink. "It will singe your bloody ears, it will."

"She was laughing at me," Stanley said, sounding close to tears. "I was telling her about my father, and she laughed."

"Gertie, how could you, after what happened to his father? How could you do such a thing?"

Sighing, Gertie turned to face Mrs. Chubb. As she did so, a slight movement over by the stove caught her attention. At first she thought she'd imagined it, but then a faint clink confirmed it.

"'Ere," she said, pointing with a shaking finger, "that saucepan lid moved all by itself."

Mrs. Chubb's mouth tightened. "Don't think you're going to put me off like that, my girl. That was a terribly insensitive thing you did—"

Gertie squeaked as the lid popped again, settling with

another clink. "There! Didn't you bloody hear it? I told you I saw it. Look at it."

"Don't be daft," Mrs. Chubb said, flicking a glance over at the stove. "Lids don't—" She stopped short as the lid raised a half inch, then settled again with a loud clink.

"Oh, Gawd," Gertie said in a hushed voice, "we've got bleeding ghosts."

Mrs. Chubb snorted. "There are no such things as ghosts."

"Miss Pengrath says there is." Gertie stared at the lid and squeaked again when it popped up.

Mrs. Chubb clicked her tongue and marched across the kitchen, making Gertie's insides go cold and clammy.

"Don't touch it!" she yelled. "If you let it out we'll all be cursed."

"Nonsense." Mrs. Chubb grasped the lid and raised it, then dropped it on the floor with a crash as something leapt from the saucepan and landed on the floor.

The little green thing sat for a moment, blinking slowly in the light from the oil lamp, then it bounded forward, heading straight for the pantry.

"Great heavens, it's a frog," Mrs. Chubb exclaimed, and dashed after it to slam the pantry door. "I'll have to get Arthur to go in there and catch it."

Slowly Gertie's heart relaxed its pounding. She turned and looked at Stanley, who sat quietly at the table, his face a mask of innocence.

"You bleeding little horror," she said, shaking her head in disgust, "you brought that back from the pond with you, didn't you?"

Stanley looked at her and opened his eyes wide. "Who, me?"

"Dear God," Mrs. Chubb said mournfully, "just look at the state of this saucepan. It's Michel's best, too. We'd better get it cleaned up before he sees it like this, or there'll be ructions, that's for sure."

She started across the floor toward the sink, then her foot

slipped on something, and she slid sideways. The saucepan flew out of her hand and skidded across the floor, smashing into the opposite wall with a resounding crash.

Gertie caught her breath as Mrs. Chubb clumsily regained her footing. "What on earth is that on the floor?" she said, peering down at her feet. Lifting her skirts, she ran a finger across the tile, then peered at it. "Butter. It looks as if someone dropped a pat of butter on the floor. Look, here's another one. And another."

Gertie looked at Stanley and gritted her teeth. "I just wonder who did that."

"Well, we'd better get this mess cleared up," Mrs. Chubb said with a sigh. She cast an eye on the clock sitting on the mantelpiece above the stove. "I think it's time a little boy went to bed."

"No," Stanley wailed, "I don't want to go to bed. It's not dark yet."

"It's going to be bleeding dark when I lock you in the coal cellar," Gertie muttered as she bent to retrieve the saucepan.

"Oh, give me that." Mrs. Chubb held out her hand for the pan. "That's Michel's favorite saucepan. It's the only one that doesn't have a dent in it."

"It flipping well does now." Gertie held the pan up to the light, revealing the large dent in the side.

"Oh, Lord, we'll pay for this." Mrs. Chubb took the pan and made a vain effort to straighten out the indentation.

Gertie didn't answer. She was busy on her hands and knees cleaning up the butter.

For once Stanley was quiet, probably afraid he'd be sent to bed if he made any more noise. With a groan Gertie climbed to her feet and moved over to the sink to empty the dirty water. "Gawd," she mumbled, "you've certainly caused me a lot of grief today, I can tell you. I'll be bloody glad when this day is over, that I will. I'm that tired—"

Yawning, she wiped her hands on her apron and sank into the nearest chair with a sigh of relief. Something beneath her cracked and rustled. Puzzled, she got to her feet again and looked down at the chair.

A giggle exploded behind her as she stared at the smashed egg, half of which she knew had to be clinging to the back of her skirt.

That was the last straw. Full of fury, she advanced on Stanley, who leapt from his chair and made for the door.

Before Gertie could reach him, he'd tugged it open and hurtled through. She heard his footsteps pounding along the hallway, and then up the stairs. Good riddance, she thought, slamming the door shut on the sound.

Mrs. Chubb emerged from the pantry and looked around the kitchen. "Where's Stanley?"

"Gone to bleeding drown hisself, I hope," Gertie said, twisting her shoulders around so she could look at the mess dripping from her skirt. "Look at this." She turned her back on the housekeeper. "That little bugger put an egg on me chair and waited for me to sit in it. I'm going to kill that bleeding kid when I get me hands on him, so help me I am."

"No, you are not," Mrs. Chubb said quietly. "We have to make allowances for him. He's had a terrible shock and he's only acting out his grief."

"Acting it out? He's bloody giving all of us grief." Gertie stomped over to the sink and grabbed a dishcloth. Holding it under the tap, she turned on the water and saturated the cloth. Dabbing ineffectively at her skirt, she added, "I'll be bloody glad to get rid of him, that I will. When is his bloody bedtime, anyway?"

As if to answer her question, the door opened, and Cecily walked in with an anxious frown on her face. "Oh, Mrs. Chubb," she said, "I'm so glad you're here. I'm afraid that Lady Lavinia is not at all well. I don't like to send Master Stanley up there while she's like that. Do you think you could find a space for him down here for the night?"

A short silence greeted her words, and she added a little sheepishly, "Perhaps his mother will be better in the morning."

"He's not bleeding sleeping with me," Gertie said, turning to show Cecily the back of her skirt. "Look what that little perisher did to me. Stuck a bleeding egg on me chair, he did."

"Gertie," Mrs. Chubb said warningly.

"And he put a bloody frog in Michel's best saucepan. Dropped butter on the floor—"

"Gertie," Mrs. Chubb said again, louder this time.

"Mrs. Chubb slipped and dropped the saucepan, and now there's a bleeding big dent in it—"

"Ger-tay!"

Gertie clamped her mouth shut.

Mrs. Chubb gave Cecily a tight smile. "I'm sorry, mum, there's been a spot of bother down here, but it's all right now. We've taken care of it."

"I'd like to bloody take care of it," Gertie muttered.

"Gertie," Mrs. Chubb said in a voice that would have cut through steel, "go and find Master Stanley at once. Bring him back here, and make sure he stays here while I go and make up a bed in Samuel's room. If there's any more trouble, it will be on your head."

Something seemed to snap in Gertie's brain. She'd taken all she was going to take. With pure murder in her heart, she went once more in search of Master Stanley Malton.

CHAPTER

❖ 10 ❖

Cecily was pleasantly surprised when Madeline called in at the hotel the next morning. The slender woman looked almost ethereal in a large-brimmed hat and a frothy gown of lavender gauze that swirled around her ankles, revealing matching silk shoes.

Madeline had never talked much about her past, but Cecily knew she had lived with a much older man for many years. Apparently he had rescued her from the streets when she was very young and had taken her in.

Although he had taken good care of her, feeding and clothing her by all accounts, Cecily suspected that Madeline had paid a heavy price for her benefactor's benevolence.

Whatever had transpired in their relationship Cecily could only guess. Madeline was now alone and without any means of supporting herself except for the handcrafts she sold to the gift shops and the occasional interior decorating she did for Cecily at the hotel.

And the potions. That was something else Madeline rarely spoke about, perhaps because her talents with herbs and flowers had earned her such an adverse reputation. People, for the most part, were afraid of Madeline and her strange powers.

There had even been times when she had unsettled Cecily, though, of course, Cecily would never admit that to her friend.

Madeline announced that she had come to discuss the flower arrangements for the ball and seemed more than eager to make amends. Pleased that the slight discord between them seemed to have been settled, Cecily gladly accepted her invitation for lunch. She was particularly gratified when Madeline added that the treat was to make up for their disagreement.

"I don't see enough of you," Madeline said as they settled themselves in the trap. "I certainly don't want to spend our time together quarreling."

"Neither do I." Cecily looked out across the crowded beach to where the sea lay shimmering beneath a cloudless sky. "I'm so glad the good weather is holding. This has been our busiest season in years, and we have the heat wave to thank for that. The city can be so miserable when it's hot."

"It can indeed." Madeline let out a sigh. "We are so fortunate to be living here on the coast, to enjoy the fresh sea breezes."

"Even if they do turn into gales in the winter." Cecily laughed. "But I do agree. Badgers End has to be the most perfect place to live in the whole of England."

She cast an appreciative eye on the elegant pastel gowns and matching parasols that adorned the ladies strolling along the sands. While the children frolicked in the ocean, several adults stood at the water's edge, chatting amongst themselves.

Further down the beach the brightly striped awning of the

Punch-and-Judy show stood outlined against the chalky cliffs, and sea gulls wheeled and swooped overhead, ever on the lookout for a tasty morsel dropped from a careless hand.

Deck chairs were scattered all across the beach, and gentlemen slept with handkerchiefs draped over their faces to protect their skin from the burning rays of the sun.

In the distance Cecily could hear the faint sound of music carried on the ocean breeze, heralding the orchestra playing in the bandstand further down the Esplanade.

Yes, she thought, feeling a little rush of pleasure, this was indeed a wonderful place to live. The only thing that was missing was someone with whom to share it.

An image of a square-cut face with cool gray eyes popped into her mind for some reason. Uncomfortable to be thinking about Baxter in that context, Cecily said brightly, "I haven't been to Dolly's Tea Shop in quite a while. This is a most pleasant surprise."

"I'm sure it will be crowded, this being the height of the season. I never can understand how Dolly gets so many people crammed into that tiny space." Madeline grabbed hold of her hat as the breeze threatened to dislodge it.

She had apparently forgotten to pin it securely, as Cecily had done with hers. But then Madeline had no bun to pin it to, preferring to wear her hair loose and flowing over her shoulders.

Cecily thought about Simani and her short hair. It would be nice to have her own hair shorn off, so much cooler and infinitely easier to manage. She could just imagine Baxter's expression should she do something so drastic. He would no doubt have a great deal to say on the subject, none of it complimentary.

"What are you looking so gleeful about?" Madeline said, sounding more than a little curious.

Cecily shrugged. "I was wondering how I would look with my hair cut off."

She almost laughed at Madeline's shocked expression. Fortunately the trap pulled up in front of Dolly's before

Madeline could comment on her friend's outrageous suggestion.

After instructing Samuel to return in an hour, Cecily led the way to the door of the tea shop. The High Street was thronged with visitors, most of them peering into shop windows or trudging along the pavement with their arms loaded with an assortment of buckets and spades, large rubber balls, fluttering paper windmills, and cumbersome fishing nets just waiting to snare an unsuspecting creature of the sea.

The tinny bell jangled on its hook when Cecily pushed the door open and stepped inside. A ripple of voices filled the room, couples murmuring over steaming cups of fragrant coffee and tea, friends enjoying the delectable cakes and pastries that had made the tea shop such a thriving business.

Dolly herself greeted them as Cecily and Madeline approached the counter. "Well, I do declare. You ladies are a sight for sore eyes, I must say. I was beginning to think you had lost your appetite for my currant buns." Her heavy jowls wobbled as her raucous laugh rang out.

"Never, Dolly," Cecily assured her and followed the bulky figure as she squeezed past the tables, muttering apologies for nudging the occasional elbow with her massive hips.

Settled at a table by the window, Cecily removed her gloves and tucked them into the prongs of her parasol. "I think I shall order the Ploughman's Lunch," she announced. "That drive along the Esplanade has really given me an appetite."

Madeline shook her head. "Not for me. I just adore Dolly's Eccles cakes, and if I eat all that cheese and pickled onions I'll have no room left to enjoy the cakes."

Cecily sighed. "You are right, of course. What is the point of coming to Dolly's if you don't sample her incredible baking? Eccles cakes it is, with perhaps a sausage roll?"

"I think I can manage that." Madeline leaned forward,

tilting her head to look at Cecily from under the brim of her hat. "You are not really contemplating cutting off your hair, are you? I mean, I know some of the women on the Continent are doing it, but it looks so terribly degrading."

The arrival of Dolly's latest assistant prevented Cecily from answering right away. After giving the girl their order, she looked back at Madeline and gave her a smile of resignation.

"I wonder why it is," she said, "that everything that seems more relaxing, more manageable, or just more plain fun is deemed to be disgraceful by our ever-watchful society? I had high hopes, once Edward became king, that the Victorian limitations would be relaxed."

"They are, to a certain degree."

"For the aristocracy perhaps. They seem to be able to get away with murder these days." Cecily smiled at the assistant as she placed the silver tray on the table.

"Don't worry," she added when the girl hurried away, "I have no intention of cutting my hair. I was thinking about Simani and how much easier it must be for her to take care of hers."

Madeline's expression changed immediately, becoming wary. Cecily waited until she had poured the tea before saying quietly, "I do think it would be kind to tell me what it is you are apparently hiding."

The other woman's eyes widened in protest. "Hiding? Why, Cecily, dear, you don't imagine I would hide anything from you?"

"If it had something to do with my new daughter-in-law, I think you might. Particularly if it was something you knew I wouldn't care to hear."

Madeline dropped her gaze and reached for a sausage roll. "I'm so glad we ordered these," she said, raising it to her mouth. "I have also discovered an enormous appetite. Just the heavenly smell of these things convinces me I'm starving."

"Madeline. I truly want to know. I think I have a right to know."

Cecily watched her friend struggle for a moment or two longer, then Madeline shrugged her slim shoulders. "Very well. If you must know, I'll tell you. I found out about it purely by chance."

Cecily tried to ignore the little flutter of apprehension. "Found out about what?"

"A friend told me he saw Simani late one night behind the inn. She was acting very strangely. When he described to me what he had seen, I knew what it was."

"And what exactly did he see?"

Madeline sighed. "He saw Simani chanting and sticking pins into a doll. Then she started to dance, and she was talking to the moon, he said. He couldn't understand it, of course. He thinks she is strange in the head. I think I managed to persuade him that she was probably sleepwalking."

"But you have a different explanation for her odd behavior?"

Madeline looked around to make sure no one could overhear. Then she leaned forward and whispered, "judging from what he told me, I am certain that Simani was practicing voodoo."

Cecily stared at her in astonishment. "Voodoo?"

Madeline lifted a finger to her lips. "Shsh. It's not something you want spread around. You know how people gossip in the village."

"I don't pay much attention to gossip. Neither does anyone else who has an ounce of sense. They gossip about you and your powers, but anyone who knows you pays no attention to it."

Madeline shook her head. "You don't understand. It's not the same thing at all. My potions and spells are created to help people. Voodoo is evil. It is used to bring curses down on the heads of unfortunate victims. A voodoo curse can make an enemy do some very strange things." She sat back, an odd expression on her face. "It can force someone to destroy himself, without knowing why, or without the power to stop it."

Cecily stared at her friend. "Like attempting to balance on a balcony railing, for instance?"

Madeline slowly nodded. "Precisely."

Although the room was unbearably stuffy, Cecily felt suddenly chilled.

With his connections as a barrister and his influence with some of the wealthiest men in London, he could easily have put me out of business. Michael's words. And what was it Lady Lavinia had said? *Black magic, if you ask me.*

"That's nonsense," Cecily said sharply.

Madeline's expression softened. "Of course it is. You know that, and I know that. But I wonder how many people would consider the possibility, if they heard the gossip? And how many people would risk patronizing the George and Dragon if they considered Simani capable of such a feat?"

Suspecting that Madeline was merely attempting to appease her, Cecily said carefully, "We shall just have to make sure that such gossip is never started."

"My friend will not say anything, I promise you. And no one will hear it from me."

Cecily leaned forward and patted her friend's hand. "Thank you, Madeline, but I never suspected they would. Now, tell me what you think about these poor suffragettes starving themselves to death in the London prisons."

Madeline had a great deal to say, much to Cecily's relief. It was high time she changed the subject. The last thing she wanted was a discussion on Simani and her questionable powers. For no matter how hard she tried, Cecily could not entirely dismiss the possibility that Simani could be involved in some way in the death of Sir Richard Malton.

It was one of the advantages of getting old, Colonel Fortescue thought as he dozed contentedly in the Rose

Garden. Nobody thought it strange if he caught forty winks now and again.

The sun felt warm on the top of his head, and the humming of the bees in the roses lulled him, soothing his nerves.

He sometimes got very tired of all the clamor and clatter in the hotel, and it was wonderful to stroll outside, find a quiet spot, and nod off for an hour or two. Did one a world of good, he assured himself, as his chin dropped lower and lower onto his chest.

After a while he found himself standing in the jungle in Kenya, rifle at the ready. He actually heard the monkeys chattering and the sound of a heavy animal crashing through the undergrowth.

Then he saw it. Two yellow eyes gleaming at him through the dark green foliage. A tiger.

There it was, standing motionless, its eyes fixed on him. He could see the muscles in its powerful shoulders bunched, ready to spring. He started to raise the rifle higher, to bring it to shoulder level. But it was damnably heavy.

The rifle wasn't the only thing that was heavy. His eyelids felt as if they had weights hanging on them, dragging them down. He couldn't afford to close his eyes. He had to watch for the tiger, wait for it to spring, then aim and fire.

He just couldn't keep his eyes open. They closed of their own accord, and he tensed, his hands gripping the rifle that suddenly seemed very slippery in his hands.

He heard the rustling noise, and the brute prepared to leap. Frantically he struggled to open his eyes. The noise got louder; the damn animal must be walking toward him. He waited for the next growl, hoping to pinpoint the monster's position.

What he heard instead was more like a giggle.

Startled, the colonel's eyes popped open. Right in front of his face, nose to nose, was another face, with wild, staring eyes.

He jumped back with a loud yelp. The face broke into

crazy laughter, and the colonel was jolted wide awake. It was that dratted boy, Master Stanley Malton.

"Here, here," the colonel protested lustily. "Where are your manners, young man? How dare you creep up on me like that. Dashed bad form, you know."

Stanley's face dropped. "I do beg your pardon, sir, but I was merely trying to find out if this is your watch. I found it lying near the fish pond, and since I saw you there yesterday, I wondered if it belonged to you."

Ashamed of his curt manner in the face of such consideration, the colonel was immediately apologetic. "Oh, jolly decent of you, my boy. But I don't wear a watch. Never have. Pesky things, they are."

"It's a very expensive watch," Stanley said, pulling a bright gold object from his pocket. "Are you quite sure it doesn't belong to you?"

"Quite sure. Quite, quite." The colonel was beginning to get a little irritable. This was, after all, his siesta time, and he did not want to miss it. He wanted to be thoroughly refreshed in order to toddle off back to the hotel for his gin before dinner.

Always had a snifter or two before sundown in the tropics. Of course, the sun went down at such dashed odd times out there. One had to start drinking in the afternoon, or nightfall could easily creep up on one, what?

"Take a good look at this watch, Colonel," the boy said, holding up the gleaming watch by its chain. "Even if it doesn't belong to you, you might remember seeing someone with it and can tell me who it belongs to."

The colonel peered at it. "Never seen it before. Better take it back to the hotel. Mrs. Sinclair will soon find out who it belongs to."

"But it's such a handsome watch. Look at it, how it shines in the sun."

"Why don't you run along now, sonny," Colonel Fortescue said, waving a languid hand in the direction of the hotel. "They are probably looking for you, old chap."

"Oh, no, they are not," Stanley said, beginning to swing the watch slowly back and forth. "They are quite busy at the moment and don't even know I'm gone."

The colonel blinked as the sunlight caught the shiny watchcase and sent a shaft of brilliant light into his eyes. He saw the watch swinging back and forth through a sort of hazy glow, pretty much as he saw things after a snifter or two of gin.

"Look at this watch, Colonel," Stanley was saying in a low soft voice that was strangely soothing. "Keep your eyes on the watch. See how good it makes you feel. Back and forth, back and forth. Just keep your eyes on the watch."

Actually the colonel didn't think he could tear his gaze away if he tried. The swinging, shining object seemed to mesmerize him, and it was far easier to watch the pendulum swing back and forth than to try to look at something else. Very pleasant, in fact. Very pleasant indeed.

"That's right, Colonel," Stanley's voice said, sounding a long way off. "Just watch it swing. Your arms are getting heavier . . . heavier. . . . Your body is relaxing, you are so tired . . . so tired. . . ."

By george, the boy was right about that. The colonel had never felt so dashed tired in his entire life. Once more his eyelids felt weighted down, and no matter how hard he struggled he couldn't lift them.

He could hear Stanley's voice in the distance but couldn't fathom a word of what he was saying. It just felt so good, dozing there in the warm sun, just a little doze . . .

He thought he heard himself say something, but that couldn't be. He had to be dreaming . . . dreaming . . .

Suddenly he was wide-awake. His eyes snapped open as if someone had cut the ties that held them. He sat up straight, a little dazed, but very much alert.

He looked around, noticing the sun playing on the leaves of the rose bushes and the bees weaving in and out of the blossoms. Above his head a blackbird sang its achingly sweet song, accompanied by the chirping of sparrows. The garden was heavy with the scent of roses, and a breeze rustled the branches of the weeping willow.

But of Stanley there was no sign. He had completely disappeared from sight. And, the colonel thought with amazement, he never heard him go.

CHAPTER

✥ 11 ✥

The sultry day had faded, and the welcome dusk brought cooler breezes to dispel the heat from inside the hotel. Windows stood ajar along the front of the Pennyfoot, as perspiring guests aired out their rooms. The front door stood open, while Arthur loitered outside on the steps, resplendent in his doorman's uniform with its gold braid and buttons, completed by a lofty top hat.

Phoebe Carter-Holmes, approaching the hotel from the Esplanade, thought she had never seen a better sight in all her born days.

She had waited until the evening to take her stroll along the seafront. Walking in the direct sunlight made one perspire, and she definitely did not want to meet up with handsome Arthur Barrett with beads of moisture on her brow. Most unbecoming.

She had dressed with care in one of her gowns from her better days. The pale lemon silk tea gown had gone through some changes according to the fashion. The tiny pearl buttons from neck to waist had been painstakingly sewn by Phoebe's own hand five years ago.

The appliqué lace and embroidery above the deep frill had been added when a copy of *The Tatler* had professed such an adornment to be sheer necessity for haute couture.

Phoebe was particularly fond of that phrase. Ever since she had discovered it in the magazine, borrowed from Cecily, she had taken advantage of every opportunity to say those delicious-sounding words.

Of course, when dear Sedgely was alive, she had dressed in the height of fashion all the time. But when the poor dear man had suffered that terrible accident, having been thrown from his horse during a wild fox hunt, that had been the end of Phoebe's life as she had known it.

The Carter-Holmes family had never deemed her worthy of their name. They couldn't wait to get rid of Phoebe and her son, considering them both to be far beneath their station.

It was true, Phoebe thought, patting the overloaded brim of her hat to make sure it was securely fastened, her background as a child left much to be desired. But she was a quick study and had done her best to become the lady dear Sedgely had always professed her to be.

Of course, Phoebe thought, as she sidestepped a small pile of excrement left on the pavement by some inconsiderate dog owner, dear Sedgely was incredibly stupid not to make a will.

In fact, now that she thought about it, he was also incredibly clumsy to have fallen from that ridiculous horse in the first place. If he had been a more experienced rider, he would have easily taken the fence. It really was most uncharitable of him to have left his wife and son in such an unfortunate predicament.

Shocked by the way her thoughts had progressed, Phoebe

paused for a moment at the railing to catch her breath. In all the days since dear Sedgely's accident, she had never once put any blame on his shoulders for her misfortune. Until now.

Phoebe glanced across the street to where Arthur stood, his face tilted to the sky in obvious enjoyment of the cool breeze from the ocean. Could it be that her heart was beginning to accept a new interest? Could it be time to let go of dear Sedgely and try to find a new love with whom to finish out her life?

Phoebe's pulse fluttered madly at the mere thought. How would it feel to share a bed with another man after all these years? What would Algie say? His mother and the doorman of the Pennyfoot? He would no doubt be shocked right out of his plimsolls, which would upset him no end. Some kind soul had recently given Algie a pair of the newfangled shoes, and the vicar practically lived in the dratted things.

Phoebe shook her head. She felt quite dizzy at the prospect of a liaison with the delectable Arthur Barrett. She dug into the pocket of her gown for her lace-edged handkerchief. Drawing it out, she waved it in front of her face to cool the warm flush that had spread over her cheeks.

At that moment Arthur Barrett turned his face in her direction. He must have mistaken her gesture, assuming she was waving her handkerchief at him. He doffed his top hat and gave her a low sweeping bow.

Phoebe had never seen any man bow to her that way before. A polite nod of the head or a slight dip of the shoulders, perhaps, but never a full, grand, majestic bow such as the doorman just executed. It quite took Phoebe's breath away. So romantic. She couldn't quite remember ever being so enchanted.

She tilted her head at a graceful angle, no easy feat considering the weight of her hat, loaded down as it was with stuffed doves and a mess of silk leaves and flowers, not to mention the wide satin bow in the front.

It was even more difficult to hold the pose as she crossed

the street, but somehow she managed it, determined to present the best picture possible as she stepped daintily across the cobblestones.

It was unfortunate that at that moment the driver of a motorcar chose to thunder down the street toward her at a good ten miles an hour, the car belching smoke, its horn blaring. Phoébe thought suddenly that the devil himself was out to flatten her into the ground.

She froze, staring at the oncoming vehicle, knowing she could not possibly escape those dreadful wheels. She saw a man bounce up and down in the hoodless compartment, shouting something at her she couldn't comprehend.

Then, as if sent from heaven, two strong arms clasped her about her waist and lifted her bodily from the ground. She felt herself swung to one side, and closed her eyes as the motorcar hurtled past her, the draft of it swirling her skirt about her ankles.

Very gently she was set upon the ground, and a deep voice said in her ear, "Faith and begorra, dear lady, that was the closest shave I ever did wish to see."

Phoebe's knees slammed into each other as she looked up into Arthur's heavenly blue eyes. "Oh, my," was all she could manage to say.

"Ah, 'tis the shock of it all, to be sure," Arthur said kindly. "Let me be helping you into the hotel, and I'll find you a chair to sit yourself upon."

Phoebe nodded weakly, her flesh still throbbing from the grasp of those manly hands. In fact, she wouldn't have minded at all if the hands had still held her. Arthur had let go of her and was now guiding her with decorous fingers under her elbow up the steps of the hotel.

Nevertheless, Phoebe thought as her senses quickly restored themselves, it was a very auspicious beginning to what could turn out to be an interesting relationship. Very interesting indeed.

Cecily leaned her hands on top of the wall that guarded the edge of the roof gardens and looked down into the courtyard below. Strains of a waltz floated up to her, making her feet tap in time. How she longed to dance again, as she once did, clasped in James's arms, floating across the floor of the ballroom as if her feet had wings.

The sound of soft laughter drifted from the balcony, and she could hear the murmur of a deep voice mingling with the hushed tones of a feminine companion.

This was indeed a night for love, she thought, her gaze drifting across the gardens. Miniature gaslights strung from the branches swung to and fro in the evening breeze.

The roses still filled the night with their fragrance, not at all overpowered by the fresh salty air. Lights twinkled in the harbor from the windows of the thatched cottages and pinpointed Lord Withersgill's estate high on the hill above Putney Downs.

How James had loved the roof garden. He had enjoyed the quiet times, standing side by side with his wife, touching hands, watching the night creep across the ocean until it blanketed his beloved village.

Something stirred behind her, and Cecily's heart skipped a beat. For an instant she thought it could be James's ghost, come to share his most treasured moments with her once more.

Then Baxter's voice dispelled the notion. "Madam? I trust you are feeling well?"

She relaxed in the gathering darkness, comforted by his concern. She was well aware that he had made a special trip to reassure himself. "Quite well, Baxter, thank you."

She kept her back to him, her gaze still on the restless ocean, and after a moment or two she heard him breathe a faint sigh.

"Very well, madam. I will leave you alone."

"No." She turned to look at him then and was struck by his expression. It reminded her of when her sons were small and she had been thoughtlessly curt when one of them had interrupted her at an inopportune moment.

She smiled at him, and the wounded look vanished. "I'm

feeling a trifle melancholy, Baxter. I would appreciate your company for a moment or two, if you have the time?"

"Of course, madam."

She turned back to the view of the ocean, and he moved to stand beside her. She wondered what he would say if she touched his hand, and was immediately ashamed of the thought. How could she stand there and miss one man so sorely, and in the next instant feel a need to make contact with another?

Was she missing James? Or was she merely missing the warmth and comfort of a man's love? Was it her dead husband she mourned or the loss of security, the intimacy of a familiar body lying next to her in bed?

"It is a beautiful night," Baxter said softly.

She gave him a swift glance, half afraid he had read her thoughts, and embarrassed by the notion. But his face was tilted at the stars and the cloudless sky.

"It is indeed." Deciding it was time to banish her wayward thoughts, she added, "I heard some disturbing news today. It's troubling me a great deal."

"Would you care to share it with me?"

She paused, wondering just how much she should tell him. Then she shrugged off her doubts. She had always confided in him in the past, and she saw no reason not to do so now.

"It's Simani," she said, tracing around a large stone embedded in the wall. "Madeline says she has been practicing voodoo."

"Well, Madeline should know all about that."

He sounded amused, and Cecily felt a flush of resentment. "Madeline says that Simani is capable of putting a curse on someone. Of making them do something they wouldn't normally do."

This time she waited for several seconds before Baxter answered. "Does this by any chance have anything to do with the death of Sir Richard Malton?"

She looked up at him, silently entreating him to understand. "Sir Richard threatened Michael a few nights ago. He told him he was going to close down the George and Dragon Michael was quite worried about it. Business has not been good at all, and Sir Richard could have done him a great deal of harm."

Baxter raised his eyebrows. "Why would Sir Richard want to close down the George and Dragon?"

"Apparently he was rude to Simani, and Michael practically threw him out."

"I see." Baxter clasped his hands behind his back and rocked on his heels. "That would no doubt annoy him. But I'm sure it would have been an empty threat. I doubt that he would have done anything quite so drastic. Just the anger of the moment, I should say."

"Perhaps. But would Simani know that?"

Baxter stopped rocking. "Are you suggesting that your daughter-in-law placed a voodoo curse on Sir Richard, causing him to fall to his death?"

Put into so many words, Cecily had to admit it sounded ridiculous. "I don't know what I'm suggesting," she said, turning back to look at the gardens. "But I can't stop thinking about the wedding, presided over by a witch doctor. I have spent time in Africa, and I have heard of voodoo and the harm it can do."

"If I may say so, madam, with all due respect, I would suggest that you have been paying a little too much attention to Miss Pengrath and her mumbo jumbo. Whatever caused Sir Richard to choose to end his life in that manner, I feel reasonably certain it couldn't have been anything to do with magic. Black or otherwise."

Cecily looked at him sharply. "You still believe that Sir Richard ended his own life voluntarily?"

"I can think of no other explanation. It is the only one that makes sense."

She was inclined to agree with him, except for one thing—the odd little dance that Phoebe described so graphically. She couldn't dismiss that so easily. It seemed such a strange thing to do when contemplating suicide.

Thinking of Phoebe jolted her memory. "Oh, good heavens," she said, picking up her skirt, "I have to run. I have a meeting with Phoebe and I must be at least half an hour late."

"The last time I saw Mrs. Carter-Holmes," Baxter said, moving to open the attic door for her, "she was engaged in a most animated discussion with our intrepid doorman."

Cecily grinned. "Was she, indeed? In that case I had better hurry before he sweeps her off her feet and carries her off into the sunset. I need her able assistance for the Saturday night ball, without which I fear the event would be very mundane."

"If there is one thing we can be sure about," Baxter said as Cecily passed through the doorway, "with Mrs. Carter-Holmes in command of the entertainment, the evening will be anything but mundane."

Reaching the foyer a few minutes later, Cecily was surprised to see Phoebe happily chatting with Arthur. In fact, Cecily noted with some amusement, it looked very much as if the two of them were engaged in a mild flirtation.

Cecily had thought at the time that Baxter was being facetious when he mentioned Phoebe's discussion with Arthur, but by all accounts they were both enjoying the conversation.

Across the foyer Colonel Fortescue stood talking to the grandfather clock. Cecily gave him no more than a cursory glance as she started toward Phoebe, who was seated in a chair by the front door.

Baxter had gone back to his office to finish the bookkeeping for the week, and most of the guests were either in the ballroom or strolling outside in the balmy evening.

Phoebe looked up as Cecily approached, a look very akin to disappointment crossing her face. "Oh, there you are, Cecily," she said without too much enthusiasm. "I was beginning to think you had forgotten our meeting."

"I am so sorry to keep you waiting," Cecily said with a quick glance at Arthur. "I see my doorman has kept you well entertained in my absence."

Phoebe's face flushed a bright red. "I'll have you know that this brave gentleman saved my life," she announced, loud enough for everyone in to the hotel to hear. "I am most grateful to him."

"Poppycock," the colonel muttered, still addressing the clock.

Arthur sent him a startled look, but since the colonel had his back to him, he returned his attention to Phoebe, who sat gazing up at him as if she'd found paradise.

Cecily wondered what Mrs. Chubb would say when she discovered that Arthur was spreading his favors around to more than one lady. She and Phoebe had been close if unlikely friends for years.

After Sedgely Carter-Holmes's untimely death, Phoebe had returned with her son to Badgers End, with nothing more than a trunk full of clothes and a few personal possessions.

Mrs. Chubb and her husband, who was still alive then, had taken Phoebe and the boy in until the estate had been settled.

The meager sum that the Carter-Holmes family had grudgingly given to Phoebe had been barely enough to feed even one mouth for more than a few months, but Phoebe's pride wouldn't allow her to accept charity any longer than necessary.

She had moved into a rented cottage and begun working for the local vicar, cleaning the church and the vicarage until Algie had subsequently inherited the position, with a great deal of help from his persistent mother.

Phoebe had never forgotten the housekeeper's kindness. She was one of the few people allowed to call Mrs. Chubb by her Christian name. And now, apparently, she was a rival for the attention of an attractive Irishman with more than his fair share of blarney.

Cecily looked down on Phoebe's sparkling face and hoped fervently that the woman would not be hurt. She had been hurt enough in her life. She couldn't help wondering if perhaps Baxter had been right in his assessment of the new doorman.

At that moment the clock began to chime the hour. "Good heavens," Cecily exclaimed, "I hadn't realized it was that late. I do beg your pardon, Phoebe, for keeping you so late. Perhaps we should have our meeting tomorrow instead."

"Oh, no, not at all." Phoebe fanned her face with her handkerchief. "The wait has been most interesting, I can assure you." She sent a coquettish glance up at Arthur, who gave her his one-sided grin.

"It has that, sweet lady. A pure pleasure, to be sure."

"Well," Cecily said, a trifle impatiently, "would you like to come down to the library, Phoebe? We can have our meeting there. I don't suppose it will take that long—"

She was interrupted by a bloodcurdling howl. The last of the chimes died away, and a shocked silence settled over the foyer as everyone turned to look at the colonel.

He stood with his back to the clock, his hair standing out on each side of his head as if he'd crawled through a hedge backward.

His eyes were wide and staring and appeared to be fixed on Arthur's face, while the doorman stood as still as a lighthouse.

"You are not going to shoot me down like a mad dog," the colonel howled, taking a step forward. "I'll cut you to pieces first."

He brought his hand from behind his back, and Phoebe screamed. The light from the gas lamp fell across the blade of the saber, illuminating the deadly razor edge.

"Colonel!" Cecily's horrified voice rang out as she started forward. She had taken only one step when Arthur's arm was thrust in front of her.

"No, ma'am. I'll handle this."

Cecily wasn't so sure anyone was going to handle the

situation. She had never seen the colonel look so wild, and it was the first time she had ever seen him with any kind of weapon.

"By george," the colonel said in a strange, choked voice, "I'll cut you into tiny pieces and feed them to the wolves. Don't think I don't know what you're up to, you blithering bastard. You can't fool me. I know you have a blasted gun tucked away in the corner, just waiting to shoot me between the eyes."

He brandished the saber as Phoebe screamed again. "Don't deny it!" he shouted.

"Colonel," Arthur said with amazing composure, "I am your friend, that I am. I have no wish to harm you. I don't even know how to use a gun. Never did like the blasted things."

"Don't lie! I know your sort. Think you can fool me, what? What? Damn you, sir!"

The colonel took another step forward, and Cecily looked wildly in the direction of the hallway. She had to get help and quickly. It looked very much as if Colonel Fortescue had finally gone over the edge. Apparently he had every intention of running Arthur Barrett through the heart, and the onlookers were powerless to stop him.

CHAPTER
❈ 12 ❈

It was fortunate, indeed, that Baxter, upon hearing the commotion from his office, arrived promptly on the scene just as the colonel crouched for his final charge.

Cecily was most impressed with the way her manager grasped the colonel's upraised arm, narrowly avoiding being sliced by the saber. She did have a nasty moment or two when it looked as if the colonel's strange fit had endowed him with extra strength and would overpower the larger man.

But then Arthur leapt into the fray, drawing a gasp of admiration from Phoebe. Her eyes glittered with all the excitement.

Between them the two men managed to subdue the crazed colonel, who seemed to deflate right in front of their eyes once he was relieved of his weapon.

"Baxter," Cecily said, feeling a trifle shaky at the knees, "would you be so kind as to escort Colonel Fortescue to his room? I'll go and ask Mrs. Chubb for one of her powders. It will ensure him of a good night's sleep, at least. I will see how he is in the morning before I decide what should be done."

Baxter nodded his agreement and took hold of the now complacent, if somewhat dazed-looking, colonel. "Come along, sir," he said quietly, "please allow me to assist you to your suite."

"Dashed decent of you, old chap," Fortescue murmured and obediently accompanied Baxter to the staircase.

Footsteps scurried down the stairs to the kitchen as Cecily approached them, and she sighed. No doubt one of the maids had witnessed the entire scene. She knew, only too well, how such things became exaggerated out of all proportion.

She couldn't imagine what had come over the colonel, or why he had chosen to attack Arthur, who was surely the most congenial member of her staff. But she was going to find out as soon as possible.

Down in the kitchen she found Mrs. Chubb busily engaged in a discussion with Michel about the next day's menu. Gertie and Ethel were at their usual posts at the sink, stacking wet dishes and whispering amongst themselves.

Cecily wondered which of them had seen the colonel's attack. She could only hope the housemaids would adhere to the hotel rules and keep all gossip to themselves. She strictly enforced the rule, and she would hate to be put in the position of having to let someone go for breaking it.

Michel and the housekeeper cut off their conversation as she approached. "I don't wish to interrupt," Cecily said with a smile of apology, "but I wonder if I might have one or two of your powders, if you please, Mrs. Chubb?"

The housekeeper looked at her in concern. "Are you not feeling well, mum?"

"Perfectly well, thank you. One of our guests, however, is

a little under the weather and needs something to help him sleep."

"Oh, right away, mum." Mrs. Chubb hurried into the pantry, while Michel twirled the end of his mustache with his fingers.

"I do 'ope, madame, ze gentleman is not feeling ze collywobbles from my cooking tonight."

"No, Michel," Cecily said with a reassuring glance at her chef, "I am quite sure that no one could have a single complaint about your excellent cuisine."

"Ah, I thought not. One can find no complaint with the greatest chef in the British Empire, *non*?"

"Blimey, 'ark at him," Gertie muttered, clattering a plate loudly onto the pile.

Michel sent a smoldering glance across the kitchen, but at that moment Mrs. Chubb bustled back with two small envelopes in her hand.

"Here you are, mum, one of these and the colonel will be sleeping like a baby."

So the news had already begun to spread. Cecily hoped passionately that rumors of a madman running berserk in the hotel would not generate a panic.

Just to make sure, she said loud enough for everyone to hear, "I sincerely hope that the unfortunate incident which took place tonight will not be mentioned outside of this room. Since no harm was done, I see no reason why it should not be forgotten."

Mrs. Chubb nodded with a great deal of vigor. "Rest assured, mum, I shall see that no one tattles on the poor man. What was it, do you think? A bit too much sun? Sunstroke can do terrible things to you, I know."

Seizing on the excuse, Cecily hastily agreed. "I'm sure he'll be a new man in the morning," she added, without too much conviction.

She glanced around the kitchen. "By the way, where is Master Stanley?"

"Oh, he's with Samuel, mum." Mrs. Chubb looked

anxious. "I do believe he's out in the stables, helping to muck out the horses."

Cecily rolled her eyes. She could just imagine the state the boy must be in by now. "Well, I think it's time he came inside," she said, glancing at the small clock on the mantelpiece. "It's past his bedtime."

"Yes, mum, I'll go and fetch him. He'll more than likely want something to eat before he goes to bed."

"Just don't let him get his sticky little hands on my ptarmigan pie or the smoked salmon in the larder," Michel said darkly, forgetting his French accent.

Mrs. Chubb gave him a scathing look. "As if I would."

Anxious to see the colonel settled for the night, Cecily left them arguing and made her way up the stairs to the third floor. She wasn't too sure what she was going to find, but she hoped fervently that Baxter had managed to get the old gentleman into his bed.

"I tell you, Ethel, it were a bleeding sight for sore eyes all right." Gertie clasped a plate to her bosom and grinned. "There he was, standing in the middle of the flipping foyer, waving that sword around his head and bellowing like a sick cow. I thought he was going to bloody chop his ear off, so help me I did."

Ethel nodded, her arms moving through the soapsuds as if she were searching for a lost tiddlywink.

Gertie grunted with exasperation. She was relating the juiciest story she'd had in days, and Ethel was acting like she was hearing the laundry list.

"Well, anyway," Gertie went on, determined to get her friend's attention, "Arthur stood there facing him, looking like he'd just shit in his drawers. Never moved a muscle, he didn't. Then the batty old colonel lunges forward"—she thrust her hand toward Ethel to demonstrate—"and bugger me if he doesn't run that blade right through Arthur's blinking heart."

The gasp came from the wrong direction. Gertie had been

testing her friend to find out if she was really listening. What she hadn't expected was for Mrs. Chubb to come rushing at her, arms waving and face as white as a bag of flour.

"You didn't tell me that!" the housekeeper cried. "Why didn't you tell me that?"

"It ain't true, that's why," Gertie said, taken aback by the hysterical note in Mrs. Chubb's voice.

She was even more astounded when the housekeeper stood for several seconds, her mouth opening and shutting as if she'd forgotten how to use it. Then she said in a tone Gertie had seldom heard her use before, "Gertie Brown, if you ever, and I mean *ever*, say anything like that again when it isn't true, I'll wallop you on your behind, big as you are. Do you understand?"

Gertie could feel her face growing warm. Ethel still wasn't saying anything, but she'd heard it all right. It would be just like her to go and tell everyone what Mrs. Chubb said.

Gertie put down the plate she was holding and undid the strings of her apron. "I'm not staying around here to be talked to like bleeding muck, that I'm not. I was only having a bit of fun, that's all."

She glared at the housekeeper and threw the apron at her. "You can't bleeding talk to me like that, so there. I'm not some bloody little guttersnipe, stealing and thieving everything I can lay me hands on. I'm a respectable woman, I am, and soon to be a mother. And no one bloody talks to me like that."

Mrs. Chubb folded her arms. "Is that so? Well, listen to Miss Hoity-Toity. Where do you think you are going if you walk out of here? Answer me that. You have a room here for you and the baby when it comes, and plenty of people to help keep an eye on it when you're working. How many places can you go and do that, hey?"

Gertie struggled for several seconds, her boiling temper pitted against her common sense. The old witch was right.

She had no bleeding choice. It was stay there and take whatever they handed out to her, or starve on the streets.

She stared belligerently at Mrs. Chubb, longing to tell her what she thought of her, and knowing she was powerless to do anything.

Finally the housekeeper handed her apron back to her. Without a word, Gertie tied the strings and turned back to the sink.

She waited until Mrs. Chubb had left the kitchen before muttering, "One day I'll have the last laugh on the lot of 'em, you wait and bloody well see."

"What are you going to do, marry a toff?" Ethel said with more than a touch of scorn in her voice.

Gertie felt tears prick behind her eyes, but the look she turned on Ethel was full of defiance. "What's so bleeding strange about that? It's happened before, you know."

"Yeah? But not to a grown woman with a kid in her arms, it hasn't."

Gertie put the plate down so hard she thought it would crack. "Look, Ethel, I don't bleeding know what's the matter with you, and if you don't want to tell me, then I don't bleeding care. But don't take your troubles out on me. I've had enough of it as it is, what with the old bat out there," she said as she jerked her head in the direction of the kitchen door, "and that flipping Stanley is driving me bonkers, and now you being sarky with me—"

Ethel dropped a plate back into the suds. "I'm sorry, Gertie, I really am, it's just I . . ." The rest was drowned in a flood of tears.

Gertie immediately forgot her resentment. She put an awkward hand on Ethel's shoulder and gave her a damp pat. "'Ere, 'ere, don't carry on, then, luv. What's the matter? You can tell me, I won't say nothing to no one, honest I won't."

Ethel gulped and sniffed for a moment or two, then said between sobs, "Joe's asked me to marry him."

Gertie stared at her in amazement. "Is that all? Blimey, I thought you was going to say he'd chucked you. I thought that was what you bleeding wanted, weren't it? To marry him? Don't you love him, then?"

"Of course I love him. That's just the problem." Ethel wiped her nose with the back of her hand, leaving a little cluster of soap bubbles behind.

Gertie dug in the pocket of her apron and took out a grubby handkerchief. "Here, wipe your nose." She waited until Ethel had delivered a resounding blow into the square of cotton, then said gently, "Why don't you tell me what's the real problem?"

Ethel handed back the crumpled handkerchief. "Joe is selling the farm. He wants to move to London and sell produce at Covent Garden. He says there's no money in farming anymore, and he says that soon there won't be no farms around here at all. He wants to sell his while he still can."

"Oh, blimey." Gertie held her breath for a moment to let the shock subside.

"So that means if I want to marry him I'll have to go to London with him." Once more the tears spurted from Ethel's eyes. "I don't know what to do . . . hoo. . . ."

Gertie took a trembling breath. First her bleeding husband, now her best friend. Swallowing her own hurt, she said briskly, "You bloody well marry him, that's what. Christ, girl, what are you waiting for? You waiting for him to go to bleeding London without you? Don't be blooming daft, luv. Grab him while you can, before some other bugger gets her mits on him."

Ethel turned watery eyes on her friend. "But I'll miss everyone . . . I'll miss you. . . ."

Gertie patted her again. "I'll miss you, too, Ethel, luv, but you can come down and visit, and I'll come up there. Me dad lives there, remember? Not that I go to see him much, but it will give me an excuse, won't it. Besides, you'll love the Smoke. All those fancy shops and theaters—we ain't got nothing like that down here, now, 'ave we?"

Ethel shook her head, looking a little less miserable.

"Look," Gertie said, carried away by her success, "tell you what. Why don't you knock off a bit early tonight? I'll finish up here. Go and see Joe and tell him you'll bloody marry him and go to London with him. All right?"

A smile crept over Ethel's face. "Yeah," she whispered, "I think I will. Thanks, Gertie."

Gertie nodded. "Go on with yer, then."

Without warning, Ethel wrapped her two arms around her neck and gave her a hug tight enough to cut off her breath.

After a moment's hesitation, Gertie returned the hug, giving her friend a quick squeeze before dropping her arms. She held onto the tears until after Ethel had left, then let them fall into the dirty water in the sink.

She had composed herself by the time Mrs. Chubb returned. She wasn't too happy, though, when she heard the shrill voice of the person accompanying the housekeeper.

"I don't want to go to bed yet," Stanley said, stomping his foot. "It's too early."

"It's way past your bedtime, young man. Now, go and wash your hands in the sink this minute. You smell like a field of manure."

Gertie could smell the little rotter before he came and stood next to her. Jostling her out of the way, he thrust his hands into the soapy water.

"Don't you bleeding do that, you little twit!" Gertie yelled. "There's blinking dishes in there. Whatcha want to do, poison everyone with horse shit?"

"Ger-tay!" Mrs. Chubb marched across the floor and pulled Stanley's hands from the water. "How many times do I have to tell you not to use that language in front of the child? Now, take those dishes out of there and run some clean water. Only let him wash his hands first, all right?"

"Bloody hell, all that work for nothing." Gertie started slamming plates down on the draining board while Stanley watched, smug satisfaction in his beady little eyes.

"Keep an eye on him while I fetch him something to eat."

Mrs. Chubb flew off with a rustle of skirts, while Stanley poked his tongue out at Gertie.

"Keep an eye on him, be blowed," Gertie muttered. She bent down, thrusting her face up to Stanley's. "Rotten little bastards like you belong at the bottom of the sea, that's where."

Stanley opened his mouth and yelled, "Mrs. Chu-u-u-bb!"

Gertie straightened, her mouth tight, waiting for the next onslaught from the housekeeper. If he was her kid, she thought fiercely, she'd let him feel the weight of a bloody rolling pin, that she would. Right where it would do the most good. On his fat bottom. Then he could go and cool it off in the bloody ocean. And drown there. And bloody good riddance.

First thing the following morning Cecily cornered Baxter in his study. "I'd like to check in on Colonel Fortescue," she said as Baxter rose from his chair, hastily buttoning his coat. "I'd like you to come with me, if you will."

"Of course, madam." Baxter shuffled the papers on his desk into a neat pile, then followed her out into the hallway. "Ethel tapped on his door earlier this morning," he added as they made their way to the staircase.

"Did he answer?" Cecily felt a pang of apprehension. "I can't help wondering what would have happened if he'd had another turn like the one last night and attacked Ethel. The man really isn't safe to be around people anymore."

"Regrettably I had come to the same conclusion, madam."

Cecily began climbing the stairs, with Baxter following behind her. She felt sad at the thought of losing one of her most valuable customers. But the safety of her guests was paramount, and she couldn't afford to take risks.

"We'll see how he is this morning," she said as they reached the landing. "He is due to leave at the end of the week. If he seems to be stable, we'll let him stay until then. After that, we'll have to refuse to accept his reservation."

"And if he comes down without a reservation?"

"Then we'll have Arthur stop him at the door."

"Of course. Sir Lancelot to the rescue," Baxter muttered.

Cecily sent him a surprised look. "Really, Baxter, this isn't like you at all. I do wish I knew why you seem to take offense to this man."

"My apologies, ma'am. Please put it down to a sour stomach. I did not sleep well last night."

Cecily paused at the colonel's door. "I'm sorry to hear that. Was it something you ate? If it was, for heaven's sake don't tell Michel, or I'll have another crisis on my hands."

"If I might be so bold, madam, there are times when I have the distinct impression that my needs come far behind those of the other members of this staff. I have to wonder what it is I am doing wrong to suffer such neglect."

Cecily looked at his pained expression and felt immediate remorse. "Oh, Bax, I'm sorry. It's just that I don't think of you as a member of the staff. You are my right hand, my business partner, my confidant, and my friend. I'm very much afraid that at times I do take you for granted. Please forgive me?"

In the dim light of the hallway she saw an odd gleam in his eyes as he looked down at her. He was standing quite close. Too close, if the fluttering of her pulse was any indication.

His expression softened, and he said gently, "Madam, it is my lot in life, and my pleasure, to forgive you anything."

She swallowed, and turned quickly to the door, lifting her hand to rap on it. "Thank you, Baxter," she said, sounding a trifle prim.

"No. Thank you, madam."

To her immense relief, the colonel answered sleepily. "Who's there?"

"It's Mrs. Sinclair and Mr. Baxter," she called out. "May we come in?"

"Yes, yes, come on in, old bean."

Opening the door, Cecily peered in.

The colonel sat propped up in bed, his red silk pajamas a startling contrast against the pale blue sheets. He made an effort to smile when she entered, with Baxter on her heels. She could see that the man in the bed looked drawn, and his eyes had some trouble focusing on her.

"I'm sorry to disturb you, Colonel," she said, taking a chair by the bedside, "but I'm afraid your little outburst last night could have had some serious consequences. I feel we must demand an explanation for such unwarranted behavior."

In the tense silence that followed, Cecily saw nothing but confusion on the colonel's face. Her heart sank as she stared at the elderly gentleman. She was going to miss him, she thought sadly. She was going to miss him a great deal.

She was startled when he suddenly sat up straight, looked her full in the eyes, and said clearly, "He sings, you know."

CHAPTER

❖13❖

"Who sings?" Cecily said, already anticipating the answer.

"That blasted doorman. He sings."

She frowned. "Is that why you attacked him?"

He stared at her, bewilderment in his pale eyes. "Attacked him? Great Scott, dear lady, why would I want to attack the doorman?"

Baxter moved to the bottom of the bed. "You do not remember attacking Barrett last night?"

"Of course not. Utter rubbish." He sank back against the pillows, muttering, "Damn kid. Ought to be in school, not running around bothering people."

Cecily exchanged a worried glance with Baxter. "Arthur doesn't go to school, Colonel. He works here, remember?"

Fortescue waved a weak hand back and forth. "Not him. That blasted boy. Never seen such an ill-behaved brat in my

131

life. Put him in the army out in India for a spell. Teach him some damn manners, that's what. What?"

Cecily sat back with a sigh. "Stanley." She glanced up at Baxter. "I found him tormenting Colonel Fortescue the other day and sent him packing. He really is a problem child. I'll be so very happy when his mother is fit enough to take care of him again."

Baxter nodded, his gaze still intent on the muttering man in the bed. "Colonel, do you remember me helping you to bed last night?"

The colonel blinked furiously and twitched his mustache. "By Jove, now that I think about it, I do remember a stout arm assisting me up the stairs. Had a drop too much, did I?"

Baxter shook his head. "No, I don't believe so. You would not have recovered so fast had that been the case."

The colonel shook his head. "Dashed if I know, old boy. Touch of the sun probably. Saw a lot of it in the tropics. Our sergeant major—big chappie, he was. Had a chest like a grand piano and biceps hard as cricket balls. Stood to attention one day at a parade . . ." He smacked his hand down on the bed, making Cecily jump.

"Went down like a wounded rhino," the colonel finished. "Thought he'd been blasted shot." He peered up at Baxter and nodded his head slowly up and down. "Sun got him. Poor fellow never was the same again. Took all the guts out of him."

Baxter cleared his throat. "Colonel, please think back to last night. You were wielding a saber, and I took it away from you. Apparently you wanted to use it on Arthur Barrett."

The colonel stared at him in horror. "Are you insane, old chap? A saber is sharp enough to cut off an ear with one slice. If I'd used it on Barrett I would have darn near cut him in half."

"Precisely," Baxter said grimly.

"Colonel." Cecily leaned forward, fixing an intent gaze

on his face. "Why did you want to harm Arthur Barrett? Did he do something to upset you?"

"Upset me? Upset me?" The colonel lay back, seemingly exhausted. "That damn child upsets me, that's what. What? Can't abide a child who won't do what he's told. Told him I didn't wear a watch, and he insisted on swinging that dashed thing around. Made me quite dizzy. Then he disappears." He flicked his middle finger against his thumb. "Just like that. Into thin air. One minute he's there, the next he's gone." He closed his eyes and went on mumbling words that were unintelligible to Cecily.

She shook her head. "I think we'll have to let him rest," she said, rising to her feet. "He obviously doesn't remember anything about last night."

"Perhaps he doesn't want to remember," Baxter muttered, starting across the room to the door.

Cecily was about to follow him when the colonel said distinctly, "He sings."

She turned back to the bed. "Arthur Barrett? Yes, I know he sings. I have heard him sing and whistle about the place. I think it's very nice."

"Madam—" Baxter began, but she silenced him with a quick raise of her hand.

"I think it's wonderful that a man can feel happy enough to want to sing all day," she continued, watching Colonel Fortescue's face.

He slowly shook his head. "Not all day," he mumbled.

"Most of the day. Is that what bothers you? His singing and whistling?"

"Bothers me?" The colonel opened his eyes and blinked at her. "No, doesn't bother me, old bean. Not at all. I like it. Just couldn't remember where I'd seen him before, that's all."

Her interest caught now, Cecily moved closer to the bed. "You've met Arthur Barrett before?"

"Yes, long time ago. On the stage. Music Hall."

Cecily made a small exclamation of surprise. "You were on the stage?"

This time he gave a violent shake of his head. "No, no, dear lady. He was. Barrett."

"Arthur was a performer? What did he do?"

The colonel mumbled something Cecily couldn't hear. Then he added something else, and this time she caught it. "Damn fine singer. Wasting his time." The words were followed by a loud snore.

"And the top o' the morning to you," Arthur sang out as Mrs. Chubb hurried across the foyer. "My, but aren't you the very picture of health, with those roses blooming in your cheeks an' all."

Mrs. Chubb gave a breathless laugh. "I don't know so much about good health. But if you had to run up and down stairs as often as I do, you'd have roses in your cheeks, too."

"Ay, and I'd love to run up and down stairs with you, that I would."

"I'll pretend I didn't hear that." She couldn't help giving him a smile as she passed him, though. "A quick cuppa later on?"

Arthur glanced at the grandfather clock. "I can come down now, if it's all right with you, lovely lady. It's time for my elevenses."

Mrs. Chubb followed his gaze. "It's not yet ten," she said, trying to sound stern.

"So I'll take it a bit early this morning. It's quiet at the moment, and I don't want to miss the chance to gaze upon your sweet and lovely face."

Mrs. Chubb grinned. "Go on with you," she said. "I can tell you've been kissing the Blarney Stone."

Arthur staggered backward with a hand on his heart. "Oh, dear lady, how you wound me. When every word I've spoken is the truth, to be sure."

"Well, I have some time myself, so come along." She

raised a hand as Arthur bounded forward. "Just a few minutes, mind. That's all I can spare."

He reached out and took her hand in his. "Altheda, me darling, I'll take whatever you can offer."

Snatching her hand away, Mrs. Chubb shot a look around the empty foyer. "You'd better behave yourself, Arthur Barrett, if you don't want to be the object of malicious gossip. There are too many eyes around this place, with flapping mouths to go with them."

Arthur placed his palms together as if in prayer. "Ah, and sure I'll be a perfect saint, I promise."

Smiling in spite of herself, Mrs. Chubb led him down the stairs to the kitchen.

She had to admit she felt warm and cozy seeing Arthur seated at her table again. It had been so long since Fred had died that she had almost forgotten the sheer pleasure of feeding a man and watching him enjoy the meal.

Happily she cut off a thick slice of jellied veal and pasted it between two hefty slices of a fresh farm loaf. After decorating the sandwich with pickled onions, sliced tomato, and cucumber, she carried the plate to the table and stuck it in front of him.

"Here, get that down, you. You look like you don't eat enough to keep a sparrow alive."

Arthur licked his lips, his hand roving over his stomach. "Just tell me one thing. What is the matter with the men around here that they haven't snatched up a good woman like you? Why aren't you at home feeding a husband, that's what I want to know."

Cutting a huge wedge of Dundee cake, Mrs. Chubb tried to keep her hand steady. This was getting to be serious talk, indeed. She had better watch her tongue before she let it run away with itself and get her into trouble.

"I had a husband once," she said, slapping the cake onto a plate. "He died and left me to bring up a daughter alone. I didn't have the time or the inclination to look for anyone else."

She picked up the knife and took it over to the sink. "That's if anyone would have had me," she added almost under her breath.

Arthur's quick ears had picked up on her words, however. "Sure, and why wouldn't they have you, Altheda? You are a good woman and a fine-looking colleen. Why, any man would be only too happy to be so blessed."

Laughing, Mrs. Chubb returned to the table. "Don't you think I'm just a little too old in the tooth to be a colleen?"

Arthur reached up and touched her cheek with his fingertips. "You are never too old, Altheda. It is what is in your heart that counts. Always remember——"

The door swung open, cutting off his words. Mrs. Chubb swung around, feeling guilty for some strange reason. She relaxed when she saw Phoebe standing in the doorway, looking like the Gibson girl in a pale orchid gown with a waist so tight it looked as if the woman would snap in half.

The gown clung lovingly to Phoebe's ample bosom, while the skirt fitted over her hips like wax, falling in graceful folds to flare out above her dainty feet. A parasol dangled from a gloved elbow, while the ever-present hat sat at a rakish angle, appearing ready to dump on the floor the entire garden of flowers that decorated the brim.

Beneath the luxuriant foliage, Phoebe's face seemed to be frozen in mid-smile as her gaze rested on Arthur's beaming face.

"Well, now," he said softly, "isn't this a little bit of heaven, to be sure. It isn't every man who is lucky enough to be entertained by two such lovely women at the same time."

Mrs. Chubb felt a painful lurch in the region of her heart. Something she must have eaten, she assured herself as she watched Phoebe glide forward, letting the door swing to behind her.

"So this is where you are," Phoebe said, her tone obviously implying that it was the last place on earth she expected to see the doorman.

"Ay, so it is," Arthur said, his gaze traveling over Phoebe's voluptuous body with obvious appreciation. "And it's happy I am that you found me, to be sure."

Phoebe sniffed, tossing her head in the air and setting the flowers on her hat trembling in apprehension. Transferring her cool gaze to Mrs. Chubb, she added, "I arrived a short while ago to find no one at the door. I'm sure Cecily would be most put out to know that you were deliberately keeping her employees from their duty."

Still smarting from Arthur's blatant transfer of interest, this added insult was too much. Shocked, Mrs. Chubb could only stare for a moment. Then she found her tongue. "What I do in my kitchen and with whom is no concern of yours, Mrs. Carter-Holmes. I'll thank you to keep your acid comments to yourself."

Arthur sat back in his chair with the air of someone about to enjoy some exciting entertainment.

"It is my business when it concerns my welfare," Phoebe announced imperiously. "I needed assistance when I reached the door of the hotel, and no one was there to help me. Because the employee concerned is sitting down here in your kitchen—" She jerked her arm up to point at Arthur, apparently forgetting the parasol hanging from the crook of her elbow. The long, pointed tip shot up in an arc. It deftly caught the handle of a pewter jug on the low shelf of the dresser and hooked it into the air.

With a deafening crash the jug landed on the table and sent Arthur's cup flying. A large puddle began spreading over the edge to drip on to the floor.

Mrs. Chubb, battling with indignation and resentment at Arthur's fickle nature, dug her fists into her hips. "Now look at the mess you've made. You did that on purpose, Phoebe Carter-Holmes. I've a good mind to make you clean it up."

"Why don't you make him clean it up?" Phoebe snarled, glaring at Arthur. "It might do him good to do some honest work, instead of whiling his days away charming whatever lady has the misfortune to cross his path."

"Ah, you don't mean that, sweet lady," Arthur murmured. "Sure, and there's enough of me to go around, is there not?"

Phoebe's eyes looked like they would explode right out of their sockets. She took a deep breath, expanding her bosom even further, to Arthur's obvious enjoyment.

Then, in a voice that trembled with quiet rage, she said, "I have no wish to associate with another person's discards. Mrs. Chubb is welcome to your doubtful charms, Mr. Barrett. Personally I find them, and you, quite despicable. Good day to you both."

She swept quite magnificently out the door, and Arthur sat back in his chair with a sigh. "Ah, the good Lord save me from a jealous woman." He looked up at Mrs. Chubb with an impish smile. "Now, how about filling me cup up, Altheda, me darling? I had only a small mouthful of that delicious brew before the dragon sent it flying."

Mrs. Chubb folded her arms across her breasts. It was bad enough to see Phoebe mortified in front of her eyes. The fact that she had been just as gullible and as foolish as her friend, responding with such immature naiveté to a heartless rake, added fuel to her wrath.

"If you want any more tea, Arthur Barrett," she said, fixing him with her darkest scowl, "you can darn well lick it up off the floor. And I'll thank you to address me by my proper name in future. I'm Mrs. Chubb to you, sir."

Arthur pushed back his chair, his smile rapidly fading. "Surely you don't mean that, lovely lady? I was only being nice to everyone, the way Mrs. Sinclair instructed me. Sure, and isn't that what she pays me for?"

"She pays you," Mrs. Chubb said carefully, "to greet the guests at the door and assist them with their luggage, or whatever help they might need. You are not paid to dazzle every woman you meet with your so-called charms and cause trouble."

Arthur's jaw dropped. "But—"

"I'll tell you this, Arthur Barrett," Mrs. Chubb went on relentlessly, "if I have lost a good friend over this, I suggest you stay out of my way and pay very close attention to your job. Or I might be tempted to see that you lose it."

Arthur stared at her for a moment, while she steeled herself to resist that roguish twinkle in his eye. Then he shrugged, touched his forehead with his fingers, and quickly left the room.

Mrs. Chubb sat down rather heavily in the chair he'd vacated. She felt a strong urge to throw her apron over her head and bawl like a baby. But that wouldn't solve anything. And it was her pride that was hurt, more than her heart. She just hoped she could say the same for Phoebe.

Fifteen minutes wasn't a long time to take a breather, and Gertie was determined to make the most of it. After the sweltering heat of the kitchen, she relished the moments in the cool fresh air, smelling the seaweed and roses and the salty breeze from the ocean.

Today, however, she had Jack the Ripper with her in the form of one Master Stanley Malton. And she was going to need her bleeding wits about her to keep him in line. If she'd had her way, she'd have put a dog lead around his neck, hoping he'd bloody strangle if he tried to hop it.

Mrs. Chubb had nearly had kittens when she'd suggested it. Just let the housekeeper try to make the little bugger behave like a human being instead of some horrible monster. See how she'd like it.

"Why is your belly sticking out like that?" Stanley said as they tramped across the grass together, his hand imprisoned in her strong grip.

"'Cause it's got a blooming baby in it, that's why."

Stanley laughed uproariously. "That's stupid."

"You're bleeding telling me. Stupidest thing I ever did, I can tell you."

"Have you got some deadly disease? My father says that there are diseases that make you blow up like a balloon until you explode." He poked a finger into her belly, making her yelp. "Are you going to explode?"

Gertie gritted her teeth. "If I do, I'll make bleeding sure it's all over you," she muttered. Eyeing the pagoda up ahead, she changed her tone. "I'm going to sit down for a minute or two and rest. Did you bring your pegboard with you?"

"It's boring. I brought a knife to practice mumblety-peg." He pulled a dinner knife from his pocket and waved it at her. "If I stick this in your belly, will it explode?"

Gertie halted and, twisting around in front of him, grabbed his arms and gave him a shaking so hard his teeth rattled. The knife fell from his hand to the ground, and she put her foot on it.

"If you so much as think about sticking that knife into anyone, Master Stanley-bleeding-Malton, I'll tell the constable to come and take you away, and lock you up with all the rats in a dungeon for the rest of your bloody life."

For a moment she saw stark terror cross his face and was immediately ashamed of her outburst. She let him go and picked up the knife. "You may be a little monster," she said, struggling to calm her temper, "but even a twit like you knows not to stick a knife into someone."

"I won't," Stanley said sulkily, kicking at the grass with the toe of his boot. "I was just teasing you."

"Well, I don't like to be bloody teased. Especially about things like that. So are you going to behave, or do I have to take you back to the blinking hotel and lock you in Samuel's room for the rest of the afternoon?"

He looked up at her with such an anxious expression she felt like a witch. "I'll behave," he promised. "I will, I will. I promise."

"All right, then." Feeling pleased with herself for getting the upper hand, Gertie trudged toward the pagoda. She reached the welcome shade and plopped down on the seat, puffing out her breath. "We have to go back in a minute, so don't go running off, all right?"

"Can I have the knife back?"

She stared at him suspiciously. "Whatcha going to do with it?"

"I told you, practice mumblety-peg."

Gertie looked at the knife. "This ain't the kind of knife you use for that. You need one that will stick in the ground when you throw it down." Looking at his crestfallen face, she decided to make amends for her earlier fit of temper. "Tell you what. When we go back, I'll pinch a proper knife and I'll show you how to do it, all right?"

Stanley immediately looked more cheerful. "That would be very nice."

Gertie studied the smiling face. The kid wasn't that bad after all. Just needed a firm hand, that was all. And if anyone could give it to him, it was bleeding Gertie Brown. Maybe it wouldn't be so hard to bring up a kid as she imagined.

She watched Stanley dig into his pocket. After a moment he fished out a large gold watch on a chain. "Isn't this a pretty watch?" he said, holding it up to where the sunlight bounced off the case and flashed in her eyes.

"Whose is it?" she said, guessing that it was his father's.

"I found it." Stanley started swinging the watch back and forth in front of her eyes. "Watch it. See how the sunlight shines on it? See it swing to and fro . . . to and fro. . . ."

Gertie narrowed her eyes. The elusive memory, the scene she couldn't quite capture in her mind, was hovering just out of reach again.

"It's a lovely watch," Stanley was saying, his voice getting low and very quiet. "Look at it. Do you recognize it? Does it belong to you?"

"Course not," Gertie said. "It's a man's watch."

"Do you know who it belongs to?"

Gertie yawned. "I ain't got the slightest idea." She was getting sleepy. The pagoda was hot, even with the shade from the roof. The smell of the flowers made her head feel heavy. She couldn't hold her chin up any longer.

"You're getting sleepy," Stanley said, reading her mind. Again something nudged her memory. The voice . . .

the swinging watch . . . reminded her of something . . . someone . . .

Gertie sat up straight, blinking her eyes to clear her mind. The woman doctor. She'd used the very same tone and almost the same words. Only she hadn't swung a watch, she'd used a pendant.

"'Ere," Gertie said, giving Stanley a hard stare. "Where did you bleeding learn how to hypnotize people?"

CHAPTER

❊ 14 ❊

Stanley stopped swinging the watch and stared at her with a look of pure innocence. "What does hypnotize mean?"

Gertie waved an impatient hand. "You know, sending people to sleep so you can talk to their bleeding minds, that's what."

"You don't have to send people to sleep to talk to their minds."

"You do if you want them to believe what you tell them." Gertie scowled at him. "That's what you were bloody trying to do to me, weren't you? Send me to flipping sleep so you could run off and do something horrible, and I'd be none the wiser."

Stanley opened his eyes as wide as they would go. "Who, me? I don't know how to send you to sleep."

"You don't, huh? Then what were you swinging that

watch for and saying all those things about getting sleepy?"

"I just thought you looked sleepy, that's all. I was trying to wake you up by flashing the sun in your eyes."

"Oh, yeah? Well, I don't believe you. I think you were up to no bloody good, that's what I think." She stared at him, and he stared back, his mouth set in a defiant line.

Gertie decided it was waste of time trying to get him to admit anything. She got slowly to her feet, groaning as pain spread down her back. Another bloody three months of this yet, and she was already as big as a house.

"Come on," she said, "we'd better bleeding get back to the hotel before they send a search party."

"Race you!" Stanley shouted, and darted off before she could stop him.

"Like blue blazes, I will," she muttered, trudging after him. It was all she could do to walk with her back aching that way. She just hoped the little bugger had gone back to the hotel. If not, she'd bleeding box his ears. Or worse.

Cecily leaned back in the trap and gazed across the sands, unaware of what she saw or heard. Her mind was on her daughter-in-law and how best to introduce the subject of voodoo.

She hadn't been able in get her conversation with Madeline out of her mind. It was true, as Baxter had said, that Madeline's interest in the supernatural was a little excessive at times. But she had been genuinely concerned about Simani's strange pastime, and Cecily was inclined to agree with her.

It wouldn't hurt to ask Simani about it, she assured herself as the trap left the Esplanade and turned onto the Dover Road. As long as she was diplomatic and didn't say anything to offend the woman.

She shivered, wondering what Simani might do if she did offend her, then dismissed her fears as nonsense. Baxter was right, she was letting Madeline's beliefs cloud her mind and her judgment.

She would wait until she'd discussed the matter with her daughter-in-law before forming an opinion one way or the other. After all, she had only the word of Madeline's friend, whoever he might be. And since the man was leaving the George and Dragon at the time, it was quite conceivable that he'd consumed a fair amount of ale. In that case he most likely didn't see what he thought he saw.

The trap halted with a creaking jerk, and Cecily sat up. So absorbed had she been in her thoughts, she hadn't realized where she was.

She had deliberately arrived at lunchtime, using that as an excuse for the visit. Even so, she saw only one other customer in the private bar when she entered.

Michael stood behind the counter, his nose buried in the local newspaper. He looked up at the sound of her voice, a frown crossing his face. His greeting sounded offhand, and Cecily felt a pang of apprehension.

"Is everything all right?" she asked anxiously.

He folded the newspaper, nodding at the empty tables. "Take a look for yourself. I ordered two dozen Cornish pasties from Dolly's, and I haven't sold one of them. They'll go bad before tomorrow. What a frightful waste of money. I might just as well have thrown it in Deep Willow Pond."

Cecily's heart ached for him. "I'm sorry, dear. I know how worrying it must be for you."

"Well, there's one good side to it." He gave her a stern look. "There's no one here to see my mother walk into a public house unescorted."

Cecily sighed. Why was it, she wondered, that everyone was so concerned about her reputation? Was this not the twentieth century? The Victorian days were long gone, and good riddance to them.

"I'm in the private bar, Michael," she said patiently. "As you well know, it's quite acceptable for a lady to visit nowadays."

"If her escort is in the public bar, yes. Not to walk in here totally unaccompanied."

"I am well chaperoned by my son, darling. Doesn't that make it all right?" Cecily patted his hand. "Besides, as you pointed out, there is no one but old Billy Gates over there to see me, and he is too engrossed in his farming magazine to take much notice of me."

Her eyes fell on the back page of the newspaper Michael still held in his hand. Struck with an idea, and thankful for the change of subject, she said, "Since you buy so much merchandise from Dolly's, perhaps she'd allow you to put up a poster advertising the inn?"

She didn't really expect to get much response to her suggestion. Michael surprised her, however, by slapping the paper on the counter with an exclamation of delight.

"Hey, that's a spiffing idea! It might just work. After all, we sell a lot of the pastries that make Dolly's so popular. If people were aware that they can get the same product here at the inn, plus enjoy a change of scenery, and Dolly doesn't sell beer or spirits . . ." His face split into a grin. "Thanks, Mother. I'll go down this afternoon and set it up. Now, what can I write on the poster?"

He gazed thoughtfully at the ceiling, and Cecily laughed. "That's something you'll have to work out for yourself. Perhaps Simani can help you." She looked around the room. "Where is she, by the way?"

Michael gave her a vague look, his mind obviously on the poster. "Oh, she went off somewhere. To the High Street, I think. Shopping."

Disappointed at her wasted journey, Cecily said casually, "I don't imagine you know what time she intends to return?"

"No, I don't." Belatedly absorbing the question, Michael gave her a sharp look. "Why?"

"I was going to invite her to Dolly's for afternoon tea." Cecily tapped her fingers thoughtfully on the counter. "I suppose I'll have to do it another time."

"Any special occasion?"

She shook her head. "I'd simply like to get to know her better, that's all."

Michael looked relieved. "That's wonderful. I'm sure she would like that. She admires you, you know."

Amazed by the statement, Cecily stared at him. "She does?"

"Yes, she does. She thinks you are very brave to go on running the hotel all by yourself."

"Well, I assure you I can't take all the credit for any success in that respect," Cecily said modestly. "Baxter is a tremendous asset and a very great help to me. I really don't know what I would do without him."

"I'm quite sure you would manage admirably, Mother. In fact, more than likely you would do even better if you were left to your own devices."

Cecily smiled. "I doubt that very much. Baxter is my right-hand man. He has helped me out of more trouble than you could possibly imagine."

"Trouble?" Michael's eyebrows shot up. "What kind of trouble?"

"You don't want to know, darling. Nothing too drastic, though, I promise." She gazed at him, wondering how to phrase the question uppermost in her mind. "You've been out in Africa," she said finally. "Tell me what you know about voodoo."

Michael narrowed his eyes. "Why? What could you possibly find interesting about that nonsense?"

"Is it nonsense? Don't you think there could be some truth to the theory that the practitioners of voodoo can achieve some very startling results with their curses?"

"Perhaps, but only if the person involved is overly superstitious and believes all that rot. Anyone who absolutely refuses to believe that black magic is possible would not be affected at all."

Cecily looked at him thoughtfully. "You may have a point."

"It's all a load of tommyrot, anyway. No one can really put curses on anyone. It's a lot of religious balderdash."

"Maybe Simani doesn't share your opinion." She'd said it carelessly, but Michael's chin shot up.

"What has this got to do with my wife?"

Inwardly cursing herself for her tactless words, Cecily said hurriedly, "I only meant that having come from Africa, she might be more inclined to believe in the ancient customs."

"I know what you meant." His eyes were cool when he looked at her. "You mean that because Simani is colored she's more likely to indulge in all that mumbo jumbo, isn't that it?"

Distressed that his words had cut a little too close, Cecily said defensively, "I most certainly did not. Voodooism originated in Africa, did it not? I merely wondered if Simani might have knowledge of it, that is all. Having lived there all her life, it is possible she would know about it from her people."

Michael passed a hand across his eyes. "I'm sorry, Mother. This lack of business has made me a little testy. And there are too many people who treat my wife as if she were a creature that had escaped from the zoo. Forgive me if I have taken out my frustrations on you."

Feeling a little guilty, Cecily patted his hand again. "It's all right, Michael, I understand. I must return to the hotel now, but please tell Simani that I would like to issue an invitation to her to Dolly's in the near future."

"I will, Mother. And thank you. You're a brick."

Cecily left him staring at the newspaper, no doubt still composing the wording for the poster.

Arriving back at the hotel later, she heard the most awful caterwauling as she climbed the steps to the front door. Arthur stood in the doorway, his face turned toward the foyer, where the noise seemed to originate.

He spun around when Cecily said sharply, "Whatever is that dreadful noise?"

"Ah, madam, 'tis a sorry sight, I must say. Whatever is today's youth coming to, that's what I want to know. We were never allowed to cause such a scene in my young days."

Frowning, Cecily stepped past him into the shade of the foyer. She was just in time to see Baxter leading a screeching Stanley by the ear toward the kitchen stairs.

"Baxter!" She strode toward him, all her senses set on edge by the earsplitting squeals from the struggling boy.

Baxter halted and turned his face toward her. Two spots of high color stained his cheeks, and his eyes glittered like icicles.

Cecily felt a jolt of dismay. She couldn't remember ever seeing her manager quite so furious. He looked ready to erupt any minute. Even so, she couldn't condone his harsh treatment of Stanley, whose face was as red as a beetroot.

"Is it really necessary to manhandle the child in that manner?" she said, putting her hands over her ears as Stanley emitted another shriek.

Baxter's voice cracked when he answered. "This . . . child . . . has just demolished my office in spite of repeated demands that he leave. This was the only way I could get him to come back to the kitchen."

"Don't want to go back to the kitchen!" Stanley howled. "It's too hot. It's boring. I want to go to the beach."

"You can't go to the beach on your own. Your mother would never allow it, and rightly so. But if this gentleman will be so kind as to let go of your ear"—Cecily gave Baxter a meaningful stare—"and if you will promise to come with me quietly to the kitchen, I'll see if I can find someone to go down on the sands with you. All right?"

Stanley nodded his head as best he could with Baxter still holding his ear. "Just get him off me!" he yelled.

With a sound of disgust, Baxter let go of the ear. "If I ever see you in the vicinity of my office again," he said harshly, "I'll lock you in the cellars."

"I'd give him a sound thrashing," said a voice behind

Cecily. No one had noticed the colonel creeping up on them.

Cecily gave him a disapproving look. "That doesn't solve anything," she said, including Baxter in her condemnation. "Bad behavior is a symptom of something deeply troubling a child. It is far better to discover the cause and try to remedy it than punish the child for doing his best to draw attention to the problem."

"I'd like to draw attention where it does the most good," Baxter said grimly. "In the space of half an hour this boy has managed to disrupt my entire office." He ran a hand through his hair, leaving it ruffled on his forehead. "My ledgers are a shambles," he said, glaring at the flushed face of the boy. "He managed to pour the entire contents of my inkwell over them. He pulled over the cabinet containing my records. It will take weeks to get them straightened out and back in order."

"I was trying to climb up to the window," Stanley said. "It's not my fault if the cabinet was wobbly."

"Wouldn't have wobbled, no doubt," the colonel muttered, "if it had not been forced to bear so much weight."

Stanley stuck his tongue out at him.

"Pesky little devil," Colonel Fortescue muttered. "The child needs a firm hand. Let him feel the bite of a belt strap, that'll soon put him in order, what? What?"

"I don't think so, Colonel," Cecily said firmly.

She looked up at Baxter, upset to see the anger still burning on his face. "I'm sorry about the mess in your office, Baxter. Perhaps I can give you a hand to straighten it later on."

He gave a brief shake of his head. "Thank you, madam. But I will manage perfectly well on my own." He stalked off, holding his back as straight as a chimney stack.

Cecily felt a stab of irritation. Darn the man. He was getting far too sensitive lately. She looked at the colonel, who stood staring at Stanley, his lids flapping urgently up and down.

"Discipline, my boy," he roared suddenly, causing Stanley to back off a step or two. "Do you some damn good. Never have been the same since you waved that dashed watch in my face."

Anxious to avoid another outburst like the one the previous evening, Cecily grasped Stanley's arm firmly above the elbow. "Come, Stanley," she said, "let's see if Mrs. Chubb can find some more blancmange."

They started down the stairs, leaving the colonel to grumble his way across the foyer.

"What do you like best about the sands?" Cecily asked as Stanley stepped with maddeningly short paces down the stairs.

He shrugged but didn't answer her.

"Do you like the Punch-and-Judy show?"

Again a shrug.

"Donkey rides?"

The pudgy shoulders rose and fell.

"Boat trips?"

This suggestion produced the same response.

Reaching the bottom of the stairs, Cecily decided to try another tack. All the boy really needed was love and understanding. By all accounts he got little of either from his parents.

Now he was left to deal with his father's death while his mother languished in bed. It was no wonder Stanley was always in hot water. He was starved of affection and did everything he could to attract the attention he craved.

Determined to let the child know that at least one adult understood him, Cecily said quietly, "Stanley, I know how you must be hurting inside because of what happened to your father. You will find as time passes that the pain will gradually lessen—"

"He was stupid."

She looked down at him in surprise. "I beg your pardon?"

"My father was very stupid. I hate him. I'm glad he's dead."

Hardly able to believe her ears, she said gently, "Stanley, you don't mean that."

"Yes, I do. Oh, yes, I do." Stanley started skipping ahead of her, chanting in a singsong voice, "Jack and Jill went up the hill to fetch a pail of water. Jack fell down and broke his crown and Jill came tumbling after."

Cecily felt a cold chill as she watched the boy. There was something about the words of that rhyme that unsettled her. She couldn't help wondering if perhaps they were prophetic.

CHAPTER
❈ 15 ❈

Stanley arrived at the kitchen ahead of Cecily and had disappeared inside by the time she reached the door. She heard Gertie's voice the minute she pushed the door open.

"You get away from me, you nasty little monster. I don't want you bloody near me again."

Sighing, Cecily walked into the kitchen in time to see Gertie making threatening motions at Stanley's throat with her curled fingers.

She sprang back when she saw Cecily. "Afternoon, mum," she said, bobbing a slight curtsey. "Can I get you something?"

"I'd like a bowl of blancmange for Master Stanley." Cecily patted the boy on the head. "He has promised me to behave, haven't you, dear?"

Stanley nodded his head up and down, his eyes intent on Gertie's face.

The housemaid shot a look of pure hatred at the boy. "I'll get it, mum," she said, through gritted teeth.

Stanley grinned. "Thank you so much, Miss Gertie," he said politely.

Gertie made a growling noise and went off to the pantry to get the pudding.

Cecily looked down at Stanley. "I need to have a word with Gertie outside. I trust you will sit quietly at the table and eat your blancmange while we are gone? We shan't be long."

"Yes, Mrs. Sinclair. I will be most happy to do that."

She gave him a suspicious look. The angelic pose did not suit the boy at all, and she had the uneasy feeling that the moment their backs were turned, Stanley would be up to mischief again.

Gertie returned with a bowl of yellow blancmange and slapped it on the table. "There you go, Master Stanley."

"Thank you so much, Miss Gertie." Stanley struggled onto a chair and grabbed up the spoon. He started shoveling mouthfuls of the slippery pudding into his mouth, and Gertie tutted in disgust.

"Hope it bleeding chokes you," she muttered under her breath, but not quite soft enough to escape Cecily's keen ear.

"Gertie, I'd like a word with you out in the hallway," she said. Then, turning to look at Stanley, she added, "Now, remember what you promised me. We shall be only a moment or two."

"Yes, ma'am," Stanley mumbled, dribbling yellow blanc-mange down his chin.

"Oh, strewth," Gertie said, lifting her face to the ceiling. "Give me bleeding strength."

She followed Cecily out of the door and closed it with more force than was necessary. "That kid will be the death of me," she said in a voice of impending doom.

"I do wish you would have more patience with the boy,"

Cecily said quietly. "It might not be too apparent at this point, but Master Stanley is suffering from very real grief and rejection. His father has died a tragic death, and his mother has more or less forsaken him in her own suffering. Stanley's mischief is a cry for help. He is simply looking for someone to notice him."

"Can't bleeding help noticing him," Gertie mumbled, digging her toe into the carpet. "He's upset everyone in sight. He's caused more flipping trouble in three days than a dozen bloody monkeys could do in three months."

Cecily sighed. "I know he's been a handful, Gertie, and I do sympathize. Children like that can be extremely trying. But I do wish you would attempt to use a little more understanding in this situation. Try to be his friend, and you might be surprised how well Master Stanley will respond."

"I'd be bloody well shocked out of me drawers if that little bugger responded to anything," Gertie said, with some heat. "He's bleeding dangerous, he is. He bloody well scares me, if you want to know."

Surprised by the vehemence in Gertie's voice, Cecily frowned. "I hardly think an eight-year-old boy could be much of a threat."

"Oh, yeah?" Gertie stuck out her chin. "Well, he tried to bloody hypnotize me this afternoon. Gawd only knows what he would have made me do, if I hadn't been on to him and stopped it before he blinking put me under."

"Hypnotize?" Cecily suppressed a smile. "I doubt very much if Master Stanley is capable of hypnotizing anyone."

"Well, begging your pardon, mum, but that's where you are wrong. 'Cause Master Stanley started swinging a watch in front of me eyes, and he was talking real slow and quiet, telling me how I was getting sleepy and that me head was heavy and me eyelids were closing. Almost nodded off, I did, until I remembered."

Cecily's smile faded. "Remembered what?"

"About hypnotism. How you can send someone to sleep by making them watch something swinging back and forth, and then you can tell them things, and the subcon . . . sub something-or-other mind stores it and makes you think you was the one what thought of it."

It was a garbled but fairly accurate description of hypnotic suggestion. Impressed, Cecily asked, "How did you learn all this about hypnotism?"

Gertie puffed out her cheeks, obviously pleased with her aired knowledge. "Well, it was when that woman doctor stayed at the hotel. Thought I was bleeding pregnant, I did, and I was worried about it, and she found out and hypnotized me into thinking I wasn't pregnant, and lo and behold"—Gertie held up her hands—"I wasn't." Her cheeks turned a faint pink. "If you know what I mean, mum."

Cecily smiled. "Yes, I know very well what you mean."

"Well, anyway," Gertie went on, "I got interested in it, like, since it happened to me, so I read up on it. Saw something in a magazine about it. And that's what Master Stanley was doing, trying to hypnotize me."

She looked at Cecily with a thoughtful frown. "Though how the hell he learnt it I can't imagine. The magazine said that usually one only sees a hypnotist in the Music Hall, and Master Stanley's much too young to have been there."

Cecily stared at her without speaking for several seconds. *Never have been the same since he waved that dashed watch in my face.* "Thank you, Gertie," she said at last. "Perhaps you should go back to the kitchen and keep an eye on Stanley."

"I'll keep an eye on him, all right," Gertie said, turning back to the door. "I'll watch that little twit like a mouse watches a cat."

"I told him someone would take him down to the beach," Cecily said, remembering her promise to the child. "If Mrs. Chubb can spare you for a little while, perhaps you could take him on the sands?"

Gertie looked as if she'd been asked to stoke coal for the

devil himself. But she tightened her mouth and said, "I'll ask permission from Mrs. Chubb, mum."

Cecily nodded. "Thank you, Gertie." She left quickly, anxious to find Baxter. There was something she wanted him to do, and it could take her a while to persuade him.

She found him in the conservatory, examining the leg of the chaise lounge. "This needs tightening," he announced when he saw her. "It has a definite wobble. I'll get Samuel to see to it."

"As soon as possible," Cecily said. "We don't want the thing to collapse with one of our guests seated on it."

"Precisely, madam. That was my concern, too."

Cecily moved over to a huge fern and began fingering the leaves. "I should get Madeline to take a look at these plants out here. They are beginning to look a little droopy."

"Probably the unusually warm weather, madam. Plants like lots of fresh air, and it has been unbearably stuffy in the conservatory of late."

"Yes, I know. It's all this glass. It holds the heat." Keeping her gaze on the fern, she said casually, "Speaking of fresh air, do you have any special plans for tonight?"

She could hear the wariness in his voice when he answered. "Not any special plans, no."

"Good. I should like to go out tonight, and I will need an escort. I should appreciate it very much if you would accompany me."

There was a long pause, while she pretended to scrutinize a feathery leaf.

"May I enquire as to where we would be going, madam?"

"You may, Baxter." She drew in a breath. "I would like to visit the Hippodrome in Wellercombe."

After what seemed an eternity, Baxter made a small choking sound. "Is madam aware that the Hippodrome is a . . . Variety theater?"

He'd said *Variety* in almost a whisper, as if afraid to be caught uttering such profanity.

Cecily braced herself and looked at him. "Yes," she said

calmly. "Madam is fully aware of that fact. Which is the reason I wish to visit it."

He drew himself up to his full height. "Am I given to understand that this has something to do with the fact that Arthur Barrett was once an entertainer?"

"It might," Cecily said cautiously.

"Madam." Baxter coughed, cleared his throat, and tried again. "I simply cannot allow it, madam. Mr. Sinclair would most certainly not approve."

"Mr. Sinclair is not here, Baxter," she pointed out gently.

"Nevertheless, I gave him my promise—"

"To see that no harm shall befall me," Cecily cut in. "Yes, I can hardly forget that, since I'm being constantly reminded of it. I fail to see, however, what possible harm could befall me in a perfectly legitimate, well-lit theater."

"Madam, the kind of people who patronize that sort of disgusting entertainment are not the sort with whom you should be seen associating."

"I have it on very good authority that members of all classes visit the Music Halls, including the aristocracy." Cecily met his affronted gaze with calm assurance. "Why, only the other day I read that Lord Winterfield and his new bride were in the stalls."

"That was probably in a West End theater. The Hippodrome in Wellercombe is much more likely to be filled with the lower-class element of the population."

"Really." Cecily raised a delicate eyebrow. "And, as such, they are little more than animals to be avoided at all costs. Is that it?"

Baxter ran a finger around his stiff collar. "That is not what I was inferring, madam. I feel compelled to point out, however, that because of the nature of the audience, the content of the entertainment is likely to be . . ."

He paused, apparently searching for the right word.

Cecily waited patiently, interested to hear what he would say next.

Finally he said a little desperately, "They are likely to be . . . vulgar, madam."

"So I understand." She fought the urge to smile. "But I am not exactly a naive young girl anymore. I venture to think the entertainment might not be too risqué for my tender ears."

"You are making fun of me," Baxter said stiffly.

Cecily burst out laughing. "Only when you become deplorably stuffy, Bax. Come on, admit it. Don't you think it might be fun?"

"Fun, madam, is not a term I would use for the kind of behavior that goes on at such places. Not only can the performers be offensive, the hecklers sometimes drown them out with their obscene remarks."

Cecily shook her head. "You worry too much. The hecklers are usually up in the balconies. We shall be in the stalls, all perfectly proper and correct."

"I don't know how proper and correct it will appear, madam, if you are seen at such a place escorted by an employee of your establishment."

"Piffle. Since when, pray, have I ever worried about what other people think?"

"Which is precisely why I gave my promise to Mr. Sinclair to take care of you."

"Very well, then. Since I have every intention of going to the theater, it would seem that the best way for you to keep that promise would be to accompany me."

He sent her the kind of direct look that had made more than one housemaid shake in her shoes. Even Cecily felt intimidated by it at times.

"Baxter," she said firmly, "I have a very good reason to visit the theater tonight. Please believe me when I say I would not go if I didn't feel it was desperately important. Please humor me in this, and I will explain everything afterward."

Confusion crept into his face. "I don't understand."

She patted his arm. "I know you don't, Baxter. As I said,

I'll explain it all later. I'll leave you to order the trap, shall I? I do believe the show begins at eight o'clock. We shall have to leave here by half past six in order to get a good seat. I shall meet you in the foyer at twenty-five past."

Baxter still wore a slightly dazed expression, but to Cecily's relief he slowly nodded. "Very well, madam."

"Thank you, Baxter." She gave him a brilliant smile, then left him. She still had to decide what to wear. Although she would never have admitted it to Baxter, she was really looking forward to seeing the show.

She'd read in one of her magazines that the female singers used their songs to show support for the suffragettes. In Cecily's book, any woman who was willing to stand in front of an audience and use her talent to foster the Women's Movement was well worth patronizing, vulgar or not.

Feeling a small rush of excitement at the prospect, she hurried up the stairs to begin preparing for the event.

Gertie was not happy at all. It was late afternoon, and she'd been sitting in the boiling sun for almost an hour. Stanley was still in the sea, slopping up and down and every now and again sloshing water over some poor kid.

She had hoped a big bully would come along and smack Stanley on the nose, but no one seemed inclined to take him on. Not that Gertie was particularly surprised about that. Fatty Stanley must weigh a ton. It would take three kids to even push him out of the way.

Gertie scooped up a handful of sand and let it trickle through her fingers. She still hadn't forgiven him for the mess he'd made in the kitchen when she'd gone in after talking to madam. Stanley had drawn pictures all over the kitchen table and the floor . . . in blancmange. It had taken her ages to clean it all up.

If madam had seen that mess, Gertie thought bitterly, she might have had more sympathy and locked up the flipping kid.

Groaning, she climbed to her feet. It was time to get back

to the hotel, and for once she was bloody glad. She wasn't feeling at all well.

She straightened her back, and a tiny movement in her belly made her catch her breath. She stood perfectly still, her eyes glued to her body. Another movement, then another.

Her eyes widening, she put her hand on her belly. Something thumped against her palm, and she snatched her hand away with a small yelp. It must be the baby. Gawd Almighty, it wasn't getting ready to be born, was it?

She'd read about how it was born. The details had made her feel sick, but at least now she knew where it came out. She'd been afraid they would have to cut her open to get it out. But no one told her she'd be able to feel it move.

Another light thump had her worried even more. She'd better get back to the hotel, before she dropped the blinking thing right there on the sands.

Anxiously she scanned the water's edge for Stanley. Her heart skipped a beat when she couldn't see him. Where the bloody hell had he gone? It wasn't as if she could miss him. He was three times the size of anyone else.

Panic spread over her fast. He couldn't have drowned. Surely not. Someone would have seen him or heard him.

She tried to calm herself. She couldn't be having the baby yet, it was too bleeding early. And Stanley had to be around somewhere. He had to be.

Shading her eyes with her hand, she started walking toward the water. A young boy almost ran into her, and she grabbed his arm.

"Watch where you're bloody going," she said crossly.

"Sorry, miss." He would have darted off, but she held on to him. "Have you seen a fat boy wading in the water along here?"

The child shook his head. "I haven't been here very long."

"Strewth." She let go of the boy and watched him race along the sands. What was she going to do? She couldn't go back without him. Mrs. Chubb would cut her bleeding head off.

Without much hope she began moving between the bodies lining the water's edge. Putting her hands up to her mouth, she yelled at the top of her lungs, "Stanley! Stanley!"

Several minutes later she was out of breath, even hotter than before, and almost at the breaking point. Her throat ached with yelling, and everyone was looking at her as if she was bleeding daft.

She retraced her steps, still shouting as loud as she could. "Stanley!"

"I'm here, stupid."

She almost jumped out of her skin as the voice spoke right at her feet. Looking down, she saw a mound of sand, and Stanley's head sticking out one end of it.

As she stared at him, he opened his mouth and exploded with raucous laughter.

She waited, fists dug into her hips, until he had to stop laughing to get his breath. "I've been watching you for hours," he said finally, gasping for breath. "You walked right past me lots of times."

"Get up."

He eyed her warily, apparently alerted by her tone. "I can't," he said, moving his head from side to side. "I'm trapped in here. That's why I couldn't get up before."

"I said get bleeding well up before I kick you to kingdom come."

"You can't do that. You're not allowed to kick me."

"And who's going to know?"

"I'll tell Mrs. Chubb if you do."

"All right, then. I'll . . . stuff your mouth full of sand so you can't talk to no one. How would you like that, Master Stanley-bleeding-Malton?"

Stanley's face assumed a haughty look. "You wouldn't dare."

"Oh, no?" Gertie squatted down and grabbed a handful of

sand. "I'm going to count to five. If you're not on your bloody feet by then, you'll have sand for your supper tonight."

She got to four before Stanley sat up, spraying sand everywhere. "All right, spoilsport," he muttered. "I'm coming. I'm coming. But I'm going to tell everyone how rotten you are to me. Even Mrs. Sinclair."

Gertie waited until he was on his feet, then she bent over him and thrust her face close to his. "I wish you'd bleeding drowned, you rotten little bugger. It would serve you bloody well right. Feeding the fish at the bottom of the sea. That's where you belong."

She grabbed his arm and began dragging him across the sand. "Come on, I've got better things to do than to stand here arguing with you. But I tell you, Stanley, one of these fine days I'm going to really lose my temper with you. Then you had bloody well better watch out."

For once Stanley didn't give her a back answer. Which was just as well. She could feel the baby kicking inside her again, and she couldn't wait to get back to the hotel and tell Mrs. Chubb about it.

CHAPTER

❖ 16 ❖

Although Wellercombe was a little less than seventeen miles from Badgers End, it took Cecily and Baxter the best part of an hour to arrive at the Hippodrome. Here the motorcars invaded the streets in far greater numbers than in the villages.

It made navigation in a horse-drawn trap a hazardous experience, not only from the aspect of maneuvering past the bulky machines, but also the sudden bangs and pops that erupted from them could startle a frisky mare into rearing onto its back legs—or worse, racing down the street in terrified flight, dragging its helpless victims with it.

Baxter sat in tense silence once they reached the outskirts of the town. Cecily had complete faith in Samuel's capabilities and was more inclined to be fatalistic about the situation.

Deciding that Baxter needed something to keep his mind from imagining any number of dire mishaps, she kept up a stream of chatter, talking about anything that came into her head.

"You know," she said as they moved in a series of stops and starts down the High Street, "I have been reading about all these kinemas opening up. It would seem as if the moving pictures industry is growing very fast. It has certainly come a long way since it was first seen in the fairgrounds. Have you ever seen one?"

Baxter looked at her as if she'd lost her mind.

"They really are quite fascinating. A little bit hard on the eyes at times, since they do jump around a lot, but it really is amazing to watch actors acting out a drama without the audience actually having to be there in person. Just think of the number of people they can reach, and they only have to do the play once."

Baxter grunted.

"Some believe the pictures will take over the theater eventually," Cecily continued. "I hear that now the passion for roller skating has abated, all these skating rinks are standing empty. Some astute entrepreneurs are buying up these places and turning them into kinemas. Actually they used to be called kinemas. I believe now they call them cinemas. For twopence one can view an hour's film, and for another penny, they'll serve you tea and biscuits."

The trap jerked to an unexpected halt, and the bay whinnied. Baxter made a muffled exclamation, but Cecily blithely ignored him. "I do hope that won't mean the death of the theater. Somehow I can't imagine that those flickering images on a screen can possibly compare to a live performance. Can you, Baxter?"

He mumbled an answer she didn't understand.

"I read about a film called *The Great Train Robbery*. And apparently filmmakers are issuing new programs as fast as they can turn them out. They even have a pianist in the cinemas to give the story more atmosphere. Though I must say I would prefer a full orchestra, wouldn't you?"

Baxter looked as if he would like to turn the trap around and return to Badgers End. "Madam—" he began, but she interrupted him with a raised hand.

"Look, Baxter, there's the Hippodrome. It certainly is a magnificent building, wouldn't you say?"

The trap slowed to a halt a short distance from the theater, as people streamed along the pavement toward the doors. "I think this is as close as I can get, mum," Samuel called out over the roar of motorcars.

"I'm afraid we will have to walk, madam," Baxter said, his tone suggesting that they were about to walk into the valley of death.

"So we shall," Cecily said brightly and allowed him to assist her out of the trap. "Please return for us in two hours," she told Samuel. He touched his hat with his whip and moved off.

Once inside, the theater looked even more impressive, with its brass railings lining the balconies and the thick crimson carpeting underfoot. Crystal chandeliers hung from a ceiling covered in plaster nymphs, who appeared to be playing all manner of musical instruments.

Cecily found it all fascinating, but the moment the orchestra struck the first chords of the overture, the decor was forgotten. Amidst loud cheers, an occasional boo, and lots of good-humored advice from the upper circle, affectionately known as the gods, six young women tapped their way energetically across the stage and performed various gyrations that made Cecily feel dizzy to watch them.

Act followed upon act, from a comedian whose jokes made Baxter visibly squirm, to a third-rate soprano who fought desperately for the top notes, and closing with a quite spectacular magician whose talent for making things disappear made up for his stoic and sometimes unintelligible patter.

By the time the show came to a boisterous finale amid

thunderous applause and much cheering from the balconies, Cecily felt quite exhausted.

"We have to make our way backstage," she told Baxter as they prepared to leave their seats.

Baxter, obviously horrified at this latest suggestion, opened his mouth to protest, but she forestalled him.

"I don't have time to argue, Baxter. Either come with me or wait for me in the lobby."

Snapping his mouth shut with an expression that boded trouble for her later, he rose from his seat and followed her up the aisle.

It took much less effort than she had anticipated to reach the backstage area. She merely told the doorman that she owned the Pennyfoot Hotel and was looking for entertainers, while Baxter stood looking aghast at her.

She was ushered into a narrow passageway fraught with ropes and pulleys, ladders of all kinds, and huge screens with painted backdrops on them.

"Madam," Baxter said behind her, "I must strenuously object to us being here in this environment."

"Baxter, I have to be here if I want to speak with the performers."

"*Speak* with them, madam?"

She stopped and turned to face him. His expression mirrored his alarm, and she almost felt sorry for him. "I'm sorry, but I have to question these people if I'm to find out what I want to know."

"Surely there is a less distressing method of procuring information?"

Cecily smiled. "Please try to relax, Baxter. I will be as quick as possible."

She caught sight of one of the dancers climbing down a circular stairway. "Ah, there is someone now," she said and hurried over to the young woman before Baxter could protest further.

The girl's face was streaked with dust and perspiration, which left tiny rivulets in the heavy greasepaint. Bright blue circles surrounded her eyes, which were fringed with long, thick black spikes for eyelashes. Her skirt barely skimmed her ankles, and her arms were bare from the shoulders.

Cecily could almost feel Baxter's look of disapproval. Trying to ignore his stone-faced presence, she greeted the girl and complimented her on her fine performance.

"I happen to be acquainted with an entertainer myself," Cecily said casually after the girl had thanked her. "He used to be in the Music Hall, I believe. His name is Arthur Barrett. Have you heard of him, by any chance?"

Blond curls bounced all over her forehead as the dancer shook her head. "Never heard of him, ducks. But then, if he was in Music Hall, I probably wouldn't know him. Variety is what is in now. Bit different than the old Music Hall. Got a bit more meat to it, if you know what I mean."

She gave Cecily a hearty nudge in the ribs with her elbow. "Lot more saucy. The crowds like that. Lot better than that hoity-toity crowd in the West End. You can have a laugh with these audiences. Bit of all right, this lot. They know a good joke when they hear one."

The dancer looked over at Baxter, whose face looked as if it was about to crack. After running her gaze over him from head to foot, she said, "Enjoy the show, did ya, luv? Want me autograph, then?"

Baxter made a noise deep in his throat as if he were drowning. The dancer let out a deep, coarse belly laugh, then spun around to wind her way through the passages and disappeared.

Cecily risked a glance at her manager. His face was scarlet, and he studiously avoided her gaze as he said, "I trust we can leave now, madam?"

She felt sorry for him, but she was not about to give up that easily. "I won't be much longer," she assured him and prepared to venture further into the strange world of backstage theater.

From somewhere off to her left she heard voices and followed the sound, stepping over more ropes and around boxes crammed with strange-looking objects. Finally rounding a corner, she saw a group of people laughing at a man who appeared to be the center of attention.

Recognizing one of the comedians, Cecily prudently waited until he'd finished his joke before coming forward. Baxter had been embarrassed enough.

The huge stage lights reflected on the man's bald head, and his smile appeared to stretch all the way across his face. "Ay, up, lass, what can I do for you?" he asked in a thick north-country accent.

The group fell silent as Cecily asked her question. "Does anyone here know of a performer by the name of Arthur Barrett? He was on the stage in the Music Hall for a while, I do believe."

The comedian shook his head. "Sorry, luv, never heard of him. They come and go fast in this business, you know. Maybe you should ask one of the old-timers. Like Harry Mattson. He might know."

"Or Dennis," someone else piped up.

Cecily turned to the young man who had spoken. "Dennis?"

"He's Denmarric, the magician."

The young man was one of the acrobats, and Cecily was sure she had never seen anyone so skinny in her entire life. "Do you know where I'll find him?" she asked.

The young man jerked his head backward. "He's in his dressing room. Second door on the right. Can't miss it, he's got a star on the door."

"Harry should be wandering around somewhere, too," the bald man added. "He has the room next door. He might be able to help."

Thanking them, Cecily followed the direction she'd been given, with Baxter following in silence behind. No doubt he was saving all his additional objections for later, she thought. But she couldn't worry about that now.

Finding the magician's door, she rapped on it. It was opened abruptly by a heavyset man in a faded silk dressing gown. Without his turban and robe the magician looked a lot less impressive. He had removed most of his makeup, but traces of yellow and brown greasepaint still clung to his mustache and eyebrows.

Cecily was surprised to see the deeply etched lines on his face. He had looked much younger from the stalls. His gray hair sprang defiantly from his head in all directions, and his dark eyes darted back and forth between her and Baxter like twin mosquitos on Deep Willow Pond.

"Please excuse me for disturbing you," Cecily said, feeling a little unsettled by the man's quivering impatience, "but I would like to ask you a few questions, if I may?"

"Certainly. Certainly. Why didn't you say so?" His voice boomed out as though he were still trying to be heard in the back of the stalls.

He opened the door wider. "Come in, come in." Giving Baxter a scathing look, he demanded, "Is this your camera-man? Tell him to get his equipment. Hurry, hurry! I haven't got all night."

Confused, Cecily stepped into the tiny room. The magi-cian's stage clothes had been thrown over the top of a screen in the corner, while his turban sat on the table in front of a large mirror. Gas lamps burned all around the frame, sending odd shadows across Cecily's face as she glanced at her reflection.

She turned to face the magician, who was still inspecting Baxter as if he were a particularly nasty insect.

"I wanted to ask you if you had heard of a performer by the name of Arthur Barrett," she said, finally getting his attention.

He swung his head around and scowled at her. "No, I haven't. Should I?"

Cecily was beginning to feel most uncomfortable. The man's attitude left a lot to be desired. "He is an acquaintance of mine, that's all. I was interested in talking to anyone who might have known him when he was performing in the Music Hall."

"Good Lord, woman, is that all you wanted?" Denmarric bellowed. "You're not a writer? You're not here for an interview?"

Cecily shook her head in mute apology.

"Then why in the hell are you wasting my time?" He waved an arm furiously at the door. "Get out of here before I turn you both into sniveling little frogs. Out, out, I say!"

Baxter stepped forward, his eyes burning with outrage. Before he could speak, Cecily said hastily, "I'm sorry, sir, I did not mean to mislead you. Am I to assume that you have not heard of Arthur Barrett?"

"I not only haven't heard of him," the magician roared, "I don't give a fig about him. Now get out and leave me alone."

Cecily moved fast, straight at the door, forcing Baxter to step back before she collided with him. "Phew," she said, pretending to mop her brow as the door slammed behind her. "What a nasty-tempered man."

"I did warn you, madam," Baxter said, his face arranged in an *I-told-you-so* expression.

"So you did, Baxter," Cecily said cheerfully. "I am most grateful that you were here with me."

A look of relief crossed his face. "May we leave now?"

"Not yet." She moved over to the next door. "Just allow me to question one more person, then I promise I will leave."

She tapped on the door quickly before Baxter had time to dissuade her. A moment later the door opened and a sad-faced man looked down at her. "Yes?"

"Mr. Mattson?"

"That's my name."

"I enjoyed your performance very much tonight," Cecily said, trying to remember exactly which act he'd performed.

"Oh, thank you." He looked a little brighter. "Did you come for an autograph? If so, you have to have Bessie's and Poppy's, too."

"I do?" Cecily looked at Baxter for help.

Her manager shrugged and lifted his gaze to the rafters as if to tell her she was on her own.

"You want to see them?" Harry Mattson opened the door wider, and Cecily peered in. In a large basket lined with pink silk, two poodles looked solemnly back at her, one black, one white.

Now she remembered. The performing dogs. They had pranced back and forth on their hind legs wearing dresses and carrying parasols. "Oh, how sweet," she said, wondering how happy a dog could be in such an environment.

"They won't bite you," Mattson said, looking as if he were about to cry. "They never bite."

"I'm sure they don't." Cecily gave him a smile. "I would love their autograph, and yours, too."

Mattson's face crumpled like a baby's, and a large tear rolled down his cheek. "That's so wonderful. No one has ever asked before. The girls will be so happy."

"Madam," Baxter said, sounding desperate.

Cecily gave him a reassuring nod. "I won't be a minute."

She followed Mattson into the cramped quarters and gave him her program.

The entertainer sniffed and wiped his nose with the back of his hand. Then he sorted through an assortment of bottles on his dressing table until he found what he was looking for. Opening the lid of the jar, he took hold of the white poodle's paw and dipped it into the pot.

The dog sat there with a bored expression on her face while her owner pressed her paw to the program. He did the same thing with the black poodle, who seemed equally bored with the entire procedure. Then he found a pen, dipped it into the ink, and scribbled something underneath.

Handing the program back to Cecily, he said tearfully, "We will remember you for the rest of our days."

"Thank you," Cecily said, glancing down at the words he'd written. *Mattson's Mutts, with deep gratitude from Harry, Poppy, and Bessie.* "I'm sure I'll remember you, too."

She turned toward the door, then paused. "I don't suppose you know of a man named Arthur Barrett, by any chance?"

Mattson sniffed and wiped at his nose again. "Barrett? Arthur Barrett? Sounds familiar." He creased his forehead in concentration while Baxter fidgeted from foot to foot. "I seem to remember something . . ."

Cecily held her breath while the poodles yawned. Then Mattson snapped his fingers. "Now I remember!"

Both dogs immediately leapt from the basket and began walking across the floor on hind legs.

"No, no," Mattson said sternly to them, "not now. Go lie down."

The poodles obediently dropped on all fours and padded back to the basket.

Cecily hardly noticed them. Her attention was fully on Harry Mattson's mournful face. "You remember Arthur?"

"Yes, I do. Only that wasn't the name he used. It was . . . let me see."

He struggled with the memory some more, then his face cleared. "Yes, that's it. His stage name was Mervin the Mysterious."

Cecily's pulse leapt. "That's an odd name for a singer," she said carefully.

Mattson looked at her in surprise. "Singer? Oh, Arthur Barrett didn't sing. At least not professionally. Mervin the Mysterious was a hypnotist. A darn good one, too, if I remember."

CHAPTER

❊ 17 ❊

Cecily heard Baxter give a little grunt of surprise. Wondering if he'd come to the same conclusion she had, she asked Harry Mattson, "How well did you know Arthur? Did you work with him?"

Mattson bent down to fondle the dogs' ears. "Not that well. He kept pretty much to himself. I was under the impression that his career was all that he lived for. I don't think he was married. I never saw him with a woman, anyway."

He looked at Cecily with his sad eyes. "Most of us are like that, you know. Something happens to us when we get bitten by the performing bug. We throw ourselves into show business, neglecting everything else in our lives. We live only for the applause. It's our sustenance, our bread and water."

How sad, Cecily thought, to give up so much for such dubious glory. "It must be a hard life," she said, "though an interesting one. I understand you travel all over the country?"

Mattson nodded. "Me and the girls." He laid a hand on each dog's head. "It's not easy finding digs. Most landladies won't have animals in their establishments. I have to take what I can get. Sometimes it's a park bench or the sands. But then, it's only a place to sleep. The theater is our real home. And the artistes become our family, even if only temporarily."

"Life on the stage must be quite lonely without the companionship of a woman," Baxter said unexpectedly.

Intrigued by this uncharacteristic comment, Cecily glanced up at him. His attention, however, was concentrated on the entertainer.

Mattson shrugged and wiped away another tear. "Few women want to marry an entertainer. But then, show business is very like a woman in many ways. Unpredictable as a summer storm, yet exciting, challenging, and deep down you know you are tied to her for life. Once the theater is in your blood, you can never ever let go."

"Some people do," Cecily said with a smile. "Arthur Barrett, for one."

"Ah, but Barrett was forced out. I suppose we all were at the time."

"Forced out?"

Mattson sighed. "It was about three years ago. Things are changing, you know. They don't call it Music Hall anymore. That appeals to a smaller, more sophisticated audience and is more or less confined to the West End. Variety is the name of the game now. The acts are more slick, more direct, more for the working man than the toffs."

He shook his head and looked mournfully down at his dogs. "It will only be a matter of time now and we'll be out. Unless I can come up with something new. That's all they scream for now, you know. Something new. Something different."

"About Arthur?" Cecily prompted.

Mattson started. "Oh, yes. Where was I? Yes, it was the old Theater Royal in Bodlington. We had a six-month engagement. Nine acts. We worked as a troupe . . . one manager, one booking for the entire ensemble." He looked up at Cecily. "Most of them work solo now, like we do." He patted the dogs again. "Don't we, girls?"

Poppy yawned, while Bessie curled up in a ball and closed her eyes.

Cecily made an effort to curb her impatience. As fascinating as she found all this, the man really did have a most annoying habit of straying from the point. "And Arthur was part of the troupe?"

"That's right. He'd worked with them long before I joined up with them. He was quite a bit older than I. Older than all of us, actually."

"Is that why he had to leave?"

Mattson looked at her blankly for a moment. Then he shook his head. "Oh, no. Someone ordered the theater closed down. A couple of months into the engagement. We were all out of work. For a time, that is. That's when the girls and I went solo. It took a while, but we started picking up bookings again."

"And Arthur?"

"Never saw him again. I bumped into most of the others on the rounds, but I never saw or heard of Mervin the Mysterious again."

"I see." Cecily thought for a moment. "Do you happen to know who it was who closed the theater down?"

Out of the corner of her eye she saw Baxter's quick glance at her, but kept her attention on Mattson.

The entertainer shook his head. "Never did know who or why."

"Well, thank you, Mr. Mattson. You have been most kind, and we won't take up any more of your time." Cecily bent down to pat the sleeping dogs on the head. "I did enjoy the act very much and I will treasure the autographs."

Mattson actually looked as if he were going to smile. "Come and see us again. We'll be here for another six weeks."

Cecily straightened. "I should like that very much." She moved toward the door, ignoring Baxter's scowl. "I wish the very best of luck to you and the girls."

"Thank you," Mattson said mournfully. "We most certainly are going to need it."

"I do feel sorry for the man," Cecily said as Baxter followed her into the cool night air. She was relieved to see Samuel parked close to the theater. He must have been there some time, as the chestnut was stamping his feet with impatience.

"If I may say so," Baxter said as they approached the trap, "anyone would feel a great deal of sympathy for a man who always wore such a somber expression."

Cecily sighed. "It really must be quite a different life. I'm not sure I would be happy with it."

"Madam, I assure you, that kind of employment would be most unsuited to someone of your caliber."

"I'm not sure I should thank you, Baxter." She lifted her eyebrows at him. "Are you suggesting I have no talent?"

She could see his perplexed expression in the glow of the lamplight. Amused, she waited for him to extricate himself from his blunder.

"Madam, I would suggest that your talents are far superior to any of those I had the misfortune to watch tonight."

It was her turn to feel unsettled, and she was thankful when they reached the trap.

Samuel sprang down to open the door for her, and she climbed up, settling herself on the worn leather seat. The trap creaked with Baxter's weight as he sat down opposite her, taking great care not to bump her knees.

Samuel had drawn the hood over, enclosing the two of

them in the cozy warmth. Cecily could barely see Baxter's face, and for once she was strangely glad of the dark shadows.

To break what threatened to be an awkward silence, she said, "I assume you understand the purpose of my questions tonight?"

"Yes, madam. I understand that people do remarkable things when under the influence of posthypnotic suggestion."

"Why, Baxter," Cecily said in amusement, "you impress me. Where did you learn about such hocus-pocus?"

"I do read, madam. I understand that the technique has been widely used in medical science. It hardly has anything in common with voodoo."

He'd sounded offended, and Cecily relented. "You are quite right, Baxter. It is an approved science and quite different from black magic, which is why I am more inclined to believe that someone hypnotized Sir Richard. I must retract my earlier theory."

Baxter seemed mollified when he answered, "It would appear that Arthur Barrett could possibly be our man. It would certainly explain why Sir Richard Malton acted in that strange manner."

"It would indeed." Cecily leaned back with a sigh of satisfaction. "Especially in view of the fact that Sir Richard could also have been the man who closed down the theater and threw Arthur out of work."

"I admit that it does seem a remarkable coincidence, since the man threatened to close down the George and Dragon, but"—Baxter paused for a moment—"are you certain it could be the same man?"

"Certain?" Cecily laughed. "No, of course not. When have I ever been certain about anything? I am guessing, of course. But since Sir Richard did tell Michael that he had closed down a business once before, and since Arthur presumably lost the career he loved because of a closed theater, and Sir Richard Malton is now dead, having lost his life in the presence of our doorman, I would say it is a fairly accurate guess, wouldn't you?"

There was a short pause, then Baxter said softly, "As I already mentioned, madam, your talents are far superior to those of anyone I have met."

"Thank you." She laughed a little self-consciously. "I do believe it's time we had a word with Arthur, don't you?"

"I think it would be far more prudent to call in the inspector and tell him what you have discovered. Then he can question Arthur, through the proper and, I must add, safer channels."

Cecily heard the words, but she had heard them so often that she paid no attention. She was remembering something else. Her conversation with Gertie that afternoon.

Though how the hell he learnt it I can't imagine. One only sees a hypnotist in the Music Hall, and Master Stanley's much too young to have been there.

"Stanley," Cecily said, abruptly leaning forward.

"I beg your pardon, madam?"

"That's where Stanley learned how to do it. By watching Arthur."

"But Barrett would have had to be using it on someone at the time, wouldn't he? And if he used it to cause Sir Richard's death, I hardly think he would advertise the fact."

Cecily nodded. "Exactly. What if Stanley has actually seen Arthur hypnotize his father?"

She heard Baxter's indrawn breath. "Then we have a witness."

"If I'm right, then indeed we do. Let us just hope that we get to Master Stanley Malton before Arthur discovers that fact."

Earlier that evening, Stanley had become bored with his game of mumblety-peg. He had practiced and practiced until he could flip the knife into the ground from a number of positions and made it stick.

But it was no fun doing it on his own. He would even

have played the game with that lumpy housemaid with the big belly if she hadn't been too busy.

He rather liked the way she talked. His mother's ears would drop off if she could hear that language. He was storing it up to shock her with when she finally got out of her bed.

For a moment he felt an overwhelming sense of misery and loneliness. It wasn't fair. He had no one to play with, and soon it would be dark and he'd have to go back to that stinking kitchen and listen to Gertie and Mrs. Chubb scream at each other.

He looked longingly across the lawn to where he could see just a faint glimmer of the sea. How he'd love to be down there. There were always other children to play with or to watch, and it was so much fun to splash in the water and dig sand castles and . . .

He felt in his pocket, smiling as his fingers closed over the watch. There was something he could do all by himself. He would have to find that daft colonel, of course. He was the only one who would sit with his eyes on the watch long enough to let Stanley send him to sleep.

Stanley laughed out loud as he remembered the colonel's attack on Arthur. It was so easy. He went to sleep just like that, and all Stanley had to do was tell him he was going to fight Arthur at nine o'clock, then order him to forget what he'd been told when he woke up.

Yes, he decided. That's what he'd do. He'd find the colonel and get him to do something really fun. Like take off all his clothes in front of the ladies. That was bound to cause a good laugh.

Stanley looked across at the hotel. He'd promised that dumpy housemaid he wouldn't leave the stretch of lawn in front of the steps. She'd been gone quite a long time, and she said she'd be back for him soon. If he wanted to leave, he'd better run now, before she came out and made him go back to that hot, stuffy kitchen.

Without further ado, Stanley broke into a lumbering trot, heading for the Rose Garden.

It was getting quite dark by the time he gave up. Everyone was at dinner, and he couldn't find the colonel anywhere, so he had to be eating his dinner, too.

Frustrated, Stanley wandered over to the fish pond. If he couldn't find anyone to work the magic on, he'd just have to try and work it on himself again.

Reaching the rockery above the pond, Stanley clambered up on the rocks and gazed moodily into the water. What if he did send himself to sleep? How would he tell himself what to do? And how would he wake himself up again if he was asleep?

All very puzzling questions, that was certain. Arthur would know, of course.

Stanley started swinging one foot and banged the rocks with his heel. It made a satisfying sound, and he did it with both feet. He liked the drumming noise it made. It reminded him of the noise the drums made at the circus when the men balanced on the tightrope.

Prissy-looking men they were, in those stupid clothes. Men didn't wear pink stuff with glitter stars on it. But he was impressed when they all balanced on the rope on each other's shoulders.

Stanley stopped drumming. Thinking about the tightrope reminded him of his father. He didn't want to think about what happened to his father. Much as he wanted to know more about this business of sending someone to sleep, he didn't think it would be a good idea to ask Arthur how to do it.

Something told him that it would definitely not be wise to tell the doorman he saw him order his father to dance on the balcony railing.

Stanley yawned. It was almost dark. If he wanted to try to send himself to sleep, he'd have to do it fast, before the night came and he wouldn't be able to see.

Carefully he scrambled down from the rocks. He didn't

want to fall in the stupid water again. He'd catch it in the neck from Dirty Gertie if he did that.

He giggled aloud, pleased with the name. He'd call her by that name when he saw her again, the next time she yelled at him. She had a voice that seemed to shiver all through his body and explode out of his head.

He knelt by the edge of the water and hooked the watch out of his pocket. Holding it by the very end of the chain, he started swinging it back and forth. Then, very carefully, he leaned forward to peer at his reflection in the water.

He had to look into his own eyes, or it wouldn't work. He'd already discovered that. If he could just keep his eyes on the watch and his own face at the same time, it might just work.

Slowly he swung the watch back and forth, concentrating intently on the reflection in the water. "Sleep," he murmured, keeping his voice soft and low, the way he'd heard Arthur do it. "Your limbs are getting heavy, your eyes are closing, you can't keep them open. Soon you will be fast asleep. Relax, keep your eyes on the watch, just relax . . ."

Something rippled the water, a tadpole, perhaps, or the breeze from the ocean.

It broke up his reflection for a moment, and he waited impatiently for the surface to smooth out again. When it did, he saw with a shock that there were now two faces peering back at him. His own and that of the doorman, Arthur Barrett.

Stanley sat back on his heels with a jerk and looked up. Arthur stood above him, looking down at him, his usual grin splitting his face.

"Well, now, me young fellow," he said softly, "you seem to be having quite a game there all by yourself. What would you be doing now, if you don't mind me asking?"

"Nothing," Stanley said quickly, shoving the watch back in his pocket.

He watched Arthur squat down beside him, not sure if he should be frightened or not. Arthur certainly looked friendly enough, and his smile seemed to warm Stanley's chilled body.

"The way I see it," Arthur said, his face now on Stanley's level. "I'd say you were doing something really interesting. Seems to me you were trying to hypnotize yourself, am I not right?"

There was that strange word again. Stanley looked into Arthur's eyes but saw only friendship and sympathy. Maybe he wasn't bad at all. Maybe it was his father who'd been bad, and Arthur had simply punished him.

Anxious that Arthur should not think he was doing anything bad, Stanley vigorously nodded his head. "I can't do it to myself," he said, then added proudly, "but I did it with that dumb colonel."

"Ah," Arthur said slowly. "Now I understand. Very clever, Master Stanley. Very clever indeed."

"He's the only one I can do it on," Stanley said, hoping perhaps Arthur would let him do it on him. "I tried to do it on myself, but it doesn't work. And no one else will keep their eyes on the watch when I tell them to."

"Well, I tell you what, young fellow," Arthur said, getting to his feet. "I can tell, just by watching you, what it is you are doing wrong. Hypnotism is a very special art, and when you learn how to do it properly, you can achieve the most amazing results."

Stanley peered up at him, his heart beating faster with excitement. "Really? Like what?"

Arthur let out a hearty laugh. "Well, me boy, you can use it to get whatever you want. Imagine going into a sweet shop and ordering the assistant to give you as many gumdrops as you can eat. Or a toy shop where you can walk out with an armful of toys, without paying one single farthing for the lot."

Stanley's eyes widened. He hadn't thought about that at all. Just think what he could do with this strange new power. He would never have to do what he was told again. He could do anything, have anything he wanted, and no one would be able to stop him.

Then he'd have lots of friends to play with, all right. They would all want to play with him when they found out what he could do. He could give all the kids toys, then maybe they wouldn't tease him about being fat anymore and would want to play with him.

"How do I do it?" he asked breathlessly. "Would you show me how to do it properly?"

"Well, of course I will." Arthur beamed down at him. "But it will take a little time. What time do you have to go to bed?"

Stanley shrugged. "Whenever they find me," he said darkly.

Arthur laughed out loud, the sound of it echoing across the darkened lawns. "Well, to be sure now, you are a boy after me own heart. Tell you what. Why don't we go back to my room? They'll never find you there, even if they searched all night, and that would give us lots of time to work on this. By the time you go to bed tonight, my fine fellow, you will know everything there is to know about hypnotism, and the world will be yours."

Stanley scrambled to his feet, eager for this exciting lesson to begin. "Where is your room?"

"It's right next to the stables, me lad. They won't see us go in there, I can promise you that. Once you have learned the magic art of hypnotism, I'll sneak you back into the hotel. How does that sound?"

"That sounds wonderful," Stanley said and put his hand into the big, warm hand of Arthur Barrett.

CHAPTER

❋18❋

Gertie knelt in front of the roaring stove, perspiration streaming down her face as she thrust the shovel beneath the smoldering grate. Another pile of gray ash emerged on the blade when she withdrew it, and she held her breath in case she should sneeze and send the lot over the hearth.

It was bad enough trying to sweep up the stray ash that fell off the shovel. The stuff seemed to have a life of its own, escaping from her in little dust clouds until she was ready to scream.

She filled the bucket with the hot ash and cinders, then straightened her back. Her last task for the day, thank God. Lifting the corner of her apron, she mopped her brow. Now all she had to do was empty the bucket, then find Stanley the Horrible, and she'd be free to go lie on her bed and rest her aching back.

The pain seemed to be getting worse lately. Not only in her back, but low in her belly, as well. She'd mentioned it to Mrs. Chubb, but the housekeeper had reassured her, saying that as long as she could feel the baby kick, she had no need to worry.

Well, she'd felt it kick all right. Right there on the sands, it had kicked so hard she thought she was going to drop it right there and then.

Gertie smiled to herself. That would have caused a right fuss an' all. Wonder what Master Stanley-bleeding-Malton would have said to that? Would have been an early lesson in how babies are born, that it would.

On her way out to the yard she met Mrs. Chubb coming in the kitchen door. "Aren't you finished yet?" the housekeeper said, peering up into Gertie's face. "Are you feeling all right, my girl?"

Gertie shrugged. "Only me bleeding back, and that pain in me belly. Otherwise I'm as fit as a spring lamb."

"Well, you don't look it. You had best get to bed and have a good night's rest. We have a big day tomorrow, getting ready for the Midsummer Ball."

Gertie groaned. "Don't bleeding remind me. I'll be bloody glad when this season is over, I can tell you. I've never been so blooming tired in all my life. I swear I haven't."

"It's your pregnancy, ducks. Drags you down a bit toward the end."

"Yeah, well, I've got another three months to go yet. Gawd knows what I'll be like by the time the little perisher gets here."

Mrs. Chubb looked shocked. "Gertie Brown, that's no way to talk about your baby. Where's your mothering instinct?"

"Got up and left, I reckon." Gertie heaved the bucket into the other hand. "There's something I'd like to bloody know. Why is it the women what have to be bleeding put up with all this shit? Why couldn't it be the blinking men what have to have the babies? They get away with it scot-free, that's what. It's not bleeding fair."

Mrs. Chubb sighed. "Gertie, love, it's time you understood that the world is not, and never will be, fair to women."

Gertie snorted. "Well, just wait until we get the vote. Then we'll vote for all women in the bleeding government and chuck all the flipping men out."

"It's a nice dream, dearie, but I'm afraid it will never happen. Men have women right where they want them." She pressed her thumb on the table. "Under there. And there isn't one of them ever going to give an inch, as long as they have slaves to do their cleaning and their cooking and bring up their children."

"Yeah, well, this woman's got to bring up her bleeding kid on her own. No wonder I ain't got the mothering instinct."

Mrs. Chubb patted her on the shoulder. "Don't worry, ducks. You'll get it. Sooner or later. And who knows, you might find a man who'll want a woman for his slave."

Gertie stepped out into the yard, shivering a little at the contrast of the cool breeze after the stifling heat of the kitchen. "Well, not me," she said, sticking her chin in the air. "I'll bring me bloody kid up on me own, with no help from no man, thank you very much."

With that she stomped across the yard to the dustbins. Lifting the lid of the dustbin, she emptied the bucket. A cloud of dust enveloped her head, provoking a fit of coughing that left her breathless.

"Strewth," she muttered when she'd regained her breath, "I've probably got a filthy face now." She started back to the kitchen, then something dawned on her. It was no longer daylight. Stanley was still out on the lawn. At least, she bleeding hoped he was.

God knows what he was up to, now that the sun had gone down. Probably terrorizing the moths that hovered around the gas lamps. The little monster wasn't happy unless he was upsetting someone.

Back inside the kitchen, the air seemed even more oppressive than it had before. Even Mrs. Chubb's cheeks had a rosy shine to them as she sat mending a lace tablecloth.

"I'm going to find that bleeding Stanley," Gertie announced.

Mrs. Chubb winced but merely said, "I was going to ask you where he is. Who's taking care of him?"

Gertie shifted from one foot to the other. "Well, nobody right now. I left him playing on the lawn, and he promised me faithfully, crossed his heart, he did, that he wouldn't leave that bit of grass."

Mrs. Chubb paused with her needle half out of the fabric. "How long ago was that?" she said in a voice that Gertie knew was just the calm before the storm.

She looked at the clock on the mantelpiece, her heart skipping a beat when she saw the time. "About three hours ago," she admitted unhappily.

Mrs. Chubb dropped the tablecloth into her lap. "Three hours? You left Master Stanley Malton alone for three hours to amuse himself, with no one to watch him?"

Gertie miserably nodded her head up and down. "I didn't realize the time slipping away."

Mrs. Chubb closed her eyes. "Well, you'd better realize the time slipping away," she said, her voice gaining volume with each word. "You'd better get out there right now, my girl, and hope to heaven that he's still there. Because if he's not, and we have to search this hotel for him at this time of night"—her voice reached an earsplitting shriek—"your head is going to be served up tomorrow night for supper with an apple stuffed into your mouth! Do you understand?"

Gertie had already begun backing toward the door. She gulped as the last words resounded in her ears like a clap of thunder.

"Yes, Mrs. Chubb," she said faintly, then tumbled through

the door and down the hallway before she could be deafened by another tirade.

Ethel stared at her as she flew past her in the foyer. "Where are you going in such a hurry?" Ethel called after her. "I've got something to tell you."

"Can't," Gertie yelled back. "I'll be back later." She reached the top of the steps and hurtled clumsily down them, her frantic glance around already telling her that Stanley was nowhere in sight.

"Damn you, you little shit!" she screamed to the wind. "Why the hell can't you do what you're bleeding told? Where the bloody blazes are you, then?"

Stanley was too far away to hear the frantic words hurled on his head. He sat on the bed in Arthur's tiny little room at the back of the stables and listened to the story the doorman unfolded.

"Now, when the wolf realized that the sheep recognized him and ran away from him, he had to think of a way to get close to them, without them knowing who he was."

Stanley yawned. He was feeling very tired. It had been a long day, and all the sun and fresh sea air on the sands had made him feel very sleepy. He wanted to hear the rest of the story, and he especially wanted Arthur to teach him how to do the hypnertiz, or whatever it was. But he was very much afraid he was going to fall asleep before he learned a single thing.

"Anyway," Arthur said, taking off his uniform jacket, "the wolf hit on a very clever idea. He went back to the first sheep he'd killed, and he took the coat off the sheep and covered himself with it."

Stanley jerked his eyes open. "Oh, I know that trick," he said scornfully. "I did that myself. I pretended I was a bear with the rug from the drawing room."

"So you did, me boy," Arthur said quietly. "So you did. Ay, and more's the pity. The world could use more imaginative people like yourself."

"What's a pity?" Stanley mumbled. Arthur had the brightest blue eyes he'd ever seen, but they gave him a strange tingly feeling when he stared into them. "When are you going to teach me how to hypnertize?"

"Right now," Arthur said, pulling a glittering glass object from his pocket. "The first thing you have to know is how to speak. You must keep your voice low and smooth, so you don't have a jarring note to wake the victim up."

"I know that," Stanley said, opening his mouth wide for another yawn. "I did that to the colonel."

"Ah, you did that, me fine friend." Arthur started swinging the glass back and forth. It looked a little like the glass pieces of the chandeliers hanging from the ceiling in the hotel. It was long and narrow and had ridges in it, which caught the light, turning them into a rainbow of dazzling colors.

Stanley watched the brilliant stone swing back and forth, until they were swirling arcs of red, blues, greens, and yellows. He tried to separate them but couldn't.

"You are getting sleepy, Stanley," Arthur's voice said.

"I don't want to get sleepy," Stanley protested, dragging his gaze away from the dazzling stone. "I want to learn how to do it."

"Ah, but isn't that just what I'm going to tell you?" Arthur's smooth, quiet voice murmured. "I'm going to send you to sleep first, you see, then I'll put all the instructions into your mind. When you wake up, you'll know everything that I know. And you'll be as clever as Mervin the Mysterious. Now isn't that the best way to learn something?"

"Who's Mervin the Mysterious?" Not that Stanley really wanted to know. He was too busy thinking about the new, simple way to learn something. No struggling with books and with hard words he didn't understand.

He'd just go to sleep and wake up with the most wonderful, exciting power anyone could possibly have. The world, and everything in it, would be his.

He'd have cars, and boats, and even one of those newfangled aeroplanes that his father showed him a picture of one day. Imagine being able to fly a machine in the air! He could soar with the birds above the mountains and the ocean, something he'd always longed to do.

No more worries about friends to play with, there'd be a million things he could do. He could . . . even . . . go . . .

With a soft sigh, Stanley stopped resisting and drifted into the welcoming darkness.

"I've looked everywhere," Gertie said, her eyes brimming with tears. "I can't think where he could bleeding be."

"Just calm down," Cecily said, giving the distraught girl a comforting pat on the shoulder. "He can't be far. I'll send out some people to hunt for him. You look exhausted. Just go to bed and stop worrying. We'll find him."

"I can't. I can't," Gertie said brokenly. "It's my fault. I shouldn't have left him alone all that time. What if he wandered off and is lost somewhere on Putney Downs? The gypsies could find him and take him away."

"Gertie," Cecily said firmly, "you know very well the gypsies left Putney Downs some time ago."

"No, they didn't." Gertie vehemently shook her head. "I've heard people say you can still hear their music at night. They just pretended to leave, but they're there, deeper in the woods on Putney Downs."

"Well, even if they did take Master Stanley, I'm quite sure that after an hour or two of his company they would be only too glad to send him back."

Gertie showed a glimmer of a smile. "What if he went in the sea and got drowned? No one would see him in the dark."

Cecily shook her head. "That's the last place he'd be," she said, trying to sound confident of that. "I'm sure we'll find him somewhere in the hotel. Most likely he'd been hiding from you, and that's why you couldn't find him."

Gertie nodded, looking a little better. "Well, maybe I will go and lie down for a little while. But I won't sleep. I won't even close my eyes, I know it."

"I'll send someone to tell you as soon as we find him," Cecily promised, praying that wouldn't be too long. She felt quite sorry for the girl as she watched her walk down the hallway to her room.

Hurrying up the steps to the foyer a minute later, Cecily thought about whom she could send to search for Stanley. Not too many of the staff were still up at that hour of the night. She would have to ask Baxter to wake up Samuel, and perhaps she could enlist the help of Mrs. Chubb if she were not yet asleep.

Arthur stood at his usual spot in the doorway when she reached the foyer. He would remain there until midnight, then lock up for the night. Anyone wanting to enter the hotel after that would have to ring the bell, whereupon the night porter would open the door.

Cecily glanced at the clock as she crossed the foyer. It was not quite eleven o'clock. She longed to speak to Arthur and confront him with what she had learned, but right now wasn't the time. Her priority had to be Stanley.

Hurrying down the hallway to Baxter's office, she prayed they would find the boy, and soon. She hoped with all her heart that Arthur Barrett was not responsible for Stanley's disappearance.

"It is such a lovely night," Ethel whispered as she strolled along the Esplanade with her hand tucked in the crook of Joe's elbow. She felt so daring, being alone with a man in the dark without a chaperon. True, they were on the street, but she couldn't see another soul, which made her virtually alone with the man she loved.

Even now, as she looked up at him, she could feel her throat fill with emotion for this strong, handsome man. She still found it so hard to believe that he cared for her enough to want to marry her.

How could she have had any doubts about what to do? Gertie had been right. She would never have been happy if Joe had gone to London without her. No, she'd made the right decision, though she would miss Badgers End dreadfully.

"A penny for them," Joe said, and she looked up at him to find him smiling down at her.

"A penny for what?" she asked, momentarily confused by her rush of love for him.

"Your thoughts, of course." He lightly pinched her cheek. "Where were you, sweetheart?"

She gave him a smile of sublime happiness. "I was just thinking how wonderful it will be to be starting a new life with you in London."

Joe looked down at her and thought he had never seen a sight more beautiful than the woman he was looking at right then. Moonshine glowed in her lovely eyes as she gazed up at him, and the curve of her mouth made him want to forget he was a gentleman.

Soon, he told himself. Soon she would be his, and he wouldn't have to fight to control his desire for her. Just thinking about it made him hot under the collar.

Tearing his gaze away, he tucked her hand closer into his elbow. It would be worth the wait, he knew it. He loved his shy, lovely woman with all his heart, and he wanted to spend the rest of his life doing nothing more than making her happy.

He kept his gaze steadily on the sands as they walked toward the Pennyfoot Hotel. It was a lot safer than looking at his bride-to-be.

The moon created a shining path of light across the smooth ocean, and he fancied himself walking along it, arm in arm with Ethel, toward a new horizon. Chuckling to himself at his romantic thoughts, he transferred his gaze to a moving shadow on the sand.

Curious, Joe kept his eye on the moving object, only half

listening to Ethel's excited chatter. As they drew nearer, he could see now that it was a child. A boy.

Joe frowned. It was a little late for a child to be walking along the sands alone. In fact, now that he came to think about it, it was odd that anyone would allow their child to be out alone this late.

Joe squinted his eyes to get a better look. Probably a boy playing truant. He'd done it himself when he was a child. Just for the adventure of it. Climbed out of his bedroom window and shinned down the old apple tree without anyone knowing he'd even gone.

"What are you looking at?" Ethel demanded, as Joe kept his gaze on the child.

He nodded toward the short plump figure and paused at the railing. "Out there. Looks like a young boy walking down to the water."

Ethel stared into the darkness. "Where? I can't see anyone."

Joe could barely see him now. The child had moved beyond the glow of the lamplight and had merged with the darkness of the ocean and the night sky.

The swish of the waves breaking on the shore seemed to echo in Joe's mind as he peered into the shadows. He could just make out the boy now, walking slowly, steadily, toward the water as if in a trance.

The small figure reached the edge of the waves, and Joe waited for him to halt. It was almost as if the boy were sleepwalking, his body held stiff and his arms straight at his sides.

Then Joe felt as if his heart had leapt to his throat. The boy had not stopped at the water's edge, but continued to wade steadily into the sea.

Joe waited a moment longer to see if the cold water would wake the child up, but still the boy moved forward, the water steadily rising up his body.

With a muffled exclamation, Joe tore his arm from Ethel's

grip and vaulted over the railing. He heard her shocked cry but took no heed to it.

In his mind was the memory of another day. A cold winter's morning, a thin layer of ice on Deep Willow Pond, and a lone boy, struggling in the freezing water.

He had saved the boy that time, Joe told himself as he pounded across the soft sand that seemed to grab at his feet with every step. He had done it then, when it had seemed an impossible feat.

He reached the edge of the waves and quickly unbuttoned his boots. Already the waves were closing over the boy's head. Wading into the cold water, Joe prayed that he could be of help again. He had to save the boy. He took a long, deep breath, and dived into the black ocean.

CHAPTER 19

Cecily heard the Westminster chimes of the grandfather clock strike the midnight hour as she returned from searching the roof garden. Arthur was nowhere to be seen when she entered the foyer. She was relieved when Baxter came striding toward her, a look of urgency on his face.

"Has anyone—?" Cecily began, then broke off as Baxter shook his head.

"I'm sorry, madam. We have made a thorough search of the grounds and every room in this hotel. There is no sign of the boy."

"You don't think he could be hiding from us somewhere?"

"If he is, it's a secret hiding place that no one knows anything about." Baxter passed a hand across his forehead. "I simply don't know where else to look."

"The tunnel? Has anyone searched the tunnel under the cellars?" She was grasping at straws, she knew, but she refused to believe Stanley was not somewhere in the vicinity. They would find him at any second.

"Madam, if you remember, we had the entrance to the tunnel blocked from the beach and the trapdoor securely bolted from underneath. Even if the boy got into the card room and found the trapdoor to the tunnel, it would be impossible to open it. In any case, as you well know, the doors to the card rooms are kept locked."

"Yes, I am aware of all that," Cecily said, feeling helpless. "I am just trying to think of everything."

Baxter looked over at the front door. "Where is Barrett? Has he left already?"

She nodded. "I think it's high time we went and had that discussion with him. If he has had anything to do with Stanley's disappearance, he must tell us where to find him." She shuddered. "If he has done anything to harm that boy, I shall never forgive myself."

She heard the wobble in her voice and cleared her throat.

Baxter moved closer. "Madam," he said softly, "please do not upset yourself. I am sure we shall find Master Stanley safe and sound."

"Oh, Gawd, I bloody 'ope so," a soft voice said behind them.

Cecily turned to look at Gertie, who stood in her long white nightgown, clutching a shawl around her shoulders.

"Whatever shall I do, mum, if they don't find him?"

"We just have to pray that they will," Cecily said, wishing she could give the girl more hope. "He has to be somewhere on the grounds. We'll have to make another search at daybreak. Thank the Lord it's a warm night. If this had been winter, we would have had even more to worry over."

"Mum?" Gertie swallowed a couple of times. "Has anyone told Lady Lavinia yet?"

Cecily flinched as she thought about the unsuspecting

invalid lying upstairs. "I don't see any need to worry her unnecessarily."

"Well, I just wanted to say . . ." Gertie paused and gave Cecily a stricken look. "I want to be the one what tells her, if we don't find him, or if something bad happened to him. It was my fault, you see. I should have looked after him better. I should never have left him alone like that."

Cecily grasped Gertie's cold hands and held them. "Let's not worry about what might happen. Never trouble trouble till trouble troubles you, remember?"

Gertie nodded, obviously deriving little comfort from the adage.

"Go back to bed, Gertie," Cecily said gently. "I will be sure to inform you if there is any news."

"Yes, mum." Gertie moved away, looking more despondent than ever. She had gone just a few paces when the front door flew open.

Gertie screamed as the cool breeze from the sea flowed into the foyer and a figure stepped through the doorway. Water dripped steadily from Joe's sodden clothes and the soggy, limp bundle he carried in his arms.

Ethel's face appeared behind him, peering around his shoulder with a look of stark dread on her white face.

Cecily covered her lips with the tips of her fingers as Baxter strode past her, heading straight for Joe, who looked as if he were about to drop to the floor any minute.

"Take him," he gasped when Baxter reached him. "He's right heavy, this lad."

Baxter just had time to take the soaking boy in his arms before Joe collapsed on the floor in a spreading puddle of seawater.

Ethel uttered a shocked cry and dropped to her knees beside Joe's still form. Cecily heard Gertie moan and started forward herself as the housemaid rushed to be by her friend's side. They each took one of Joe's hands and began to rub frantically.

"He's freezing cold," Gertie said as Cecily reached them.

Looking up at Baxter, Cecily framed the question she was almost afraid to ask. "Is he alive?"

Baxter stared down at the child's frozen face. "Barely," he said in a tight-lipped voice that betrayed his distress. "I will send Samuel for the doctor. He can bring him back in the trap and take him home afterward."

Ethel sobbed quietly at Joe's side, tears chasing each other down her wet cheeks.

Cecily leaned down and pressed her fingers to Joe's neck, relief spreading over her when she felt a strong pulse. "He's going to be all right," she told the weeping girl. "It's probably exhaustion. A night's rest and he will be fine. I'll have the doctor take a look at him, just to be sure."

Ethel gave a shuddering sob. "Thank you, mum," she whispered without taking her eyes from Joe's face.

"Can you tell me what happened?" Cecily asked gently.

Ethel's shoulders shook, but she answered in a low, halting voice, punctuated by an occasional sniff. "Joe saw him walking along the sands. He was going straight for the sea. We thought he would stop when he got to the water but he didn't. He kept on walking, right into the ocean. He wouldn't stop. And Joe . . . he went in after him . . ." She started weeping again.

"It's my fault," Gertie howled. "It's all my fault. I told him he belonged in the bottom of the sea. Oh, my Gawd, I never thought he'd do it." She threw her shawl over her head and rocked back and forth on her knees.

"I should get the boy into a bed," Baxter said, raising his voice to be heard above Gertie's bawling.

"Yes, please do, Baxter. I'll ask Mrs. Chubb to keep an eye on him until the doctor gets here." Cecily gave him a grave look. "You can put him in Samuel's room, and please ask Samuel to bring P.C. Northcott back with the doctor, will you?"

Baxter nodded, his face a stone mask. "Certainly, madam."

She watched him carry the boy across the foyer, then shifted her attention to Gertie, who howled louder.

"Oh, I'm sorry, mum, I'm so sorry. Do you have to tell the constable? What if he puts me in the clink? How am I going to take care of the baby if I'm in prison?"

She was making so much noise Cecily had to shake her to command her attention. "Gertie, I am not sending for the constable because of anything you've done or haven't done. This doesn't concern you in any way. So please, calm yourself and return to your bed."

Gertie stopped bawling. In the blissful silence that followed, Joe made a sound like a loud sigh.

All three women stared at him, then as he began to stir, Ethel threw herself down on his chest, sobbing wildly. "Oh, Joe," she kept saying, over and over again.

Cecily took hold of the girl's shoulders and drew her back. "You must let him breathe," she said as Joe's head came up and gasped for air. "He probably swallowed a lot of water."

"Too right I have," Joe muttered. "My stomach feels like a fishbowl."

"Oh, Joe," Ethel said again, still on her knees and staring at him as if he'd arisen from the dead.

Gertie got slowly to her feet, both hands pressed over her mouth. Cecily hoped she wasn't about to be sick all over the carpet.

"Ethel told me what happened," Cecily said to Joe as he struggled to sit up. "I'd like to hear your version, if you feel up to it?"

Joe nodded, then groaned and held his stomach. "I'll never eat fish again," he muttered.

Ethel let out a nervous laugh and grabbed hold of his hands. "I thought you were going to die out there," she said tearfully.

"So did I, I'm telling you." Joe shook his head. "I couldn't see him in the dark. It was the strangest thing I ever did see. Usually when someone is drowning they fight and splash about. That's what makes it dangerous to rescue someone from drowning. They are more 'n likely to pull you right down with 'em."

He coughed, a deep rasping sound that had Ethel watching him anxiously. After a moment or two he recovered his breath and said hoarsely, "It wasn't like that with this one. He just kept walking into the sea like he thought he was still on the sands, and he never stopped. I had to guess where he was. I couldn't hear or see him. Lucky for him I bumped into him, more or less by chance. Someone was watching over him, that was for sure."

He belched loudly, his face warming as he sent a look of apology at Cecily. "Sorry, ma'am. Please excuse me."

Cecily smiled. "Quite understandable, Joe, under the circumstances. We owe you a great debt of gratitude. I'm sure Lady Lavinia will want to express her thanks herself when she is informed of the incident."

Joe shook his head. "There's no need. Once I got hold of him, it wasn't that difficult to get him back to shore. He didn't resist or struggle, just came with me. It was like I was tugging a paddleboat behind me."

"We might never have known what happened to him if you hadn't seen him walk into the sea." Cecily raised her eyes to the ceiling. "Thank God you were there at that time."

Joe looked up at her and gave her a sweet smile. "Thank God, indeed. It was Him who sent me there, ma'am."

"I think it must have been." Cecily glanced down at Ethel, who still stared at Joe as if she were afraid he'd disappear if she took her eyes off him.

"Ethel," Cecily said, a little more sharply than she'd intended, in order to attract the girl's attention. "Please take Joe down to the kitchen and get his clothes dried off in front of the stove. A drop of Michel's best brandy should help take the chill off you both."

"Yes, mum. Thank you, mum." Ethel scrambled to her feet and stretched out her hand toward Joe.

He seemed to have a little trouble steadying himself, but after a moment he wrapped his arm around Ethel's shoulders. Her face looked much brighter as the two of them walked a little unsteadily toward the stairs.

Cecily looked at Gertie, who wore a woeful expression as she drew her shawl closer about her shoulders.

"Go to bed," Cecily told the housemaid. "I'll ask Mrs. Chubb to bring you a hot drink to help you sleep."

"Why did he do it?" Gertie said, her face puckered, ready to cry again. "I didn't mean what I told him, honest I didn't. I didn't think he'd really try to walk at the bottom of the sea."

"Gertie . . ." Cecily hesitated, not sure how much she could say to comfort the girl. "Please believe that you are not at fault," she said at last. "Whatever you said to Master Stanley had no bearing on this little adventure tonight. I think I know why the child did what he did, and perhaps by tomorrow I'll be able to tell you more. But for now I'm afraid you will simply have to take my word for it."

Gertie nodded, though she looked unconvinced. She seemed to drag herself across the foyer, one end of her shawl trailing dismally behind her across the carpet.

Cecily watched her leave, then made her way to Mrs. Chubb's quarters. Someone had to watch over Stanley, while she and Baxter paid a long overdue visit to Mervin the Mysterious.

Baxter met her at the head of the stairs when she returned to the foyer after speaking with the housekeeper.

"I'm worried about the boy," he said when she asked about him. "He lies so still and quiet. His breathing is hard to hear and his heartbeat very faint."

Cecily sighed. "Has Samuel left for the doctor?"

"Yes. He's also been instructed to bring back the constable when he returns with Dr. Prestwick."

"Very well." Cecily glanced at the clock. "Then we have a little while to wait for them. Mrs. Chubb will watch over Stanley, and I have given her strict instructions not to let anyone in the room, with the exception of myself or the doctor when he arrives."

Baxter stood looking at her with a frown on his face. "A while for what, madam?" he asked carefully.

"Baxter, we simply must talk to Arthur now. As soon as he knows that Stanley has been found alive, he will waste no time in leaving. We need a confession from him."

Baxter continued to fix her with his intent stare. "But, madam, if Master Stanley is alive, we have a witness to the murder. We won't need a confession."

"If Stanley lives through the night," Cecily said softly.

Baxter's face assumed a stony expression. Only the set of his mouth indicated his anguish. "I understand, madam," he said quietly. "But I would suggest that it would be most unwise to visit the man in his quarters tonight. The constable will be here after a while. Not that I estimate his capabilities to be greater than yours or mine, but he is the proper person to handle the situation."

"We don't know how long it will take him to arrive," Cecily said firmly. "In the meantime, Arthur could return at any time and discover that Stanley has been found and is unconscious. He could even attempt to silence the boy some other way. If we tell Arthur, however, that the boy has been found alive and has told us what happened, we might be able to wrestle a confession out of him."

"I still believe—"

Cecily moved closer to him until they were toe-to-toe. "I don't have time to argue, Baxter. You are fully aware that your arguments have never prevented me before from carrying out my intentions, and it will not prevent me now. I will go and talk to Arthur. You may accompany me or not, as you please."

He ran a hand through his hair and took a pace backward. "I will come with you, madam. Under protest, as always."

Cecily gave him a grim smile. "Thank you, Baxter. I knew I could rely on you."

She wouldn't admit to feeling more than a little apprehensive as they made their way across the stable yard to Arthur's room. She had heard of the way some hypnotists could send the better half of an audience into an induced sleep, and then order several of them to perform outlandish acts, to the huge amusement of the remainder of the audience.

In this instance, however, the situation was not in the least amusing. Arthur could very well send both her and Baxter into a hypnotic state from which they might never recover.

A cloud moved over the moon as their footsteps echoed across the cobblestones of the yard. The shadow seemed to sweep over them, plunging them into darkness as it engulfed the dimly lit area.

Cecily shivered. She was becoming fanciful. This wasn't voodoo or a dangerous black magic that no one could understand or control. Hypnotism was an acceptable science, and as such they surely had some resistance to it.

Her self-reassurance didn't offer much comfort to her as Baxter rapped on Arthur's door. The sound of it faded away into the darkness, and then the door abruptly opened.

Cecily's pulse danced when she saw Arthur standing in the doorway, his face in shadow as the gaslight played on his back.

"Well, to what do I owe this very pleasant surprise, ma'am?" Arthur said, sweeping them a slight bow that was purely theatrical.

"We wish to talk with you, Arthur," Cecily said, forcing a firm tone. "May we please come in?"

The doorman hesitated. "Could it possibly wait until the morning, ma'am? I have not had time to tidy up the place, and I'd be ashamed for you to see the mess—"

"It's important, Arthur."

He stood perfectly still while long seconds passed, then he sighed. "Very well."

He stood back to let them pass, and Cecily stepped into the tiny room, followed closely by Baxter. A quick glance told her the whole story. A suitcase lay opened on the bed, halfway filled with clothes.

"Are you planning to leave us, Barrett?" Baxter enquired, his voice dangerously quiet.

"Well, I was hoping to, yes." Arthur pulled out a chair from under the tiny table and waved a hand at it. "Please, make yourselves at home."

His friendly grin looked so familiar, Cecily almost doubted what she knew to be the truth. A dangerous mistake that would be, she reminded herself.

She sat herself down on the very edge of the chair. "Where are you going, Arthur? Were you not planning to inform us of your departure?"

Baxter moved to stand directly behind her, as if ready to protect her at the slightest provocation. She had to admit it gave her a most warm and welcome sensation.

"I had thought to go back to London." Arthur sighed and directed his gaze at the ceiling. "Something tells me I won't be doing that now."

"I think you know that we have guessed the truth about Sir Richard Malton's unfortunate demise," Cecily said, clasping her hands in her lap for comfort.

"I did suspect as much, yes, ma'am."

"And we assume that his son suffered the same fate."

Arthur didn't appear to be at all surprised. "I saw the boy carried from the beach. I was watching from the roof garden. I knew it would be only a matter of time before the truth came out."

"You are a miserable cad, sir," Baxter said forcefully, surprising Cecily into silence. "To end a man's life is despicable enough, but to rob a young child of his life is beyond belief or understanding."

"As it happens," Cecily said as Arthur stared down at the floor, his face unusually solemn, "Master Stanley survived. He was able to tell us the truth."

Arthur's face seemed to crumple. "Thank God," he whispered.

"We know what happened," Cecily pressed on relentlessly, "but we'd like you to tell us the details."

Arthur sat down heavily on the bed and rested his head in his hands. "Very well," he said, his voice muffled, "I'll tell you anything you want to know."

CHAPTER

❈ 20 ❈

"I suppose," Cecily said, "that we should begin with the reason you wanted Sir Richard Malton dead. I assume it's because he caused you to lose your career."

Arthur's head shot up in surprise. "Career?"

Cecily smiled. "Baxter and I paid a visit to the Hippodrome in Wellercombe tonight. We met a man by the name of Harry Mattson."

Arthur stared at her for a moment, then slowly nodded his head. "The dog handler. I remember him."

"Yes. He told us about the theater being closed down."

Arthur got to his feet, and Baxter moved a little closer to Cecily's chair.

"Yes," Arthur said, "it was the finish of my career. I'd been in show business all my life. It was all I knew. I had nothing else. When Malton had the theater closed down, he

did more than put a few entertainers out of work for a while.
Much more."

He paused, his throat working as he struggled with his
emotion. "He destroyed me," he said at last, his voice
breaking. "That man took away the one thing in the world
I lived for, just to satisfy his wounded pride."

"So it was Sir Richard," Cecily said, beginning to feel
sorry for the dejected doorman. "I assumed as much."

"It was Malton." Arthur moved over to the window and
stood with his back to the room, his hands clasped behind
his back. "I swore that I would get even with him."

Cecily exchanged a quick glance over her shoulder with
Baxter. "Why did he close down the theater?" she said.
"What did you mean by wounded pride?"

Arthur's sigh seemed to settle over the entire room. "Sir
Richard Malton was a well-known patronizer and benefactor of the theater. He had been attending the shows at the
Royal for several months. He was also well known for using
his generosity as a means of pressuring the show girls
to . . ." Arthur coughed, appearing to be searching for the
appropriate words.

"To show him special favors," Cecily finished for him.

Baxter cleared his throat, as if embarrassed, while the
doorman turned and gave her a wry smile.

"Very delicately put, ma'am. Yes, that's what I meant. He
became interested in one of the dancers in our troupe. Pretty
little thing, she was, tiny and quick on her feet, with a laugh
as sweet as an Irish ballad."

Arthur stared into space, as if seeing the girl he was
describing. "Anyway," he said, coming back to earth with a
start, "she would have nothing at all to do with him. She had
her heart set on the stage manager, who was a good deal
younger and more handsome than Malton, though to be
sure, he didn't have his money. That didn't bother Irene, of
course. She was in love, and that was all that mattered to
her."

"And so Sir Richard resented the rejection," Cecily said, guessing where the story was heading.

"He was boiling mad." Arthur came back and sat on the bed. "He threatened to fire her, but she paid no heed to the man. Malton went to the stage manager and ordered him to fire her, and it was then he discovered who his rival was. It didn't take too much effort on Malton's part to close the theater down. It was barely breaking even as it was, and he knew where to pull the strings."

"And so you lost your booking," Cecily said as Arthur gazed moodily at his feet.

"I lost my life," he said quietly. "I couldn't get work anywhere after that. The entire concept of Music Hall was changing, and I couldn't compete with these Variety artistes. All young whips, they are, full of bright ideas, always trying something new, taking risks . . . I was a hypnotist. What else could I do but send people to sleep and make them do silly tricks?"

"You could have used your voice," Baxter said dryly. "Surely there is always work for a decent singer."

Arthur stared up at him with a faint smile. "Why, Mr. Baxter, that's indeed the very nicest thing you have ever said to me."

Cecily caught sight of Baxter's scowl and said hurriedly, "Is that the reason you applied for the job at the Pennyfoot? To find an opportunity to kill Sir Richard?"

Arthur shook his head. "The thought never entered my mind at that point. I heard about the job from an acquaintance of mine. He used to work for you. Ian Rossiter is his name."

"Ian!" Cecily felt a pang of nostalgia. "Yes, he worked for us. I hope he is happy in his new life."

Arthur shrugged. "He seems to be doing all right, though how can you ever tell if a man is truly happy?"

"You can tell when they're not," Baxter said.

Cecily lifted an eyebrow at him, but he avoided her gaze.

"So it was by chance that you came upon Sir Richard Malton?" she said.

"'Twas a stroke of ill luck for both of us, I reckon." Arthur rubbed his eyes with his long fingers. "I was attending the door one fine morning last week, and there he was. Looking just as mean and ugly as when I last saw him."

"Did he recognize you?"

"No, no." He dropped his hand. "He never took much notice of the male performers. He had eyes only for the women. But I recognized him all right."

"How did you get close enough to him to hypnotize him?" Cecily asked. It was a question that had puzzled her ever since she'd suspected how Sir Richard had died.

"It wasn't that difficult. He walked right into my hands." A look of grim satisfaction stole across the doorman's face. "He came back to the hotel late one night, and when I enquired about his well-being, he told me he had a very bad headache. He'd had an argument down at the George and Dragon and wasn't too happy about it. He kept muttering about closing the place down."

"Yes," Cecily murmured. "Michael told me."

"Anyway," Arthur continued, "him mentioning closing down a business was like setting a match to an oil wick. It was adding fuel to the fire. I knew then that I wanted him dead."

He was silent so long that Cecily thought he had said all he was going to say. But then he added, "I told him I had the perfect cure for a headache. He told me he'd tried all manner of cures, but none of them worked."

Arthur stared at the wall, his voice dropping to a monotone. "I told him I could use hypnotism on him. That I'd learned it from my brother, who was a medical doctor. I explained how they used it in hospitals to cure all kinds of ills. I told him that not only would I take away that headache, but also I'd make sure he'd never have another one."

Cecily felt a chill as Baxter made a strangled noise in his throat.

Arthur looked up at him. "Well, that much was true," he said.

"So he allowed you to put him to sleep," Cecily said, wondering how she could have misjudged this man so completely.

"Yes, I put him to sleep. I couldn't have succeeded if he hadn't been willing. A subject has to trust the hypnotist or he will be too tense to respond to the hypnotic suggestion."

"Yes, I thought as much." Even though repelled by the result, the subject continued to fascinate her. "You then told him to perform his last dance on top of the railing."

"Yes."

Arthur paused, and Baxter took the opportunity to say, "But he was awake when he obeyed your command?"

Arthur nodded. "Posthypnotic suggestion. The subject is put into a trance-like state, and his mind is then acceptable to suggestion. When he wakes up he will have no memory of the trance or what was said during that time. He will, however, carry out the command at the given time, without ever knowing the source of the instruction."

"And Stanley saw you do this to his father?"

Arthur's sigh was even louder this time. "Yes. I wasn't aware of that fact until later. I found him trying to hypnotize himself, using his reflection in the pond. He was repeating actions and phrases that he'd seen me use with his father. I knew I had to do something before someone else saw him and eventually put two and two together."

"So you decided to kill him," Baxter said in disgust.

There was a long silence, then Arthur said softly, "If it makes any difference, I'm very glad the boy will survive."

"We don't know that," Baxter said, earning a warning glance from Cecily.

Arthur looked from one to the other of them in surprise. "But I thought you said—"

"I stretched the truth a little," Cecily said, feeling no shame at all.

Arthur gave her an appraising look. "A woman after me own heart. Now, if only things had been different—"

Baxter uttered a low growl, and Arthur's shoulders slumped. "How is he doing?" he said, looking as if he were about to cry.

"I think he'll be all right," Cecily said, praying she was right. "We've sent for the doctor."

Arthur nodded. "My prayers will be with him."

"You'd better pray for yourself," Baxter said harshly.

Ignoring Baxter, Arthur's gaze sought Cecily's. "I'm glad it's over. My life was finished the day I left the theater for the last time, and I'm much too old to be running hither and thither, constantly watching over my shoulder."

"I'm sorry, Arthur," Cecily said, rising to her feet. "The constable will be arriving shortly."

Arthur nodded. "I'll be ready for him."

He seemed quite pathetic, and Cecily had to force herself not to pat him on the shoulder for comfort. "We will trust you not to run, Arthur," she said softly.

Baxter made a small sound of protest, but she shook her head at him.

"I'll not run," Arthur said heavily. "Where would I go? What would I do? I might as well face the music. I have nothing more to live for."

With an ache in her heart Cecily followed Baxter out into the night and left the doorman alone with his memories.

"You look bleeding awful," Gertie said the next morning as Ethel walked into the kitchen looking as if she'd just climbed out of bed.

"I feel awful," Ethel muttered. "I was up all night, wasn't I. All that worrying about Joe made me feel so sick I couldn't sleep. I thought I'd lost him."

"I couldn't sleep neither." Gertie dumped a copper urn onto the stove, slopping water over the side. "Couldn't get that poor kid's face out of me mind. I hope he's all right. I'm afraid to ask, that I am."

She faced Ethel, who looked at her with bleary eyes. "What if he died, Ethel? How can I live with that, knowing it was my bloody fault?"

"Madam said it wasn't your fault." Ethel yawned and sank onto a kitchen chair.

"I know, but she was just being nice, like she always is. It was my fault, I know that. I told him lots of times he belonged at the bottom of the sea. I just know the poor kid took me at me word and flipping walked in there."

"Well, Mrs. Chubb will be back soon, so you can ask her how he is." Ethel pushed herself to her feet. "I suppose I'd better get some work done or I'll be in trouble."

Gertie peered at her friend. "'Ere, what happened with you and Joe? Did you tell him you'd marry him?"

Ethel's face went through a remarkable transformation as she clasped her hands to her breast and smiled. "I did that. I told him as how I would go to London with him, or anywhere in the world, as long as I was with him."

"Oo, 'ow romantic." Gertie put a daft look on her face, clasped her hands, and gazed up at the ceiling.

Ethel snorted. "Just 'cause you're off men, Gertie Brown, don't mean you have to be so snotty with me."

Gertie lowered her chin and laid an awkward arm across her friend's shoulder. "Sorry, luv. I didn't mean it. I think it's wonderful that you and Joe are getting married, and I'm happy for both of you. But I ain't half going to miss you."

Ethel uttered a quiet sob, then thoroughly embarrassed Gertie by throwing her arms around her neck. "Oh, Gertie, luv, I'm going to miss you, too. You will come and see me, won't you? And bring the baby? I do want to see the baby."

"I'll dump the little horror on yer for a week or two," Gertie said, extricating herself from the hug. "I'll most likely need a bloody rest now and again."

"You don't sound too thrilled about the baby," Ethel said,

staring anxiously into her friend's face. "You are all right, aren't you?"

Gertie managed a fairly genuine laugh. "Course I'm all right, why wouldn't I be? I just haven't got the maternal instinct yet, that's what. Mrs. Chubb says sometimes it doesn't happen until after the baby is born."

"What's that Mrs. Chubb says?" The housekeeper's voice made both girls jump.

Gertie's heart started beating very fast as she looked at Mrs. Chubb's plump face. "What about Master Stanley?" she said nervously. "Is he going to be all right?"

Bustling into the kitchen, Mrs. Chubb gave her a look of amazement. "Well, bless my cotton socks, you sound almost as if you really care."

"I do." Gertie took hold of the housekeeper's arm. "It was my fault he walked into the blinking sea. Please, Mrs. Chubb, don't bleeding keep me in 'orrible suspense. Tell me if he's going to be all right."

Mrs. Chubb smiled, patting the hand that gripped her arm. "He's going to be just fine, don't you worry about that. He's sitting up demanding his breakfast. As a matter of fact, I was just on my way to fetch it for him. But seeing as how you are so anxious to see him, I'll let you take a tray in to him."

"I didn't say as how I was that worried about him," Gertie mumbled. "But it was my fault he nearly drowned."

"No, it wasn't." Mrs. Chubb paused, then shrugged. "You might as well know, since it will be all over the hotel before the day is out."

Gertie stared at her. "Know what?"

"It was Arthur Barrett. He used to be a hypnotist on the stage. He hypnotized Stanley and told him to walk into the sea. Madam told me all about it after the doctor and P.C. Northcott had left."

Ethel made a small sound of astonishment, while Gertie's jaw dropped. "Bloody hell," she whispered. "Why'd he do that?"

"Because Stanley saw him hypnotize his father. That's why Sir Richard fell off the balcony."

Gertie and Ethel listened in amazement as Mrs. Chubb told them the rest of the story. "Cor blimey," Gertie said when the housekeeper had finished. "Just goes to bleeding show, you can never tell about a bloody man just by looking at him."

"You never said a truer word," Mrs. Chubb said. She sighed, then added briskly, "Now, about Master Stanley's breakfast."

"I'll take it in to him," Gertie muttered, "even if it weren't my fault. Then if he gives me any lip, I can dump it in his lap."

This time even Mrs. Chubb joined in Ethel's laughter. The housekeeper's laughter died, however, when Phoebe spoke from the doorway. "I apologize for interrupting you, Mrs. Chubb, but I'd like a word with you," she said primly.

Gertie nudged Ethel as the housekeeper walked toward Phoebe and without a word joined her outside the hallway, closing the door firmly behind her.

"We have been friends a long time, Altheda," Phoebe said, looking very nervous. She twirled her parasol aimlessly in her hands and avoided meeting Mrs. Chubb's gaze. "I do not wish to spoil that friendship because of an insensitive, uncouth philanderer who doesn't have a penny to his name. I am not in the least bit interested in Arthur Barrett. You are welcome to him, Altheda, and I wish you every happiness."

"That's very decent of you, Phoebe," Mrs. Chubb said gravely, "but I am not interested in Arthur Barrett either. In fact, I don't expect to see him again."

Phoebe looked at her in surprise. "Oh? Has he left? I wondered why I didn't see him when I came in this morning."

Mrs. Chubb smiled. "He's left." She took hold of Phoebe's arm. "Come into the kitchen, Phoebe, me duck, and I'll tell you a story that will leave you absolutely breathless."

*   *   *

"I suppose we shall have to start looking for another doorman," Cecily said as she leaned against the wall of the roof garden to look down on the courtyard below.

"Yes, madam. I'll see to it right away." Baxter coughed behind his hand. "May I suggest, madam, that this time *I* select a likely candidate?"

Cecily twisted her head to look at him. "Are you saying you don't trust my judgment in this matter?"

"No, madam." Baxter stretched his chin above his stiff collar. "I was merely thinking that a man might not be so easily swayed by a charming manner and a twinkle in the eye."

Cecily clicked her tongue at him. "Chauvinism, Baxter. Most definitely chauvinism. The very attitude that we women are struggling so hard to defeat."

"Yes, madam." His eyes glinted in the sun as he looked down at her. "But true nevertheless."

For once she felt disinclined to rise to the bait. Turning away, she rested her gaze on the shimmering ocean. "He did at least keep his word and wait for the constable. And to think I suspected my daughter-in-law of being involved. I'm afraid I let my personal feelings sway my judgment." She looked down at her hands. "I don't think I shall ever be able to truly accept her as Michael's wife, I'm ashamed to say."

"We cannot always base our feelings on other people's preferences."

"Maybe not. Nevertheless, I am guilty of jumping to conclusions on both counts. I was taken in by Arthur's charisma. I blame myself in a way for what happened. Had Stanley died, I would never have been able to live with myself."

Baxter moved a little closer to her. "You couldn't possibly be responsible for that madman's actions. You couldn't have known what he was when you hired him."

She kept her gaze on the wide expanse of water, glittering

beneath a warm sun. "You did, Baxter. You never liked him."

There was a long pause. "It wasn't because I suspected him of being evil," he said finally.

She looked at him then, alerted by something in his voice. "What was it?"

He seemed to be avoiding her gaze, and she watched him, suddenly intrigued. Finally he said, "I resented the devastating effect he had on the ladies." He paused, then added quietly, "And you in particular, madam. Most immature of me, I admit."

Cecily laughed in delight. "Why, Baxter, I do believe you were jealous."

She had meant to tease, but when his gaze finally rested on her face, something in his eyes made her heart begin to pound in a quite ridiculous manner.

"Yes, madam," he said softly. "I do believe I was."

She seemed bereft of air to breathe for several seconds. When she recovered her composure enough to trust her voice, she said lightly, "You should know better than that, Bax. There is not one man alive in this world who could possibly compare to my most faithful and trustworthy manager, who also happens to be my most loyal friend."

He looked at her for a long moment, then gave her one of his rare and quite beautiful smiles. "I am most happy to hear that, madam."

She smiled in return, but then his next words gave her a very nasty jolt indeed.

"I do trust, madam, that you will remember those words, should I ever decide to relinquish my position as manager of the Pennyfoot Hotel."

With that, he turned and strode briskly toward the attic door, leaving her to stare after him, wondering what he could possibly have meant by that dreadfully cryptic remark.

THE ACCLAIMED MYSTERIES OF

DEBORAH CROMBIE

Finalist for the Agatha and Macavity Best First Novel Awards

__ALL SHALL BE WELL   0-425-14771-1/$5.50

"Written with compassion, clarity, wit, and precision, this graceful mystery amply fulfills the promise of Crombie's debut."—Publishers Weekly

"Fresh and lively."—Booklist

When his close friend is found dead, Duncan Kincaid finds himself unable to let go of the case. The Scotland Yard superintendent and his partner, Sergeant Gemma James, must search through the dead woman's past...where the key to murder lies.

__A SHARE IN DEATH   0-425-14197-7/$4.50

"Charming!"—New York Times Book Review

"A thoroughly entertaining mystery."—Booklist

Detective Superintendent Kincaid's holiday is spoiled when a body is discovered in the whirlpool bath. Now instead of relaxing, Kincaid must investigate a murder within the seemingly peaceful confines of a Yorkshire time-share.

COMING IN APRIL 1996—**LEAVE THE GRAVE GREEN**